Advanced Dungeons & Dragons®

2nd Edition

Player's Handbook

Rules Supplement

The Complete Book of Gnomes & Halflings

by Douglas Niles

Table of Contents

Table of Contents

CREDITS

Designer: Douglas Niles
Editor: John D. Rateliff
Color Artists: Larry Elmore, Keith Parkinson, and Clyde Caldwell
Black and White Artists: James Crabtree and Ned Dameron
Additional Black and White Art: Larry Elmore, Brom, Jim Holloway, Stephen Fabian
Cartographer: Dave Sutherland
Typographer: Tracey Zamagne
Graphic Designer: Paul Hanchette

TSR, Inc.
201 Sheridan Springs Rd.
Lake Geneva,
WI 53147
U.S.A.

TSR Ltd.
120 Church End,
Cherry Hinton
Cambridge CB1 3LB
United Kingdom

ISBN 1-56076-573-9

Introduction

The Small Folk

Why a book for the small folk? And what do gnomes and halflings have in common that warrants their inclusion in a tome together? The answer to the second question lies in the first, for it is the diminutive size of both these popular races that is the most significant factor in the way they cope with their environment.

The worlds of the AD&D® game can be frightening and overpowering even to characters broad of girth, potent of magic, and possessing strength great enough to face many of those worlds' challenges. Imagine how much greater the danger to beings of small stature, limited strength, and little or no magic.

This is the environment faced by the gnome and the halfling. It is a world teeming with larger races, each of whom claims its niche and jealously guards its prerogatives: prolific humanity, with its potent wizards and powerful clerics; dour dwarves, with their mighty fortresses and their doughty fighters; enchanted elves, masters of the woods; not to mention the monsters—giants, trolls, goblins, ghosts, and dragons—that lurk everywhere.

To counter these inherent disadvantages, and to make and keep a place for themselves in a hard world, gnomes and halflings long ago developed several traits that allow them not only to survive, but to flourish. Common to both races is an instinct for avoiding direct conflict when possible. Just as valuable is a gift for being unobtrusive. But most important of all, perhaps, is the open-mindedness both halflings and gnomes show in their dealings with members of other racial groups.

Despite the many traits they share, gnomes are not halflings and halflings are not gnomes: each race remains distinct unto itself. Consequently, this book is divided into two major sections—one about gnomes and the other about halflings. These sections contain all a player or DM needs to know about the society, character, subraces, and kits of these diminutive demihumans.

Still, it's worth thinking about a few considerations that apply to both gnomes and halflings, especially those that relate to their size (which is small not just in comparison with humans but most of the other intelligent creatures with which they share their world). These are the traits of the races that are most useful to players, as well as important hallmarks of any all-gnome or all-halfling campaign.

Cooperation

Gnomes and halflings both have learned the value of cooperating with members of other, larger races. Halflings typically carry this interaction farther than do their bearded cousins, but gnomes, too, understand that alliances and friendship make for more prosperous neighbors than do feuding and war. Members of both races are not inherently adverse to making business deals with dwarves, humans, and elves—or even humanoid monsters, provided there is no inherent racial antipathy. Even where such enmity exists, as between gnomes and kobolds or goblins, it is usually the result of competition for living space; in settings where this traditional bone of contention is absent (as in the AL-QADIM® setting of Zakhara), gnomes find it easy to befriend even these traditional enemies. Naturally, halflings and gnomes alike will be cautious regarding offers of mutual cooperation from those who have been active enemies in the recent past, but at least they will give such offers a fair hearing.

Alliances: The value of a military pact with a strong neighbor is an obvious one to any race. The trick, however, is to avoid the smaller partner being dominated or swallowed up by the larger. The small folk have developed diplomacy into an art and are adept at being able to negotiate mutually-beneficial pacts with a variety of their neighbors. For example, elves and dwarves might ally themselves with different groups of humans but not with each other, while the humans probably will have trouble getting along even among themselves. Halfling or gnome communities in the same area are quite likely to have mutual assistance agreements worked out with the above mentioned dwarves, elves, and several of the human nations. Of course, these pacts will apply to outside threats only, as the small folk have no desire to get involved in the internal power struggles of their neighbors.

Even in cases where no military alliance is formed, a community of the small folk will strive mightily to maintain peace with its neighbors. Halflings and gnomes will readily suggest or agree to negotiation over points of contention, and they are capable of carrying on these talks for a very long period of time. If a group of humans decides to resolve an issue by force, the small folk will probably agree to the terms without violent resistance unless a matter of strong principle is at stake. However, even in acquiescence the halflings or gnomes might find a way to make the human victory a hollow one.

Say, for example, that a small patch of forest forms a common border between a human town and a halfling village. The halflings will strive to see that the woods is preserved and shared, even to the point of bestowing upon their neighbors gifts of game, mushrooms, and nuts from the woods. If the humans suddenly claim the woods as their exclusive property, the halflings will spend a long time trying to talk them out of this selfish notion—and they'll continue to use the woods as they always have for so long as the talks last.

If, however, the local human ruler issues an order barring halflings from the forest and sets guards around it to see that he or she is obeyed, the halflings will probably resort to discreet poaching, using their skills at moving silently to evade the guards. Ironically, without the tending of Forestwalkers and Leaftenders (see the halfling kits), the forest will produce much less—and the humans probably can't even *find* the mushrooms! Within a short time, the woods will become a wilder, more desolate place. Thus, both sides suffer from the humans' greed, and—if the friendship between the communities is maintained—the halflings will hope that in a few years the human policy can be reversed.

In an extreme case, where the human ruler decides that the woods should be cut down and the lumber used to build him or her a new summer palace, the halflings might be driven to more dire resistance. If the forest is really important to the community's survival and identity they may feel compelled to fight for it. Rather than declaring war on their neighbor, they will sabotage logging operations, waylay small parties of loggers, and generally make the project too time consuming and expensive for the humans to continue.

In all cases of possible conflict, halflings will first try affability, progressing from there to passive resistance, and only resorting to guerilla warfare if all else fails. Gnomes (especially Rock Gnomes) are somewhat more quick to anger under mistreatment, but they too will never be the aggressors and will gladly end hostilities at the very first opportunity. It's easy to underestimate the small folk, but they make tenacious foes to those who insist on becoming their enemies.

Intermingling: To varying degrees both kinds of small folk are open to the cultures of other races, whether this means individual gnomes and halflings living amongst humans, dwarves, and elves or accepting members of the "Big Folk" into their own communities. Between gnome and halfling, a member of one group will be warmly welcomed and feel quite comfortable living among or visiting the other.

When gnomes or halflings live among another race, say in a populous city, they are adept at retaining their old customs while adapting them to the traits and peculiarities of the people around them. The hearth, so essential to the halfling, or the fire without which no gnome dwelling would be complete, will be found anywhere a member of the respective race calls home—even if "home" is a corner in a crowded tenement and the hearth a mere

ELMORE '92

candle or a tiny flame nourished within an oilpot.

At the same time, the small folk will venture forth, sampling the city's wonders, exploring its corners bright and dark, and as likely as not making a few friends in the process. Within a short time after their arrival, chances are that they will be productive and popular members of the urban community.

The Invisibility Factor

There isn't any magical vanishing act (with the exception of certain gnome illusionists), but both gnomes and halflings have inherent talents at "blending into the woodwork," so to speak—at least, in situations where they desire not to be noticed. This is not so much a matter of size as it is of skill; a skill they take time to cultivate (it's significant that the favorite game of both gnome and halfling children is "Hide and Seek"!).

In woodland settings, this trait is illustrated most effectively by the halfling's ability to literally disappear among the underbrush. While gnomes aren't quite so adept at this, their keen sense of hearing and ever-present diligence generally allows them to hear someone approaching and take shelter before they are discovered.

In more social circumstances, the small folk are adept at directing attention away from themselves, whether in a city street, crowded tavern, or elegant dinner party. By moving quickly and smoothly, the diminutive characters will often cause a human or elf to react with "I could have sworn there was a gnome there! Where'd he go?" And when others are asked, it turns out that no one saw him leave or arrive, but they all have some vague memory of his presence! Under most circumstances, it's possible for a gnome or halfling to slip away with little or no warning.

One skill developed by both of these races is the art of diversion, often in very subtle forms. With a quick glance off to the side, a slight widening of the eyes, or sharp intake of breath, many a halfling or gnome has successfully diverted the attention of another character. Halflings use the time thus gained for some quick picking of pockets or other sleight of hand and to escape from potentially sticky situations, while gnomes use it to buy time and to set up elaborate practical jokes.

Fighting Small

When courtesy and elusiveness both fail and the small folk are forced into combat, they are adept at using their size to their own advantage. Whenever possible, halflings and gnomes will choose to fight in an area where larger creatures are hindered by overgrowth, low ceilings, or narrow constricting passages. Gnomes are particularly skilled at fighting giant-class creatures, using their small size and nimbleness to gain the −4 bonus to Armor Class against them; halflings employ their Dexterity in other ways and have mastered the use of small missile weapons so that they can do battle with larger creatures before those hulking brutes get close enough to grapple.

In their homes, villages, burrows, and warrens, the small folk will often prepare an escape route that is only large enough to let a gnome or halfling squeeze through. If these crawlways are framed with sturdy stone entrances, they can effectively block pursuit by larger creatures—and even if they're merely dirt, the time and effort needed to expand the tunnels often allows the fleeing gnome or halfling family time to escape.

In any conflict, the rules the small folk rely on to survive are easily summed up: never lose your head, take advantage of the Big Folk's bulk and clumsiness where possible, and, when all else fails, run away.

Gnomes

The full moon cast its pure illumination across a region of rocky hills, etching each knob in coral light or black shadow. Fringes of forest clustered among the stone of cliff and pinnacle, like shaggy hair trailing from the scalp and shoulders of granite-faced giants. Higher and higher the moon climbed into the night sky, bringing more of the landscape into brilliant relief.

Yet even that brilliance did not penetrate the shadowy realms of forest in the valley bottoms, where dank cliffs glowered overhead and narrow tracks wound their way through inky shadow.

It was here, on these invisible trails, that small figures moved in steady progression. They came from everywhere, emerging from narrow cave mouths in the rocky cliffs, or dark ravines in the depths of the forest glen—and even from gaps in craggy stumps, where the hollowed shells of ancient trees provided this small folk with access to their well concealed abodes.

They remained in the shadows as they followed the secret tracks. Each figure was short, no more than half the height of a man, but these little folk walked with a confidant and steady march, as if they knew that nothing would stand in their way on this night. Small beards, neatly trimmed around the chin, distinguished the faces of the males, while the rounded cheeks of the females were framed by long, unbound locks of curling hair.

Finally the marching columns came to a gathering of the trails, and here the path entered a narrow slot between two sheer and craggy cliffs. One after the other these small folk marched into the crack, following the twists and turns that would have blocked the passage of a creature any taller or any wider.

Eventually the enclosing walls spread away, letting the glory of the moonlight reveal a rock-walled valley. A pond of cool water reflected the light in wind-rippled sparkles, while a narrow waterfall spumed like a column of ivory down the face of a towering cliff.

The file of figures marched steadily and silently into the vale, gathering by village and clan into its corners, settling themselves in grassy clearings or atop rocky outcrops. More than a thousand were already here, and thousands more had yet to come.

But enter they did, as the moon neared its zenith. Now the entire floor of the valley was washed by the cool illumination, as the last of the little fellows entered via the narrow crack. They settled themselves comfortably, and though the vale teemed with upraised faces, no sound disturbed the still, midnight air.

And then the moon began to fade.

The sturdy but diminutive gnome is perhaps the most misunderstood of the traditional AD&D® game character races. They're kind of like dwarves, of course... but isn't there's more to it than that?

Indeed there is. Gnomes do share some traits with their longer bearded cousins: they are exceptional miners, comfortable underground, and resistant to magic. Yet, to the shorter nosed dwarves, gnomes seem excessively frivolous, sometimes even weaklings. Gnomes are quite comfortable out of doors, well at home in a forest. The major rituals of gnomish life all occur beneath the stars, and no cosmic symbol is as important to them as an eclipse, in contrast to the dwarves, who prefer nothing so much as solid rock overhead and care little for cosmic occurrences of any kind.

Gnomes are also cheerful and social creatures, of good-tempered and tolerant disposition. They regard rudeness as a major fault—a characteristic which in itself is enough to mark them as very different from most dwarves! Gnomes relish the company of other gnomes and will eagerly compete in the telling of tales. Their calendar is marked by many festivals, each of which is an occasion of great feasting, drinking, singing, and dancing.

Although gnomes are friendly, they are also reticent; it is possible to know a gnome for many years without learning much about him (or her). When a gnome does become friends with a member of another race, that person is adopted by the gnome's whole family as someone they like and trust. Gnomes have much to fear from the larger creatures of the world, but they have not allowed this caution to become a compelling paranoia.

Very fond of good food, gnomes show little imagination in their recipes. They are skilled with fire, and quite uncomfortable—even forlorn—if circumstances prevent them from having an evening blaze.

Finally, the gnomes have raised the art of the illusionist to a cultural heritage that permeates many aspects of gnomish life and society. The steadfast loyalty and useful skills of a gnome character can provide fine additions to any group of adventurers.

Gnomes in AD&D® 2nd Edition

Gnomes as a player character race are introduced in the *Player's Handbook* and the *DUNGEON MASTER® Guide*.

In addition, as NPCs they have been covered with an entry in the *Monstrous Compendium*, Volume One. Two of the gnomish subraces are also covered in *Monstrous Compendium* entries—the Svirfneblin in the FORGOTTEN REALMS® Appendix (MC3) and the Tinker Gnomes (Minoi) in the DRAGONLANCE® Appendix (MC4).

New Stuff About Gnomes

This section of *The Complete Book of Gnomes and Halflings* will attempt to flesh out the gnome and his or her society. The way these little people live and interact, the things that motivate them to be brave, cautious, or shy, and the kind of world they desire for themselves and their offspring are all treated in some detail.

In addition, the various subraces of gnomes are distinguished—including the Rock Gnomes, who are the typical gnomes of the campaign world, as well as the Deep Gnomes (Svirfneblin) and the Tinkers. A new subrace, the Forest Gnome, is also introduced here. Close to Rock Gnomes in many ways, they are nevertheless a distinct group, preferring the habitat of wooded glades and deep meadows to the rock-and-dirt-walled underground lairs of their more common kin.

The section also includes a selection of player character kits for gnomes, each of which entails specific advantages and liabilities, allowing players to tailor their characters toward the specific desires of the PC's campaign and background.

The final chapter in this section briefly describes a typical gnomish village, designed so it will easily fit in any AD&D® campaign world. This warren can serve as a suitable 'home base' from which to launch an all-gnomish campaign. Finally, the Appendix at the end of the book contains several adventure suggestions for gnomish PCs.

CHAPTER 1

Myths of the Gnomes

The moon faded as the shadow of the world slipped across its surface, until the natural amphitheater—recently so brilliantly illuminated under the full circle of white glare—slipped into darker, deeper shadow. Finally, in nearly complete blackness, the masters stepped from their niches onto the stages of honor set around the gathering. Each of these stages was a pinnacle of rock, rising several dozen feet above the heads of assembled gnomedom.

One of these masters raised his hands and muttered an incantation. Immediately the midnight air around him flared into a blossom of red light, light that spilled like a shower of liquid onto the floor of the valley. Another master spoke, and green illumination grew in a spurting fountain around her. Soon other showers of light, in blues and whites and pale yellows, spread across the darkened vale. The rock walls reflected the magical flares until the whole of the bowl-shaped vale brightened under the illusionary magic.

Then the circle of lights faded again, as a file of stunted figures moved into the smooth clearing beside the lake. Abruptly, these gnomes raised their hands—and the tale of the gods began....

Unlike most other civilized races, the gnomes do not have a creation myth. Instead, they view the world—and their place in it—as a constant within the flow of time, changing only in small and insignificant ways. In the big picture, they assume that things will remain very much as they always have been. Good and evil, chaos and law, exist in equilibrium, and the preservation of this balancing act is the primary purpose of time.

A great wall of white light flickered into the sky. A fountain of golden sparks appeared in the midst of the pale illumination, and the whiteness encircled the gold like a mantle wrapping royal shoulders. Slowly a figure grew distinct—gnomish of form but enormous in size, covered with rippling golden, his eyes gleaming like twin diamonds of incomprehensible size and value.

Murmurs of appreciation and comprehension rippled through the assembled gnomes. They knew that this was the image of Garl Glittergold, the patriarch of the gnomish pantheon of deities from time immemorial. In mute confirmation, the gleaming shape of a huge, silver-bladed axe materialized in the god's hands. This, they knew, was Arumdina the Justifier, the great battleaxe that would cleave the enemies of gnomedom as easily as she might slice through water.

Other fountains of color spurted upward, and within them grew the shapes of additional gods—the mischievous and merry face of Baervan Wildwanderer; the calm, stoney features of Calladuran Smoothhands; the vibrant metal-faced visage of Flandal Steelskin; Segojan Earthcaller's benign features—until the whole cosmic family was represented in the bright vale.

Only then came the creeping white shadow, reaching forward with steel-shod claws, its shape like that of a blunt and blinded beast. It glowed like a corpse-candle, its illumination swallowing up all other light, its pale glare unmistakably pure evil.

The gnomes gasped collectively, and little ones instinctively shrank beside their mothers, for they all knew that this was Urdlen—the dark center of evil that remained, even within gnomedom, always ready to flourish in the world.

The gnomish outlook on life requires a very balanced view of the universe. Thus, while gnomes consider themselves and their race to be generally good, the force of evil in the world—and even within the gnomes themselves—cannot be denied. Indeed, only by acknowledging evil, by recognizing it as the counterpoint of goodness, can the balance of all things be maintained.

Like the gnomes themselves and the other gods, Urdlen the Evil One is assumed to have always been there, and to remain for all time to come. Yet only in the steady struggle against the creature and what it represents can the truly happy and vital nature of these people be insured.

The colors flowed and flamed. In their towering pillars they told of the great battles of life, as darkness ever strives to swallow light but always the brightness breaks through.

Thousands of gnomish throats first howled with laughter, then groaned in collective grief, as the images of the gods cavorted across the epic stage. They watched in awe as Garl Glittergold raised his axe, chopping at imaginary stantions of stone to bring a thunderous collapse—this was the tale of Garl's triumph over Kurtulmak the kobold god, in which Garl brings down the cavern that Kurtulmak would have made his prison upon his captor's head.

Next the images of a thousand gnomes, arrayed for war, marched from the cliff walls, striving toward each other with braying trumpets and drums that pounded like thunder. But again came Garl Glittergold, the goldenskinned giant of a gnome, and with a swipe of his axe he cast glittering sparks of light all across the ground. Immediately the gnomish host threw down their arms, and the audience roared with amusement as they scuttled about to collect the gems that their deity had scattered. By the time the gathering was done, the weapons were lost and the trivial argument that had once propelled them to war had been forgotten.

Central to the mythology and self awareness of the gnomes is a sense of the race's togetherness—even among the different subraces that make up the whole (see Chapter 2). Indeed, one of Garl Glittergold's main tasks in the world is to intercede in potential gnome-to-gnome conflicts, usually by humor and diversion. It is this awareness that makes conflicts among these folk—whether they be marital arguments, property disputes, disrespectful youth, bitter clan rivalries, or warfare—so extremely rare.

When they do occur, the practicers of violence (on both sides) are likely to face complete ostracism until the conflict is resolved. It is interesting to note that, once resolution is achieved, the gnomes are usually quick to forgive and to welcome transgressors back into the fold. Their patience is not limitless, however, and blatant aggressors or bullies who repeatedly hector others are not likely to be easily forgiven. Fortunately, such malefactors are quite rare.

The image of the goldenskinned gnome, surrounded by his entourage of lesser gods, cavorted from mountaintop to hillcrest, scampering around the vale that held so many of his people. They laughed and roared at his antics, cheering as he and Baervan sat together at a table and alternately stole a succulent haunch of roast back and forth from each other. The illusionary roast, which was the size of a small house, sizzled and sputtered, casting the warmth of steam and the scent of its juices enticingly across the gathering.

But then the crowd drew breath in hushed anticipation as they saw, lurking in the hollow below Garl's golden image, the hideous bulk of Urdlen, The Crawler Below. Reaching upward with steely claws, the hairless, blind beast groped for the higher gods, seeking to strike and injure them in its spite and hate. Small gnomish children, not yet initiated in the scope of the tale, shouted warnings, their squeaking voices rising above the hush and stillness of the vale.

Garl took no notice, however, instead choosing that moment to perch on one foot and do a wild, spinning dance for the edification of the crowd. Ever upward crept the monstrous mole, until those steel talons reached almost to the great god's golden boot.

Suddenly, just as Urdlen prepared to lunge at its apparently unsuspecting victim, Garl leapt into the air and did a double somersault backwards over the creeping beast, finally

coming to rest on a hilltop a full quarter-mile away. Hissing in hate and spite, the evil mole reared up to make a last desperate swipe at its escaping prey, only to overbalance in its haste and fall backward, rolling over and over like a runaway snowball as it slid down the slippery slope, not stopping until it hit the bottom of the shaded vale between the two summits. A moment later an avalanche of gems it had dislodged in its fall buried it from sight.

And then, to the echo of Garl's laughter and the relieved cheers of ten thousand gnomes, the shadow slipped from the face of the moon. As brightness again filled the vale, the performance of the illusions faded... and the celebration began.

The task of the gnome, as he or she views his or her place in the world, is a mixture of important work and equally important play. Whatever the nature of the job at hand, a gnome will apply himself or herself to it with great good humor, even carrying his or her joking wit and humorous outlook into the subterranean depths of a mine or down the forest trail.

But it is when the work is done that the true nature of gnomehood becomes apparent. No one could mistake a boisterous gathering of singing, dancing gnomes for a hard-working bunch of dwarves. Indeed, the humor that possesses them comes to the fore in these days of celebration. For example, the festival of the Lunar Eclipse described in this chapter runs until the next full moon. For a full month, the gnomes set their cares and chores aside, using the cosmic occasion as an excuse to gather from far and wide, spending their days and nights in a loud and boisterous celebration of themselves and their role in life.

Gods Of Gnomedom

Gnomes are not a tremendously devout folk, but they do have a well-developed pantheon of deities, and they like to honor their gods with frequent "observances"—rites that tend to be performed, naturally, as wild and raucous festivals. The major gods listed below are described in more details on pages 33-37 and 71 of DMGR4, *Monster Mythology*.

Garl Glittergold (Greater God) is the patriarch of the hierarchy and probably the most approachable of all the Greater Gods. He often travels the worlds looking for mischief to get into. He appears as a gold-skinned gnome with gemstone eyes that shift from sapphire to emerald to ruby.

A master of pranks, Garl is a good-humored jokester who is nevertheless proud and protective of his diminutive followers. His chief concerns are twofold: to see that gnomes everywhere cooperate and work together and to remind them that while life may sometimes be hard, it's important to always keep a sense of humor.

Garl carries his intelligent two-headed axe, Arumdina, everywhere he goes; she is more a companion than a possession. Although he is a capable fighter, he prefers to use trickery and illusions to accomplish his goals, and encourages his followers to do the same.

Baervan Wildwanderer (Intermediate God) is the most popular member of the pantheon after his friend Garl, for he is the protecter of the forests and glades that are so important to gnomish well-being. Even the Svirfneblin honor him as the "Father of Fish and Fungus." Baervan is also the patron of gnomish thieves and a mischief-maker to rival Garl himself. He is pictured as a spry old gnome with nut-brown skin and a jaunty beard. His friend and constant companion in his escapades is a giant raccoon named Chiktikka Fastpaws.

Callarduran Smoothhands (Greater God) is the master of stone, worshipped primarily by Svirfneblin. The Deep Gnomes consider him equal in might to Garl Glittergold, though he is largely ignored by the other subraces. It was Calladuran who taught Svirfneblin how to summon and befriend earth elementals. He will often send his avatar to aid his people; his appearance is that of a wiry Svirfneblin miner, indistinguishable from virtually any other Deep Gnome except for a golden ring with a star insignia he always wears.

Flandal Steelskin (Intermediate God), with his skin of mithril steel, eyes like flaming coals, and beard of silver-blue, is the patron of gnomish smiths—not just blacksmiths but also goldsmiths, silversmiths, and all other workers in metal. He is physically the strongest of the gnomish gods, and his uncanny ability to sniff of the veins of metal that thread through the earth makes him a patron of miners.

Segojan Earthcaller (Intermediate God) is a nature deity whose province is the creatures who burrow through the earth; he taught the gnomes how to befriend moles, badgers, and other subterranean animals. He appears as a grey-skinned gnome clad in armor made from grass and roots, accompanied by an intelligent stone golem.

Urdlen (Intermediate God)'s form is that of a white mole, hairless, sexless, and blind but with wicked claws of steel. A mindless force of malicious evil and destruction, Urdlen serves as a warning to every gnome to beware the taint of greed that lies within the gnomish delight in gems and jewelry. In keeping with the importance of a balance of forces, Urdlen's place in the pantheon is unquestioned, though the god is greatly feared and secretly reviled. Its few worshippers destroy gems and works of art to propitiate the god and thus are regarded as immoral villains by the bulk of gnomish society.

CHAPTER 2

Gnome Subraces

The gnome subraces are very distinct groups of these diminutive demihumans. Two of them, the typical gnome (also known as the Rock Gnome) and the Deep Gnome, or Svirfneblin, have been introduced and used in a number of AD&D® products. Hence, both have long been known to players and DMs.

The third type, the Tinker Gnome or Minoi, is a native of Krynn, encountered primarily in DRAGONLANCE® campaigns (though, distressingly, they have been known to spread to other realms through the use of Spelljammers). These beings are very much like typical gnomes in appearance, but their personality and outlook, and especially their overzealous love of technology, makes them very distinct as a subrace (and an extreme menace to themselves and their companions).

A fourth gnomish subrace, the Forest Gnome, is introduced here. These shy folk are relatives of the Rock Gnome, though they do not share their cousins' love of mining and excavation. The rarest of gnome subraces, the Forest Gnomes is most likely to be encountered in pristine woodlands and undisturbed wilderness. They tend this habitat with surprisingly fierce determination.

In keeping with the gnomes' lack of a creation myth, they have no folklore to describe the origin of the different subraces—the different branches of the racial family are assumed to have always been there. While there's no hostility between the subraces (unlike the High Elves and the Drow, or the Hill Dwarves and the Duergar), there is also little contact. Each subrace keeps mostly to itself, and it is *very* rare to find mixed communities of Rock Gnomes with Svirfneblin, Forest Gnomes, or (Garl forbid!) Tinker Gnomes.

Rock Gnomes

Big of nose, quick with a laugh, cheerful, visionary, and industrious in their approach to life, the Rock Gnomes form the picture of the gnomish race as it is viewed by most of the larger folk who know them.

"I've had some experience with the little fellows, if I do say so myself... matter of fact, I had a whole team of 'em apprenticing in my smithy a while back. They were good workers, too—though not quite serious enough for my taste. Too many jokes and pranks, not a good idea around a hot forge! And those illusions! Never did know if it was a real fire I was lookin' at or just one of them bright spells.

"Still, they caught on quick to everything I tried to teach 'em. They could shovel coal good as any dwarf—well, good as some *dwarves—and they showed a real gift for wielding the hammer and shaping the steel. 'Course, they don't have the patience to make a real quality sword or axeblade, but they had the technique down okay. They'd batter at it awhile, then one of 'em would make a joke and the next thing you know the bellows'd be idle and the metal would be gettin' cool.*

"Another thing, too—when it came to making the hilt, that's *where they really shined! I've never seen gemwork like those gnomes could do, working any kind of stone into a leather hilt, wrapping it onto the steel butt with scarcely a waver or imperfection. You know, as long as they let a dwarf do the finishing of the edge and the tempering of the blade, those gnomes could put the finishing touches on a weapon like you've never seen before!*

"When they were done with work—now that's *another story. Showed no proper respect for their teachers or elders. Sat around and drank like fish, far as I could tell. And* those *songs ! Many's the time I got up out of a sound sleep and had to kick 'em out of the place, just so I could get a little rest (I had to get the fire going before dawn, you know—that's* another *thing you couldn't count on the gnomes to do!).*

"Still, you know, I kind of miss 'em. Would have been glad to keep 'em on, too. A couple were skilled enough to be journeymen—might have even made the mastership! But that weren't for them. Nope, instead they learned what they could and then, all in a pack, just

up and left one day. I heard tell they went back to their grotto, but of course I've never been up there to check."

—Gwintroc Fanish, dwarf and master weaponsmith, on his experiences in working with Rock Gnomes

Rock Gnomes are the most common type of gnome among the known worlds, and indeed, when one speaks of a "gnome," chances are he or she means a Rock Gnome. While not a populous race in comparison to humans or other demihumans, they are encountered in a wide variety of environments, showing no particular preference for any one type of climate. They do, however, tend to make their homes in areas with an abundance of natural rock (even if it's invisible under a layer of loam and forest).

All gnomes have a fondness for gemstones of all kinds, and in fact each subrace has a stone that it reveres above all others. No other gnomish race, however, is as adept at cutting and shaping these precious baubles as are the Rock Gnomes. The gem symbol of this subrace is, appropriately, the diamond. Diamonds are used as symbols of status and accomplishment, and wealthy and highly regarded clans will often have dishes, candelabras, and other elegant possessions encrusted with these hard and precious stones.

The most distinctive physical characteristic of the Rock Gnome is an enormous nose—a proboscis that is larger than that of any dwarf or human, despite the gnome's diminutive size. Indeed, the size of one's nose is a matter of some status among Rock Gnomes, and more than one good-natured debate has resulted in actual comparisons being made. The true test of a mighty nose is the ability to poke it into your opponent's eye without having his nose do more than tickle the fringe of your beard (the use of the male pronoun is *not* generic here; females pride themselves on big noses too, but in addition to lacking beards they are less prone to such boisterous comparisons).

Rock Gnomes average about $3^{1}/_{2}'$ in height. Unlike the burly dwarves, who tend to weigh as much or more than the average human, Rock Gnomes are lightly-built. Their small frame is deceptive, however, for despite their size these gnomes are as strong as most humans.

The eye color of a Rock Gnome is predominantly blue, though shades of green and, rarely, yellow or brown are not unknown. Such unusual eye colors are apparent from birth and is considered to signify either very good fortune or very dire omens, depending on the traditions of that particular gnomish community.

The brownish color of the Rock Gnomes' skin can be encountered in many shades, ranging from a light tan to nearly black. While the race does not avoid the sun, they suffer no effects from exposure—they don't sunburn or tan, so the shade of a gnome's skin has nothing to do with the proportion of his or her life spent outdoors or underground. In mature adults, the hair and beard are almost universally white or pale gray, but in youngsters and adolescents one will find as wide a variety of hair color as among human-kind. Only the males are bearded, with facial hair growing in near the beginning of the gnome's second century of life. Unlike dwarves, however, gnome males keep their beards neatly brushed and trimmed, with a maximum length of only about six inches. Sometimes the beard will be trimmed into fashionable shapes such as a goatee, or brushed into a long, curling point (or pair of points, in a *real* statement of high fashion).

While the average lifespan of a Rock Gnome is in the area of four centuries, it is not uncommon to find an elder patriarch or matriarch who has been around for more than 600 years. The oldest of them have been known to approach the venerable age of 750 years.

The first half-century of a gnome's life is generally spent in a carefree childhood. Youngsters are indulged and benignly guided by their elders, with rarely a harsh word or punishment employed against them. The children learn by example and strive to please the adults around them. Sages attribute the fact that all gnomes respond better to praise and encouragement than threats to this upbringing.

By the time he or she has reached 50 years of age, a gnome is expected to begin applying himself or herself to the development of a useful skill and to learn the basics of self-defense and weaponcraft. However, during this half-century-long adolescence, gnomes are still not subjected to an array of responsibilities—instead, they are encouraged to experiment with a variety of trades and activities until they find those best suited to their own talents and personality.

The occasion of his or her hundredth birthday is of great significance to a Rock Gnome, for it indicates that he or she has reached adulthood. It is customary for his or her family to host a large party, with a gathering of any clans within traveling distance to celebrate the coming of age. Since the party itself is likely to run for a month or more, it is not uncommon for gnomes to travel hundreds of miles for such a get-together! Each clan will bring a practical gift for the newly anointed adult, and it is a cause for great pride if the present is judged to be the finest among the array of gifts. However, the practical nature of these tokens is inviolate—boots, a shield, a sturdy tunic, even a weapon or tool are all appropriate. Gem-encrusted baubles, works of art, or simple decorations, although highly valued by gnomes, will not be given as coming-of-age gifts.

The industrious nature of gnomes is well-documented, and probably represents their closest similarity to dwarves. Like dwarves, gnomes will organize for a task, with each individual lending his or her talents where they will be most useful. When digging a tunnel, for example, the strongest gnomes will work with picks to break up the rock in their path, while others—more nimble, if not so powerful—scamper among the flailing picks, scooping up the debris with shovels and pails. A third group of gnomes, those who are very hardy and capable of great endurance, will carry the crushed rock (often in wheelbarrows, but sometimes in leather sacks slung over the shoulder) out of the tunnel to the dumping grounds.

In their pursuit of mining, gnomes are not so speedy to excavate as dwarves, but they are more careful with what they find. Indeed, many a vein of ore that has been "played out" by dwarven standards has been taken over by gnomes and continued to yield its riches to the more meticulous gnomish miners.

Even while they work, however, these gnomes will pursue their tasks with high good humor, bawdy stories, and a succession of jokes of all types. Only rarely, however, will this frivolity interfere with the effectiveness of the group's work.

Nowhere is Rock Gnome precision more in evidence than in their stonecutting and gemwork. Their skill at cutting, polishing, and mounting gemstones is unsurpassed by any other race. They are also skilled enough metalworkers to make elaborate frames and mounts for jewelry. Indeed, gnomish metalsmiths work better with soft metals such as silver and gold than they do with iron and steel—another significant difference between them and their larger cousins, the dwarves. Gold chain belts, silver necklaces, and shining buttons are all proudly displayed by the well-accoutred gnome.

This is not to say that gnomes cannot become fine blacksmiths when they are so inclined. Indeed, every community will have at least one well-muscled resident who is in charge of toolmaking and of crafting other objects such as dishes and weapons out of iron and steel. Gnomes generally purchase steel from dwarves or humans, however, rather than smelting it themselves. The finest weapons in a gnomish community are generally of outside (dwarven or elven) manufacture, often purchased in trade with the gem and jewelry work that they do so well.

Rock Gnomes also can become skilled carpenters and (perhaps not surprisingly, given their dextrous and artistic nature) exceptional woodcarvers. Though most gnomes do not devote a lot of attention to fabrics, those that do are skilled tailors and embroiderers as well.

In the area of culinary skills gnomes are not so elaborate. In fact, their standards when compared to halflings are downright plain. Their ideal meal is boiled or roasted meat, unspiced, accompanied by potatoes and mushrooms. Also unlike halflings, Rock Gnomes rarely keep cows, so they have little milk, butter, or cheese. Their bread is unleavened and relatively unpalatable to others with more refined tastes.

In the area of brewing, Rock Gnomes believe themselves to be every bit the match of halflings and humans and insist that they make a much tastier beverage than the heavy mead favored by dwarves; some gnomes even champion their wares above the famed elvish wines. Impartial judges pronounce gnomish brews a distinctive but acquired taste. Gnomish brewers make a variety of ales and are ingenious at finding ways to chill these beverages even in the height of summer. They will employ underground storage caverns, often sealed in ice which is brought down during colder months. In fact, many gnome communities will have wooden piping systems installed from these subterranean coolers so that the amber fluid can be pumped to spigots on the surface. Any gnomish innkeeper worth his or her salt (high praise indeed for a gnome!) will have such an arrangement in the cellar, and as a general rule, the better the chill on the beverage, the higher the perceived quality of the establishment.

Rock Gnomes typically make abysmal

farmers, but they can be capable hunters and are excellent at gathering the bounty of their native woodlands, including nuts, fruits, grubs, mushrooms, and wild greens. A community will typically tend a small field of grain, which is used in about equal proportions to make bread and ale.

In one area Rock Gnomes most closely resemble elves among all the other demi-humans—in the category of music and dancing. Unlike dwarves, gnomes are very musical, and have designed and perfected a wide variety of instruments including flutes and horns, stringed instruments such as lutes and mandolins, and a great assortment of percussion. The latter range from concave rocks, rattles, cymbals, and gongs to standard drums made of hide stretched over a base of wood or metal. The most talented gnomish musicians are famed for their skill and highly sought as entertainers, and nearly every adult can play some sort of instrument; family gatherings often climax in a cacophony of music-making and merriment. Unfortunately (for non-gnomish listeners, at any rate) their vocal skills in no way come close to their instrument-playing abilities, and since they insist on singing along to most every kind of music, the resulting melodies are not necessarily pleasant to the non-gnomish ear.

A Rock Gnome's idea of an ideal setting for a home is an area of wooded hills with an underlying bedrock of limestone that can be transformed into a complicated network of lairs, tunnels, and stairways. Rock Gnomes are not so comfortable in the deep and dank recesses of the Underdark as, say, dwarves—or their own gnomish cousins, the Svirfneblin. Therefore, their settlements will almost always be found near the surface, where the steep faces of hillside or cliff can provide a number of entrances and airholes to a many-layered dwelling. Often these entrances must be reached along narrow and precarious trails—easily traveled by gnome-sized creatures but perilous to larger would-be intruders—taking one far above steep slopes of jagged rocks, or along the edge of a deep gorge, with a rolling torrent of icy water plunging below.

Rock Gnomes are very social creatures, and generally live in thriving, active communities. Such communities are organized into up to a dozen clans, and all permanent residents are member of one or another of these families. Smaller outposts may consist of a single tight-knit family, with a patriarch, matriarch, or pair of elders providing benign leadership over three or four dozen gnomes. The typical upper limit of any one community is 400-500 gnomes, mainly due to limitations in the surrounding food supply—not due to any desire for isolation from their neighbors.

Whatever the size of a Rock Gnome settlement, the chain of status will always culminate in one unquestioned leader. To this chief (who is usually, but not always, male) come all crucial decisions on matters of defense and trade, as well as the arbitration of the rare instances of discord within the community. When this chief makes a ruling or command, he or she is obeyed immediately, with a discipline that can instantly transform a pastoral community into a determined work force or warlike army at need.

Most communities of Rock Gnomes will be found within a few days' or weeks' travel of each other, with grand gatherings of the clans—often including four or five thousand gnomes—held every decade or so. These festivals can last for a fortnight or more and generally climax in frenzied musical performances, nose-measuring contests, tournaments to determine who is best at drinking, snoring, and other things, and feasting.

The individual burrows of the Rock Gnomes are small and tidy. Generally a married couple will have a small chamber to themselves, with all children (cousins as well as siblings) sharing a common room. Adolescents are segregated by sex, with a large burrow having two separate chambers for its young males and females respectively. Most of these private chambers will be connected via tunnels to a central family chamber, where the fire is kept, food is prepared and eaten, and the family members meet for the talk and socialization that occupies virtually all their nonworking waking hours. The common room will always have a chimney vented to the outside (often through a very long passage). Ideally, it will have some other access to fresh air and light as well—chambers with no window are considered oppressive and tomblike by many Rock Gnomes.

The family quarters will also connect (usually via an underground passage) to the other families that make up the clan; and similarly each clan in the community will be connected to the others. At every place junctures occur, there are large chambers. In the bigger towns these areas contain inns and shops, as well as open commons where impromptu parties (as well as many scheduled festivals) can take place.

Gnomes travel frequently among their communities, and many of them will venture into human or demihuman cities out of curiosity. They mix well with halflings and find life in a halfling village quite pleasant. Unlike halflings, they have no particular compulsion that holds them to their own homes or locales, and their long lifespans afford them the time to indulge their curiosity about how other races live.

While Rock Gnomes can survive and even flourish in a community of humans, dwarves, elves, or halflings, few would care to leave their fellow gnomes permanently. It's far more common for a gnome to live among other races for a few decades, perhaps even a century or more, before returning home to his or her own clan. Perhaps a quarter of all Rock Gnomes spend at least part of their second century "seeing the world" before returning to take up his or her role in clan affairs.

Rock Gnomes will sometimes welcome members of other races into their communities. However, humans and especially elves tend to find gnome cities claustrophobic, while the furniture and passageways between rooms are usually too cramped for the average dwarf. Halflings sometimes exchange extended visits to their gnome neighbors but it's a rare halfling who leave his or her own burrow behind forever.

Table 1: Rock Gnome Ability Scores

Ability	Minimum	Maximum
Strength	6	18
Dexterity	3	18
Constitution	8	18
Intelligence	7	19
Wisdom	3	17
Charisma	3	18

Ability Score Adjustments:
+1 to Intelligence; −1 to Wisdom

Languages: Gnome, Common, Dwarf, Halfling, Kobold, Goblin, and Burrowing Animal (the latter is a language of signs, grunts, and snorts that allows minimal communication with moles, badgers, weasels, and similar creatures, including giant versions).

Infravision: Yes (60')

Special Features: Rock Gnomes have a number of special abilities. These are described on page 22 of the *Player's Handbook* and are summarized here for easy reference:

Detect Underground Features—Like dwarves, Rock Gnomes can locate sloping passages (1-5 on 1d6), flawed stonework (1-7 on 1d10), and approximate depth (1-4 on 1d6) and direction (1-3 on 1d6) underground.

Saving Throw Bonus—The Rock Gnome gains a +1 bonus to his or her saving throws versus spell for every 3.5 points of Constitution.

Combat Bonuses—Rock Gnomes add +1 to all melee attack rolls against kobolds or goblins, their traditional racial enemies. They receive a −4 bonus to their Armor Class when attacked by giant class creatures (gnolls, trolls, bugbears, ogres, ogre magi, trolls, titans, and giants)..

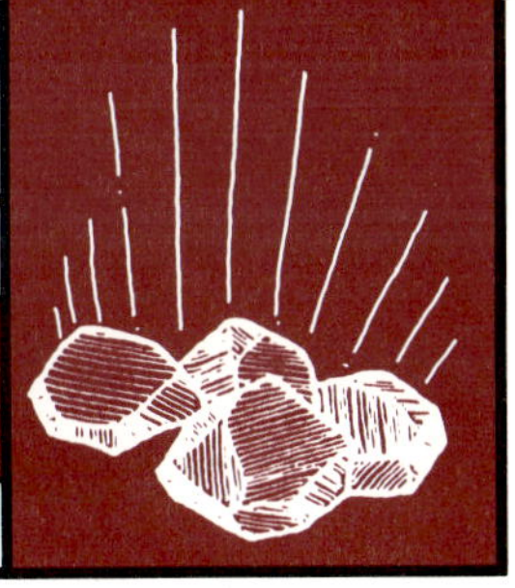

Svirfneblin (Deep Gnomes)

To most surface dwellers the gnomes of this race are mysterious denizens of the Underdark about whom little is known. Those who judge by appearance see them as stunted and gnarled creatures and believe them to be the Rock Gnomes' evil counterparts, the gnomish equivalent to the Drow and Duergar. In truth, they are no more evil than their more numerous cousins; their sinister reputation is merely the result of ignorance. The Deep Gnomes are the most reticent of all the gnomish subraces, surviving in an extremely hostile environment entirely by their own wiles.

"Svirfneblin? I loathe them—they are fit only to die on the tip of a Dark Elf's sword! They scurry about the sunless realms with tenacity. We kill them wherever we find them, and still they return! They show no fear of our Drow mages, even when dozens of them perish at a time. Even the priestesses of Lolth, while they slay the sniveling gnomes in mass, do not inspire enough terror to stop their malicious intrusion!

"And why do they come? The answer is gems. They thirst for precious baubles with a ferocity I have never seen. They will drive their tunnels into the farthest corners of the Underdark, and this is what makes them a threat to me and my people.

"I give you a tale of Desselderekathe, a great cavern network not so very far from my own home. Its mere existence was naturally a threat to us, and thus—more than a century ago—we sent an army to destroy it. I myself commanded a company of lizardriders in the assault.

"Our Drow forces struck them from all sides. My own cavalry entered through the cavern ceiling and rode down the walls, striking into the heart of Desselderekathe before the foe knew they were attacked. Our mages cast clouds of poison gas that settled into the city's low places, and into these we drove the screaming little pests.

"Within a few hours it was over—not a single Deep Gnome remained alive within the walls of Desselderekathe! We withdrew in triumph, and I myself was decorated by the matron mother of our city's greatest house! Yet within a decade we heard reports that renegade Deep Gnomes had moved into the abandoned ruins. We set a garrison in the place, but they suffered ambush and other treachery—and it proved too expensive to station a full army in what was otherwise a worthless shell. Though there were in fact some gem-bearing rock formations in the region, the excavation proved too troublesome to warrant the return. Seventy years ago we abandoned Desselderekathe, and now I hear that the place is again full of Svirfneblin! I suppose we'll have to do it all again, and I know these runts will not allow us to simply repeat our first attack. We shall have to devise a new tactic, one which may well be more costly in terms of Drow lives. And for what? Simply to insure our destiny, and our right to live in peace.

"You see now, I trust, why the Svirfneblin are fit only to be hated, loathed, and despised?"

—Fassyth Yssarial, Secondboy of House Twylleenimor, Imperial Drow City of Qaucium.

These diminutive inhabitants of the Underdark are as tenacious at survival as the just-cited opinion by their mortal enemies indicates. Unlike their Rock Gnome cousins, they have no friendly neighbors to ally themselves with, forcing them to become entirely self-reliant. Only the few who have won their trust know that they are in many ways as social and artistic as other gnomes.

Why do they endure this frankly hostile environment? The answer is simple: they are drawn by the lure of gemstones, which is more pronounced in the Deep Gnomes than in any other subrace.

The gem that most draws the interest and devotion of the Svirfneblin is the ruby, which is the predominant symbol of the race. The Deep Gnomes view these crimson stones with reverence approaching awe—so much so that they are never used for mundane practices such as ornamentation of garments, weapons, or armor. Rubies are reserved for sacred purposes and are often employed to decorate artifacts that are dedicated to the Svirfneblin gods. They are also favored by Deep Gnome monarchs, so much so that a Svirfneblin king or queen might have a full ring of rubies around his or her crown, with others of the precious stone set in the throne and sceptre.

Svirfneblin average between 3 and $3^{1}/_{2}'$ in height, rarely exceeding this norm by more than an inch or two. They are creatures of wiry muscle and tough bones, slightly thinner than their surface cousins but possessing as much strength as any other gnome.

Like their cousins of the other gnomish subraces, Svirfneblin have prominent noses. Otherwise their faces are much narrower. Many males have completely hairless bodies; most females have only thin and stringy hair, which they wear no longer than shoulder length. A Deep Gnome's skin is rock-colored, predominantly brown or gray. Eye color is always a shade of gray, sometimes so dark as to be almost black.

The Svirfneblin are not so long-lived as their surface-dwelling kin, living to an average old age of only about 250 years; a good number meet a violent demise before this time is up. They mature relatively quickly, however, with the first quarter century of life considered childhood and the next two decades as a period of disciplined adolescence. A Svirfneblin is assumed to reach adulthood somewhere around the age of 45 or 50, though this milestone is not marked by any grand ceremony such as is per-

formed by the Rock Gnomes. Indeed, the Deep Gnomes don't even keep track of the passage of days, so there is no way to record one's actual "birthday."

The most valued common skill among the Svirfneblin is that of the miner, with perhaps 75% of any given community's adult males devoting themselves to that pursuit. Svirfneblin miners are exceptionally able with pick and shovel, capable of chiseling a passage through solid stone more quickly than Rock Gnomes or even dwarves. While mining is broken into specializations, such as choppers (who do the actual pickaxe work), scouts (who locate promising veins for excavation), and haulers (who carry the tailings away from the scene), a Deep Gnome miner will be reasonably proficient at all aspects of his trade. The most alluring target of the Svirfneblin miner is, naturally, gems. However, these diligent diggers will also pursue veins of metal, including gold and silver, and they also occasionally gather a stockpile of coal or iron ore—from which they make a very passable steel.

A smaller percentage of the Svirfneblin work force (perhaps 10%) is engaged in the processing and finishing of the gemstone material excavated by the miners. These include polishers, smelters, carvers, and smiths. Though they lack a bit of the exceptional detail skill of the Rock Gnomes, in the other areas they are at least as proficient as their surface-dwelling cousins. Indeed (and unlike Rock Gnomes), Svirfneblin blacksmiths can possess exceptional skill. Their weapons and tools are generally made by Deep Gnome artisans, and these are nearly the equal of the products of the highest level of dwarven craftsmanship or Drow weaponsmiths.

Perhaps because suitable habitat is harder to find in the Underdark than on the surface, Deep Gnome communities tend to be larger than those of the Rock Gnomes. Generally the Svirfneblin live in thriving cities located in deep cavern networks, often with more than a thousand residents. However, these communities are generally separated by great distances from any others of the same subrace, and thus they tend to be more insular than the towns of the gnomes who dwell on or near the surface. Indeed, most Deep Gnomes live out their lives without ever seeing another Svirfneblin community beyond the one in which they were born.

Still, festivals and celebrations are as common among these gnomes as they are on the surface—it's just that the Svirfneblin don't travel from far distances for the gatherings. Instead, each community tends to have its own special observances, and though the whole city will turn out for many of them it is rare that any outside guest would be admitted. Also, these celebrations are not tied to recurring cosmic events, such as solstices or eclipses; instead, they occur when the city's priests declare that they are due. These instigations occur more for political and psychological reasons than by any regular passage of time.

In fact, it's worth noting that Svirfneblin don't even measure the passage of their lives in years—after all, the cycle of seasons has little meaning amid the eternal chill of the Underdark. However, if the priests notice that the production of the workers has begun to lag, or tempers are growing short among the chieftains and warriors, they will act hastily to initiate a grand festival full of pomp and song, good food and potent (one hesitates to say 'good') beverage.

Svirfneblin festivals are often invoked to recall great events of the past, though again these recollections bear no calendar relationship to the occurrence being commemorated. However, if teams of miners are preparing to embark on one of the periodic quests for new gems that propel so much of Svirfneblin activity, then the priests and illusionists will recall stories of grand expeditions in the past, even trotting out sacred objects encrusted with the jewelry made from the proceeds of these previous missions. Similarly, if a war is being contemplated, or a raid against some marauding monster becomes necessary, the warriors will be sent off with tales of great military campaigns in the past. It's interesting to note that these war stories are not all tales of victory—the Svirfneblin, perhaps because of the many defeats they have suffered over the years, have a keen interest in doomed causes and will draw considerable emotional support from the story of a dramatic last stand made by their forefathers. Even cautionary tales, such as the obliteration of a city by treacherous Drow attack, are related at these celebrations and used as a warning against future lapses of vigilance.

Another unique aspect of Deep Gnome society is that roles are far more rigidly determined by sex than in any other gnomish culture. Males perform all of the mining and warrior work that occurs beyond the borders of the community cavern, as well as most types of jobs within the city as well. Females concern themselves almost exclusively to the vital tasks of raising and preparing food (in the great mushroom farms that are a part of every Deep Gnome city) and the care of the young. In fact, females venture out of their cities so rarely that even the Drow have never encountered any in the neutral territory of the Underdark. Both sexes wear nondescript clothing which, with their ability to stand absolutely motionless, helps them avoid being spotted by enemies.

Besides the many types of fungi that are the staples of the Svirfneblin diet, Deep Gnomes sometimes maintain a small herd of rothe or other underground mammals. They are also fond of fish, and each city is likely to have several shallow lakes where blind trout and other subterranean delicacies are bred and captured. Deep Gnome women are responsible for tending of all these food sources and serve as the fishers and cooks as well as the farmers and herders. Also, salt is an important part of every Deep Gnome meal and is one of the most valued commodities in the trading of the Underdark. In fact, most Svirfneblin food is so heavily salted that a typical surface dweller would find it quite unpalatable.

As a beverage the Svirfneblin prefer for daily use a pungent brew made (naturally) from fungi, fermented by a unique process that involves great amounts of salt and not a little fish protein. It is highly intoxicating, tasting somewhat like an oversalted and watery fish chowder. It has been tasted by a few courageous non-Svirfneblins who (when they finally regain their voices) tend to decline a second serving.

The Svirfneblin also distill a strange drink known as Gogondy about which little is known other than it is deep red in color, kept in wrought iron bottles, and potent beyond belief. It has been called the finest wine in the world and is said to grant strange visions to those who drink it, but more than one human who drank it has promptly fallen asleep for decades or died after the first glass with horrified looks on their faces. The Deep Gnomes prize Gogondy almost as much as rubies and will only give or trade it to their most trusted friends, making it rare indeed.

The Svirfneblin survive in domains that are populated by many implacable enemies. The two most dire among these are the kuo-toa and the Dark Elves, who continually seek to drive these gnomes from territory they consider rightfully theirs. Illithids (mind flayers) often attack individual Deep Gnomes, considering them something of a delicacy, but never in such numbers as might drive away such tasty prey. Svirfneblin rarely encounter surface-dwelling gnomes, and the latter find them little less puzzling than do those of other races.

The cities of the Deep Gnomes are vast and complex places. Many layers of caverns, tunnels, and buildings are connected by narrow corridors and spiraling staircases. Generally, however, at least the central part of the city will occupy a single large cavern, with narrow streets winding among tall stone buildings. If large stalagmites are present, high-ranking Svirfneblin will claim these and excavate the interiors for the private homes; most residences, however, are carved into the natural bedrock of the earth.

Because of the confined nature of the environment, the home of the typical Svirfneblin family is more crowded than that of their surface-dwelling cousins. Parents and children will likely be crowded into a single, rather small, chamber. Families tend to be small, however, so this is rarely more than a half-dozen individuals. They are not so clannish as the Rock Gnomes, so that the population of a city is generally an amalgamated mass of Deep Gnomes, with overriding clan structure dividing the city.

However, they also tend to be rather quick-tempered and fractious (again, by comparison to other gnomish subraces). Every Deep Gnome city is ruled by both a king and a queen, each independent of the other yet equally powerful. The king's province is mining and protecting the community; the queen controls the food supply and is responsible for the day-to-day lives of the citizens. Both posts are determined by popular choice: when a monarch dies, a contest is held to select the best possible replacement, with the winner becoming the new ruler.

Svirfneblin worship the same pantheon as their Rock Gnomes cousins (although they conceive of these beings as Deep Gnomes). Urdlen plays a large role in Deep Gnome mythology, with cautionary tales of how he snared many an unwary Deep Gnome being a staple of any Svirfneblin's upbringing.

Table 2: Deep Gnome Ability Scores

Ability	Minimum	Maximum
Strength	6	18
Dexterity	6	19
Constitution	6	18
Intelligence	3	17
Wisdom	4	18
Charisma	3	16

Ability Score Adjustments:
+1 to Wisdom; +1 to Dexterity;
−1 to Intelligence; −2 to Charisma

Languages: Deep Gnome; Gnome Common; Underworld Common; Drow; Kuo-toan; earth elemental language (a curious "language" without words consisting solely of vibrations; each different pitch conveys a different message).

Infravision: Yes (120')

Special Features: Deep Gnomes have a number of special abilities detailed fully under the entry for Svirfneblin in the FORGOTTEN REALMS® appendix to the MONSTROUS COMPENDIUM® accessory (MC3):

Detect Underground Features—Svirfneblin are very good at determining slopes (1-5 on 1d6), depth (1-4 on 1d6) and direction (1-3 on 1d6) underground, and unsafe stonework (1-7 on 1d10).

Magic Resistance—Deep Gnomes have a base magic resistance of 20% and gain an extra 5% for every level beyond the 3rd.

Saving Throw Bonuses—Svirfneblin gain a +3 bonus to all saving throws except those against poison (for which they receive a +2 bonus instead).

Inherent Illusionist Powers—All Deep Gnomes radiate *non-detection*. In addition, all have the innate ability to cast *blindness*, *blur*, and *change self* once per day.

Freeze in Place—Svirfneblin can remain absolutely still for long periods, giving them a 60% chance to remain undetected by any observer, even one with infravision.

Surprise Bonuses—Deep Gnomes are only surprised on a roll of 1 on 1d10; they surprise opponents 90% of the time.

Defense Bonus—The typical Svirfneblin warrior has a Armor Class of 2. Deep Gnomes become harder to hit as they gain experience in dodging in combat, causing their Armor Class to improve by one point for every level beyond 3rd, to a maximum of AC −6.

Combat Bonuses—Svirfneblin make and wield *stun darts*, throwing them to a range of 40 feet, with a +2 bonus to hit. Each dart releases a small puff of gas when it strikes; any creature inhaling the gas must save versus poison or be *stunned* for 1 round and *slowed* for the four following rounds. Elite warriors (3rd-level and above) also often carry hollow darts with acid inside (+2d4 to damage) and crystal caltrops which, when stepped on, release a powerful *sleep* gas.

Tinker Gnomes (Minoi)

These unique creatures, native to the DRAGONLANCE® world of Krynn, are among the most technologically... er, perhaps we should say 'innovative' creatures among the known worlds. Unfortunately, their keen and inventive motivation is not matched by any particular talent—thus, a Tinker invention is at least as likely to cause harmful or fatal damage (probably to its creator) as it is to do what it's supposed to do. In spite of this, Tinkers are a thriving subrace that have even managed to spread beyond their native world.

"They're not real *gnomes, of course—don't know how anyone could think that they are! 'Course, they might look like us, and sound like us—but that's as far as it goes. There's not an illusionist among 'em, nor anyone else who's got a useful skill to his name, far as I can tell. Fact is, they're a menace!*

"As for getting into space, that must have been luck. One of 'em invented something that actually worked—a fluke, I assure you—and launched 'em into the stars. The only reason they're still up here is they haven't figured out how to get back down again.

"And if you ever see one of those ships of theirs, you'd know what I mean. It's got catapults that shoot nothing but air, gears and propellers that spin to no good purpose, and if you get close to it a blast of steam is liable to shoot out and barbecue you before you can say 'get me outta here!' "

—Kappelheim Gladdensnoot, famed Rock Gnome explorer and Spelljammer extraordinaire

The Tinkers are a very courageous and curious bunch of gnomes, and Gladdensnoot is no doubt exaggerating when he suggests that their attainment of Spelljamming travel is accidental. Nevertheless, he provides a good example of the attitude held by those few other gnomes who've encountered the Tinkers. Of course, it's not likely that the Tinker would stop and take notice—he or she is probably too busy working on the finishing touches of his or her newest invention (in fact, many Tinkers spend the bulk of their lives working on a few such 'finishing touches')!

In one respect the Tinkers resemble the rest of gnomedom—in the fact that they do value various types of stones, attributing to them great and supernatural powers. However, whereas the other subraces seek gems, the Tinkers hold a different substance as the grandest rock of all: coal. The Tinkers hold that coal (also known as the "Father of Steam") is the most valuable substance of the world, and those places where it can be mined quickly become Tinker Gnome warrens.

In size and stature, the Tinkers resemble Rock Gnomes—so much so that the difference is not immediately apparent, at least when based only upon appearance. Perhaps because their numbers are fewer, there is not such a variety of hair and skin color among Tinkers as is found in their more common cousins: their hair is almost always white or a slightly colored shade that is nearly white. Their skin tends toward brown, in ruddy and earthen shades. Their eyes are blue or, less frequently, violet, but the noses are every bit as prominent as those of any other gnomish subrace.

The clothing of a Tinker is likely to be representative of his or her travels and background—i.e., it will have parts of all kinds of things somehow attached together and providing a modicum of covering. As a rule, the more exotic the better, though the Tinker Gnomes tend to be fastidious about cleanliness.

Tinkers who live out their lives can attain an age of 250 or 300 years, but it must be

noted that this is a rare occurrence among the members of this subrace. If one of his or her own inventions doesn't do a Tinker in, chances are good that one of his or her neighbor's gadgets will.

Even in childhood, Tinkers are encouraged to experiment with gadgets and gimmicks, trying different means of making things to perform tasks that could otherwise be easily done by hand. The Tinker reaches adulthood at about the age of fifty (by which time perhaps 10-15% of them have already succumbed to the common fate of their kind). Despite this high attrition, it's not until maturity that a Tinker Gnome's activities begin to get *really* dangerous.

Upon reaching adulthood, the Tinker Gnome must select a guild for himself or herself. The number of guilds available varies by location, but in Mount Nevermind on Krynn—which is the center of Tinker civilization and by far the largest community of these inventive creatures anywhere—there are more than 150 active guilds. These include virtually all areas of practical endeavor, and quite a few impractical ones as well: Weaponry, Steam Power, Hydraulics, Mathematics, Agriculture, Warmaking, Animal Taming, Brewing, Carpentry, Astronomy, Ceramics (Rockmaking), Air Utilization, Historians, Coalmining, Rockcarving, Vehicle Design, and Music.

These guilds are not like the guilds common in many human and dwarven societies, however; in the latter cases, the guild's purpose is generally to impart the knowledge of the masters to a steadily growing crop of apprentices and journeymen. The Tinker guilds have a different philosophy dedicated to a righteously-held belief, to wit: whatever has been done before can be done better with a new and improved invention. Consequently, a Tinker

Gnome who enters the Music Guild, for example, will spend the bulk of his or her life trying to design a musical instrument with at least one more moving part than the last instrument designed by a guildmaster (it is not advisable to ask the guild for a performance—whole audiences have been scalded by ruptured steam pipes or deafened by ultrasonic waves of crushing sound).

A good example of the Tinker Gnome tendency of not knowing when to stop is the infamous Giant Space Hamster. Not content with this remarkable achievement, the Animal Breeders' Guild that created the creature promptly began working on developing new strains. The result include such monstrosities as the sabre-toothed giant space hamster, the carnivorous flying giant space hamster ("a regrettable if understandable line of inquiry"), the fire-breathing phase doppleganger giant space hamster, and the miniature giant space hamster (a dwarf variant the exact same size as the ordinary rodent).

However, Tinkers are nothing if not tenacious. After selecting a guild, each member of the subrace settles upon a Life-quest. The actual choice of the quest may take several decades, but once it has been decided, it becomes the reason behind that Tinker's existence. The Lifequest is an attempt to reach a perfect understanding of some device (anything from a spelljamming helm to a screw), a task at which the Tinker very rarely succeeds. Indeed, the best estimate is that less than 1% of these gnomes ever do fully grasp the nature of the object that has occupied their attention for so much of their adult lives; the rest of these easily-distracted gnomes get hopelessly sidetracked somewhere along the way.

Despite the vagaries of their existence, the Tinkers are a fun-loving and generally sociable race. Their speech is unique in both its speed and complexity. Two Tinkers can rattle off information and opinion to each other in a succession of thousand-word sentences, speaking simultaneously and yet listening and understanding (as much as is possible, given the esoteric nature of many discussions) each other even as they voice their own points of view. Those Tinkers who have had some experience interacting with other races have learned to slow the pace of their communication but never quite overcome their frustration with those who can't talk and listen at the same time.

Despite the chaotic impression given by an initial encounter with the Tinkers, these gnomes have a highly-organized societal structure. Their culture is unusual, for gnomes, in that guilds are more important to most Tinkers than their clans; the typical Tinker identifies himself or herself not by the family he or she was born into but the guild he or she joined upon reaching adulthood. The community is ruled by a council made up of the masters of the various guilds and the patriarchs of the various clans. The result is a paralyzed bureaucracy that nevertheless keeps itself going with debate, argument, near resolution, and subsequent disagreement. Following long and careful consideration (sometimes lasting for years, even decades) the various concerned parties go off and do whatever they wanted to from the beginning.

However, the debates themselves can be well-reasoned, extremely polite, and quite extensive. Just the recital of names at the beginning of a presentation can often take weeks, since the full and formal title of each gnome involved is used—and remember, this is despite the fact that Tinker Gnomes speak very rapidly indeed! For those Tinkers who come from extensive and well-documented ancestry and have themselves lived long and eventful lives, the formal introduction can last the better part of two days. Because of this inconvenience, an abbreviated form of a gnome's name (usually taking less than a minute to recite) is used in daily life.

Tinker Gnomes have the least involved family life of any of the subraces, since all adults are too involved with their Lifequests to devote much time to the raising of their children. The youngsters learn mostly by example, and of course are possessed of that insatiable curiosity that seems to take the place of so many other emotions in the lives of a Tinker. Tinker males and females accept their Lifequests with equal obsession; there is no difference between the sexes in level of recognition and attainment. For example, guildmasters and clan leaders are as likely to be female as male.

Their communities are located underground, but always close to the surface, with plenty of access to fresh air. Their penchant for burning coal to achieve steam makes good ventilation necessary—we needn't dwell on the unfortunate results of those experiments in deep subterranean quarters amid caverns warmed by vast, oxygen-devouring furnaces.

The various chambers of a Tinker community will be connected by various means of transport, powered by steam, spring-power, wind, water, gravity, and any other means available. Types include cars that run along rails or are suspended from cables and pulleys, soaring gliders, 'gnomeflingers' (i.e., catapults), elevators that run up and down through shafts bored through rock, and independently-steered carts and cycles propelled by various means. Needless to say, there is a high rate of attrition on gnomish transport—generally a character stands about a 3% chance per trip of suffering grievous injury (usually about 1-12 hit points of damage).

For private living quarters, Tinkers are inclined to settle for any old niche in the wall that can be closed off for a little privacy. They like to sleep in absolute darkness but have absolutely no trouble slumbering amid a thunderous cacophony of noise.

Far more important than his or her bedroom, to a Tinker, is his or her workshop. This area will be a private chamber, if the gnome is influential enough to warrant such a luxury, or if he or she inherits it from a deceased parent (for obvious reasons, Tinkers tend to gain their inheritance at a far younger age than do any other gnomish subrace). The shop should ideally be well-lit, by candle, coal-oil lantern, or natural light. One of the more successful gnome inventions is a network of mirrors aligned to reflect sunlight through long tunnels so that it reaches caverns far underground. Despite its utility, this invention is considered an abysmal failure by most Tinkers, due to its utter lack of moving parts.

Tinker Gnomes do not worship the usual gnomish pantheon, instead venerating the Krynnish god Reorx, patron of blacksmiths, crafters, and inventors. One of the oft-repeated pieces of evidence Rock Gnomes are wont to put forward in their neverending attempts to prove that Tinkers aren't "real" gnomes is that *"they haven't even heard of Garl Glittergold!"*

Additional details on the Tinker Gnomes can be found under the entry for "Gnome" in the DRAGONLANCE® appendix to the MONSTROUS COMPENDIUM® accessory (MC4).

Table 3: Tinker Gnome Ability Scores

Ability	Minimum	Maximum
Strength	6	18
Dexterity	8	18
Constitution	8	18
Intelligence	8	18
Wisdom	3	12
Charisma	3	18

Ability Score Adjustments: +2 to Dexterity; −1 to Strength; −1 to Wisdom

Languages: Tinker Gnome, Gnome Common, various human tongues

Infravision: Yes (60')

Special Features: Tinker Gnomes share many of the same special abilities as their Rock Gnome cousins, a fact which has led some sages to argue that Tinker Gnomedom is a culture rather than a true subrace. Whatever the truth, all Tinkers have the following innate abilities.

Detect Underground Features—Tinker Gnomes can identify sloping passages (1-5 on 1d6), flawed stonework (1-7 on 1d10), and approximate depth (1-4 on 1d6) and direction (1-3 on 1d6) underground.

Magic Resistance—The Tinker Gnome gains a +1 bonus to his or her saving throws versus spell for every 3.5 points of Constitution.

Combat Bonuses—Tinker Gnomes receive a −4 bonus to their Armor Class when attacked by giant class creatures.

Forest Gnomes

This subrace is not so common as are the others, but its members fill an important niche in their environment. Forest Gnomes are shy and reclusive, and often the mere arrival of human settlers within their wooded domain is enough to send them migrating to a new, unspoiled home. Nevertheless, they have been known to aid adventurers from other races and are particularly friendly with elves.

"For the longest time—and I speak of many *centuries—we didn't even know they were there. Of course, the Wyndhome Wood is a vast place, full of sheltered ravines and wide, hidden grottos... but we elves had always prided ourselves on knowing every inch of the place.*

"Then came the years of the Troll Tide, and we thought that the forest was lost. All of the elven clans banded together, and we fought for each tree—indeed, not a blade of grass or meadow blossom was surrendered to that horde without a fight—but it seemed that our defeat would be inevitable. There were too many of the brutes, too few of us.

"But then, when the situation had grown most dire, they *came from those ravines, from the shaded grottos and the darkest thickets, and they lent their arrows and their courage to our cause. Short and frail we judged them—harshly, I admit. But they're smaller even than halflings, and so shy that it was painful even to speak with them!*

"Yet they fought—and died, in great numbers—for Wyndhome, and their bravery was unsurpassed, their deadly skill decisive. At last, after many lives lost, many villages burned, the Troll Tide was turned away.

"In its wake the forest was left in ruins, with smoldering trunks stretching to the far horizons. Yet these shy gnomes—these tiny creatures whose aid had turned the balance of battle—joined with us for the task at hand. It was an effort that took years, but during those years we forged a lasting friendship.

"My people were stunned to learn that the Forest Gnomes had dwelled as our neighbors since the very time of our arrival in the wood—and never *had we so much as suspected their existence! Sadly, it took a war to breach the wall of their privacy.*

"But now that struggle is in the past, and for both our peoples we rest secure in the knowledge that, whatever challenges the future holds, we shall face them with our allies at our side."

—Kasseryth Daltine, Elven Captainrider and hero

The Forest Gnomes prefer a life in which no one knows who they are or where they live. They dwell in large swaths of woodland, and—unlike the other gnomish subraces—prefer to dwell in houses that are at least partially above ground. They are creatures of nature far more than any of their cousins, and to those rare folks who meet them (and pass through the walls of initial shyness) they can prove to be steadfast allies and delightful companions.

However, this subrace has not totally abandoned the love of gemstones that is so inherent to all gnomes. The emerald is the favored gem of the Forest Gnomes, no doubt because it most accurately reflects the healthy colors of their verdant homelands. While these gnomes can make excellent gemsmiths and jewelers, their work tends to be reverent images of the flowers, leaves, butterflies, and birds that are such a key part of the Forest Gnome's environment.

These are the smallest of the gnomish subraces, averaging from 2′ to $2^{1}/_{2}$′ and peaking out at a few inches under three feet. They share the stocky physique of the Rock and Tinker Gnome and the bulbous nose which is so characteristic of the race in general. They are the only gnomes inclined to wear beards and hair very long, and an older male is likely to have a beard that extends to within a few inches of the ground, and hair that, when unbound, falls all the way to his waist. These beards are a source of great pride to the venerable males, and they often trim them to a fine point or curl them into hornlike spikes that extend to either side.

The skin of a Forest Gnome tends toward a greenish cast of tan rather like bark, although often darkened and ruddy from exposure to weather. Their eyes are generally brown or blue, but green eyes are not unheard of and are considered very attractive and the omen of a good life for their owner. Their hair color is brown or black, often becoming gray or white in old age.

The Forest Gnomes are a very long-lived people, with an average life expectancy approaching 500 years. Childhood and adolescence blend together in the growing process. Since these gnomes do not generally embark upon a craft or apprenticeship as a life speciality, there is no need to differentiate a carefree youngster from an equally happy-go-lucky youth. Adulthood is granted upon the hundredth birthday, and this anniversary is a cause for great celebration.

Shy and timid when it comes to relations with other intelligent races, Forest Gnomes are very determined caretakers of their wooded domains. They are viewed with friendship by the animals of the forest and have developed a limited language of signs and sounds (similar to the Rock Gnome's 'speech' with

burrowing mammals) that allows them to communicate with these creatures, though without a great deal of detail. Thus a squirrel might chatter something about an intruder in the forest and even indicate the general direction of the trespasser, but it can provide no information as to the nature, size, or numbers of the possible enemy (as a rule of thumb, consider all such communications to consist of a single word only; i.e. "danger!" "food," "happy," and the like).

Forest Gnomes are also very adept at protecting and caring for the plant life of their woods. They gather the nuts, fruit, and other bounty of the woods for sustenance, taking meat only infrequently—and always with a reverent ceremony to the spirit of the animal slain by the gnomish hunter. They despise the use of traps, never employing snares, pitfalls, or such traps themselves. When they encounter such devices set by humans or others, the Forest Gnomes have been known to rig the traps so that they capture (with a snare) or injure (as with a deadfall or pit trap) the trapper when he or she comes along to check for game. Generally, the trapper receives the same effect that his or her trap would have inflicted upon an animal.

Aside from meat, Forest Gnomes eat their food raw, though with a great deal of ceremony and politeness. Even a nut or a berry is only consumed after the tree or bush that gave it life has been properly, albeit silently, thanked. Needless to say, meals among the Forest Gnomes are very long, quiet affairs.

These diminutive beings are exceptional woodcarvers, far more skilled than any other subrace at the working of this natural material. They can also be skilled carpenters, and their skills lean heavily toward natural-looking renditions of their structures. A storage shed, for example, might be built to resemble a clump of tightly-clustered pine trees, concealing the fact that there is any kind of structure there at all.

Priests have a higher status in this society than in any other gnomish culture. Baervan Wildwanderer is the patron deity of most of these clerics and has blessed them with a number of duties and tasks, most of which involved the protection and preservation of the forests and the wild creatures found there.

The most hated enemies of the Forest Gnomes are orcs, with troglodytes and lizardmen close behind. These creatures will be ruthlessly attacked and ambushed whenever they are encountered. Despite their shyness, Forest Gnomes have made friends with elves and halflings, though they tend to distrust humans and dwarves, who in their experience all-too-often view trees only as so much firewood. Occasionally, with great courage, one of these smallest of gnomes will venture out of his or her forest domain in a quest to see the world, though he or she will usually try to return after a few years and will never be entirely comfortable in a place that has no trees.

The gnomes of this subrace tend to live in smaller communities than do their kin, largely because their numbers are so much fewer. A Forest Gnome village will average less than a hundred residents, and the family homes that make up the "village" may be hundreds of feet apart. They are always located in a dense woods and are virtually invisible to anyone who happens to wander through—even a veteran woodsman might stroll down the main street of a Forest Gnome village without knowing he or she was in anything other than trackless wood. In part, this is because the forest gnomes disdain the use of tracks and trails—they are adept at moving through the underbrush while leaving no sign of their passage. Also, their dwellings tend to be concealed within the trunks of large, hollow trees and, sometimes, into burrows that extend below the surface of the ground.

The preferred house of a Forest Gnome, however, is above the ground and within the comfortable wooden enclosure of a tree trunk. These creatures prefer lairs of many different levels since, even to these small gnomes, most hollow trees don't provide a lot of floor space. Instead, the house will be a network of cylindrical rooms, usually no more than four feet from floor to ceiling, connected to the floors above and below by tiny trapdoors and rope ladders or, sometimes, spiraling stairways carved into the wood of the tree. Each floor will have a few windows opening to the outside, but these will be so cleverly camouflaged on the outside by bark or limbs as to be virtually invisible.

Excavated chambers are used for the commons areas of the Forest Gnomes, so that when a whole community gathers (as they do many times a year, to observe this or that celebration) they can do so in large, earthen caverns concealed underground. These chambers are connected by dirt tunnels and are often quite large, with ceilings reinforced by timber and brace. Forest Gnomes have no interest in excavating through stone, and though they will occupy a natural cave if they find one conveniently located, they will never dig into bedrock to expand or shape their surroundings.

A village of Forest Gnomes is organized very much like a large family, with the oldest patriarch or matriarch in the community generally revered as the venerable leader. As far as actual societal organization, there is very little—when Forest Gnomes act as a group (for example, to defend their woodland or migrate to a new homeland) they do so because the necessity of action is obvious to every member of the clans.

Forest Gnomes are sometimes mistaken for brownies by those humans who catch a rare glimpse of them, but the two races are not related. For one thing, brownies prefer rural settings—farms and small human or halfling villages; the very environments Forest Gnomes go out of their way to avoid—to the forest. Despite their size, brownies are more closely related to elves than any of the other demihuman races. Also, brownies are highly magical, while Forest Gnomes distrust magic and make less use of it in their daily lives than any other gnomish subrace. The two races are friendly, but their paths seldom cross.

Table 4: Forest Gnome Ability Scores

Ability	Minimum	Maximum
Strength	3	17
Dexterity	8	19
Constitution	8	18
Intelligence	3	17
Wisdom	6	18
Charisma	3	18

Ability Score Adjustments:
+1 to Dexterity; +1 to Wisdom;
−1 to Strength; −1 to Intelligence
Languages: Forest Gnome; Gnome Common; Elf; Treant; forest mammal
Infravision: No
Special Features: The Forest Gnomes have several characteristics in common with their racial cousins, as well as several unique abilities:
Pass without Trace—A Forest Gnome can pass through any kind of wooded terrain without leaving a sign of his or her passage.
Saving Throw Bonus—The Forest Gnome gains a +1 bonus to his or her saving throws versus spell for every 3.5 points of Constitution.
Hide in Woods—Like the halfling, a Forest Gnome can make himself or herself virtually invisible in wooded surroundings.
Combat Bonus—Due to size and quickness, Forest Gnomes receive a −4 bonus to their Armor Class whenever they fight man-sized or larger creatures. Also, they get +1 bonuses on all attack and damage rolls when fighting orcs, lizard men, or troglodytes, or any creature which they have directly observed damaging woodlands (e.g., a woodman chopping down a tree full of birds' nests).

CHAPTER 3

Gnomish Culture

Soon the cool wash of moonlight illuminated the vale, the disk of shadow passing across the lunar face. Brilliant in the glory of the summer solstice, the silvery orb outlined the thousands of gnomes in white light and shadow.

Then the bonfires flared into life, dozens of them flickering into the sky, silhouetting rings of small, dancing figures. Soon the rugged cadence of chant and song, accompanied by the wail of pipes and the strident beat of the drums, echoed from the looming cliffs.

Finally, the full brightness of the moon was restored; in the stark outline of light and dark, the festival commemorating the moon's rebirth began.

Living for the most part isolated from the other cultures of their worlds, the gnomes thrive and prosper. Their labors go unnoticed by mankind, their mines undiscovered by the dwarves. The Forest Gnomes, in their dense and tangled thickets, remain unseen even by their sylvan neighbors, the elves.

Who are these reclusive folk? How do they live, and what lure draws some of them from their pastoral homes and onto the road leading to adventure and peril?

This chapter looks at several aspects of gnomish life and culture. It addresses those traits that all gnomes have in common, since the previous chapter was devoted to the differences between the subraces. Where exceptions exist, these are noted where possible.

Festivals

All gnomes enjoy festivals. These celebrations typically involve much music, dancing, feasting, storytelling, illusionary magic shows, drinking, and contests of strength and wit. While the actual festival observances vary somewhat by subrace, a given community will generally gather for no less than 12 to 15 big celebrations every year.

These will be for many different occasions, including celebrations of harvests, seasonal occurrences like the solstice and equinox, and anniversaries—of birthdays, famous victories or discoveries, and even weather phenomena. Rock Gnomes have been known to hold celebrations to commemorate the date of a horrendous cyclone that once ravished their realm, the eruption of a volcano, or even a notable blizzard; anything which might serve as a good excuse for a party. The patterns can vary by subrace, since Svirfneblin don't keep track of dates and the Tinkers often forget what year it is, yet gnomes of all types seem to have a communal sense of when a gathering is needed. When the time is right, they'll get together.

The truly major festivals, however, are often years apart. The festival commemorating the total eclipse of the moon, for example, only takes place about once per century. For Rock and Forest Gnomes, this is the most significant occasion of all, and as such it calls for the grandest festival. Svirfneblin reserve similar festivities for the coronation of a new king or queen, while Tinkers celebrate the successful design and completion of an invention—now *that's* rare! Likewise, a gnome's most significant birthday in most subraces is considered his or her one hundredth.

Another trademark of the gnomish gala is that they go on for a long time—the bigger the occasion, the longer the celebration. Even the smaller festivals are generally two-day affairs, with the first day devoted to preparations (such as rehearsals of performances and cooking the wide variety of food necessary for the feast). The second day, beginning at dawn, is likely to be a sequence of songs and performances, mixed with appropriate rituals and remembrances, and liberally spiced with many opportunities to eat and drink. Ale and wine, together with the music and revelry, flows freely from dawn to dusk and throughout the following night.

The greater festivals last many days or several weeks, with the most significant lasting a full month or more. However long the celebration, the gnomes are generally quite ready to pitch back in to work as soon as the festivities are concluded. In the case of the longer celebrations this is an especially good thing, since a month of extreme partying can pretty much exhaust the food and drink reserves of a community!

Fires

Gnomes have a peculiar fascination with flame and the light it brings into the darkness in which they would otherwise dwell. One well-known gnomish nursery tale relates the story of Verpoolisch Popplepip, a typical gnomish hero:

A master illusionist and thief, Verpoolisch crept into the halls of the gods and watched the deities labor at their forges. Becoming intrigued by the shower of sparks falling from their great hammers, he substituted an illusionary brightness for a real spark and stole the actual flame. By the time the gods realized the deception, Popplepip had made it safely back to the world. There he nourished his spark, and it became the father of fire. With typical generosity, the gnomes shared this blessing with the rest of the world.

Every gnome has a place in his or her home for a small fire, and in pensive moments he or she will be inclined to sit before the flame and meditate.

Marriage and Family

Weddings, perhaps surprisingly, are not big social occasions. Instead, they are private ceremonies attended by the immediate families of the young couple—and even these guests soon depart to leave the newlyweds with a chance to get to know each other privately.

Bride and groom have generally been friends since childhood and have made the match of their own free will. Marriage commonly occurs during the decades immediately following the coming of age period for members of that specific subrace, though gnomes who choose not to wed are not ostracized or even considered odd. Gnomes marry for companionship as much as procreation, and a couple will almost always remain happily married until one or the other of them passes away. Remarriage is rare, although it has been known to occur; divorce is unknown.

Gnomish couples rarely have the numerous broods familiar to halflings and humans. A family with three children is considered large, and only sizable clans will have five or six youngsters dwelling in the warren at any one time. Even in adulthood, gnomes retain deep bonds of friendship with their siblings and parents. It is very common for brothers and sisters to join together in business endeavors, for example.

The Nose Knows

The big schnozzola is an important status symbol among all of the gnome subraces. Parents proudly point out the size of their children's noses and make enthusiastic prognostications about future growth. While the practical applications of such a facial feature are admittedly limited, gnomes will frequently embark on size contests, with heavy wagers, between members of rival clans. Svirfneblin go so far as to make this a primary determinant in the selection of a new king or queen!

Food and Drink

Gnomes enjoy feasting and drinking, but their diet and beverage selection reflects far less variety than does that of the halfling or even most communities of humankind. No gnomish subrace, for example, uses yeast in the baking of bread nor in its brewing. They don't keep cows or make cheese or butter. Sugar is unknown in their diet, and gnomes tend to avoid sweets even when they travel to places where cakes or candies are available. Also, spices and sauces are rarely employed in the preparation of gnomish cuisine.

However, those foods that gnomes do cook they cook well. They are excellent at preparing wild game and in using the natural products of their surrounding areas for salads and hot dishes. All gnomes like salt, although the Deep Gnomes carry this to the greatest extremes. They cook their meat until it's very well done. This tendency, coupled with the liberal use of salt, insures that the food keeps for a long time without spoiling.

The brewing skills of the gnomes are effective, even if the results are not exactly tempting to humans and other demihumans. Heavy meads and ales are favored. In areas where fruit can be readily harvested (apples and cherries are preferred) gnomes make passable, if somewhat astringent, cordials.

Gems

More than a medium of wealth, gems are cherished to a degree difficult for non-gnomes to comprehend. Every gnome has a small gem he or she will carry at all times, often feeling or stroking it when thoughtful or troubled. Every gnomish village will have a few particularly splendid stones that belong to the community as a whole, each with an accompanying legend, and enchanted gems are the favorite magical items of gnomish spellcasters.

Craftsmanship

The single most artistic endeavor of the gnomish craftsman (excluding Tinker Gnomes) is, of course, the carving and mounting of precious gems. These little folk are adept at every aspect of the jeweler's trade, including the smelting and finishing of precious metals. While each subrace has a special affinity to a certain type of stone (diamond, ruby, and emerald respectively for the Rock, Deep, and Forest Gnomes; coal for the Tinkers), their gemcarvers are capable of working with virtually any type of stone.

This artisanship goes beyond mere rote skill. Gnomish jewelers are capable of very creative designs in jewelry and have developed the most elegant royal crowns, sceptres, and decorative sculptures known to demihuman-kind. Stonecarving is another skill at which gnomes excel, and in those caverns where they have dwelt for many centuries intricate patterns have been scrolled into many of the walls and ceilings, enhancing the natural beauty of the rock.

Their special affinity to stone makes gnomes exceptional excavators, miners, and tunnelers. Those gnomes who seek employment among other cultures might work as gemsmiths if sufficiently skilled but are far more likely to find work in the mines of humankind. Even dwarves, grudgingly, admit that gnomes are almost as good at digging as themselves. This is, in fact, an ungenerous assessment—Rock Gnomes in particular are every bit the equal of dwarves in this profession!

Beyond the working of stone, however, the gnomes are somewhat limited in the tooling of materials into useful products. As a general rule, gnomes find it hard to produce raw materials but easy to shape it. For example, they do not weave, so all their clothing is either made of leather or of materials bartered from other folk. However, given the right fabrics, a gnomish tailor can create almost any kind of garment, often with elaborate stitching and similar attention to detail characteristic of all gnomish work.

Carpentry is another skill that demonstrates the gnomish penchant for elaboration. Whereas dwarves will hew timbers to shore up a mine shaft and at need can make rough tables, beds, and chairs for their own use, gnomes have a compulsion to cover every available inch with decoration which goes far beyond utility. Thus gnome miners will often use their breaks to carve delicate designs into the support timbers (taking care not to weaken the beams!), often having friendly contests between different shifts as each continues the other's work. Gnomish furniture is a marvel of fine woodcarving, with a multitude of baroque detail.

Trade

The primary stock-in-trade of the gnomish folk, whether on the surface or under the ground, is naturally the gemwork that is such a trademark of the race. The urge to create is so strong (in Tinker Gnomes, it has run amuck) that gnomes regularly trade finished jewelry for uncut gems, and gnomish gem traders will sometimes travel great distances in the course of their labors.

However, gems aren't the only thing gnome communities seek in trade. Salt is a necessity to the gnomish diet, and if there is no natural source available gnomish traders will go to great lengths to acquire it. Weapons, fabric, and raw steel are generally not made by gnomes but needed by the community. Delicacies, such as tender meat, dark flour, and strong liquor, are other items sometimes gained by trade.

Since these folk have little interest or capability in freight-hauling, those who would sell such bulk goods to them generally have to take responsibility for delivery as well. Human and demihuman traders know this, and many a human and halfling merchant has gotten rich simply by carting loads of textiles or steel to the vicinity of a gnomish village. Often, the trader will sell cart and pony at the same time—after all, he or she doesn't need much space to haul away a fortune in finely-cut gems!

Taboos

"Did you hear about Kasselwort Biddlestumpf? He brought some of that dwarvish black brandy to the Acorn Festival—and after he drank it, it went straight to his tongue!

"First he insulted his old grandfather, Wigglefount Biddlestumpf, who tried to rebuke him for his behavior. Kassel was betting on all the contests, showing around these little bloodstones as if they were rubies!

"Then he got into a fight with Nucklereet Shtoomiss—he called old Nuck' a "Shortnose Blowhard," and of course the poor fellow couldn't let that *pass (we all know Shtoomiss' nose leaves a little to be desired, but Kass' had no call to be making fun of it)!*

"But that's not the worst of it! Finally, when they came down to the nut-eating contest, Kass' bet on Graybeard Friggleheit to win, but the old fellow choked on a husk and had to quit the contest. And when it came time to pay up—believe it or not!—Kasselwort Biddlestumpf refused to pay!

"It'll be a long time before he can show his nose in this *village again!"*

—Lillyllotta Glindlehome, gnomish matriarch (and self-admitted gossip)

Gnomes are a fun-loving society, with a great emphasis on personal freedom. However, a cornerstone of this freedom is a respect for the rights of others—and those who tromp on those rights are considered to have committed a grave breach of gnomish etiquette. This cornerstone of individual responsibility is the key to understanding the gnomish culture.

Some of the worst infractions of this personal code that a gnome can commit involve the performance of his or her work. It is, however, a rare circumstance for a gnome to shirk a duty or to perform it at anything less than his or her highest level of ability. Those few gnomes who refuse to work are generally, after many chances to reform, cast out from their communities. They don't usually live too long on their own.

It is a little more common for offending behavior to occur in social settings, often accompanied by the consumption of alcohol. Virtually all gnomes enjoy drinking, and ale and mead are important features of gnomish festivals and clan gatherings. In most cases, gnomes become quite jolly and carefree when they drink, singing, laughing, and joking—the "mean drunk" is not a familiar character in gnomish society.

However, strong liquor is not a customary drink among gnomes—their ales and fruit wines, while strong-tasting by human standards, are not the match of brandy or whiskey in potency (Svirfneblin fish beer and Gogondy excepted). When a gnome gets hold of something stronger, trouble has been known to result. When it does, the malefactor is subjected to stern criticism from the bulk of the community—usually when he or she is in the throes of the worst hangover of his or her life. One such experience is generally enough to bring about a lifelong reform.

The contests that are an integral part of every gnomish festival are another source of pride to these small demihumans, and the honor of the participants is accepted and, for the most part, taken for granted. Wagering is a common practice, but one is not expected to bet more than he or she is prepared to lose. Welching on a bet is a gross affront to a gnomish sense of right and wrong. Similarly, a trader who cheats gnomish clients by substituting inferior goods for those promised will be marked for life; no gnome will ever trade with that individual again.

Finally, while friendly insults are commonly and frequently exchanged among gnomes, one is expected *never* to criticize lack of nose size. Those gnomes who have been cursed with small noses (those that stick out less than, say, three or four inches from the face) are assumed to suffer the curse of their shame inwardly. It is nothing more than needless cruelty to ridicule this unfortunate lack of endowment.

Emotions

Gnomes are very emotional creatures, given to laughter and joy, weeping and sorrow, in loud and affecting displays. This applies to both work and play. Despite their physical resemblance to dwarves, a group of gnomish miners can easily be distinguished not only by their smaller size but by the laughter and song that accompanies them on their task.

When given cause for sorrow, such as the death of a friend or relative, gnomes grieve openly and loudly. Natural disasters or malicious acts from enemies are likewise cause for wailing and crying—so much so that an observer might assume that an entire community has just received a sentence of painful doom. However, these moods pass quickly (perhaps *because* of the effusiveness of their grief) and many a boisterous party has resulted from what began as a funeral observance.

Very unlike dwarves (or elves, for that matter), gnomes are quite open in displays of affection and love. Hugs are frequent whenever friends, spouses, and relations meet. Parents cuddle children, and the youngsters accept the attention with no self-consciousness. While romantic couples are private with their intimacy, husbands and wives will loudly and publicly profess their affection and love.

Humor

Gnomes are famous, or perhaps infamous, for their sardonic sense of humor. All gnomes love practical jokes, the more elaborate the better. This can be very disconcerting when a gnome decides to express friendship or affection to a non-gnome by making that individual a special target for a string of practical jokes. As a rule, it's considered bad form to devise a joke which actually hurts somebody; the art comes from surprising the victim and making him or her look ridiculous.

In a way, practical joking takes the place filled by violence in many human cultures; two gnomes who have a heated argument are more likely to launch a feud of booby-traps to prove who is the cleverest than come to blows. Taking their cue from Garl Glittergold himself, gnomes extend this attitude to their military endeavors; it's considered a more courageous act to make an enemy look foolish in the eyes of his or her allies or followers than it is to kill the same enemy.

Animal Friends

A warren of gnomes will typically be guarded by several watchful mammals. In the case of Forest Gnomes or Rock Gnomes, these will be woods-dwelling or burrowing creatures. Among the most popular companions are badgers, wolverines, and weasels—in mundane as well as giant size. Svirfneblin sometimes gain similar companionship from moles, shrews, bats, and giant rats. In return for kind treatment from the gnomes, these creatures often take up residence nearby gnome dwellings.

These creatures are not domesticated as humans understand the word; they are allies, not pets. Still, they provide useful service as sentinels, quickly bringing word of any strangers in the area, and if the community is attacked the animal guardians will always fight savagely in defense of their friends. Many villages have tales of youngsters who have fallen into a stream only to be plucked forth and saved by the jaws of a giant weasel, for example, or of young climbers who have gotten into trouble on the steep and rocky slopes so common in gnomish habitat only to be carried to safety on the sturdy back of a climbing badger.

Warfare

"Dey come from da rocks of da ground, everywhere attackin' and killin', what wit dem bolts and dat majick! We din't see where dey wuz or where dey went, but when dey wuz gone all my pals wuz kilt.

"We had deez goblyns what wuz suzpozed to watch dat side—but dey run away! Da lucky ones ran, dat iz. Lots a dem wuz kilt too. Dem nomes, dey really whomped da goblyns—din't like 'em too much at all, I cud tell. Da goblyns wuz gonna turn to meet 'em, but da nomes come on too fast. Dey din't let 'em make da line or get off a shot. 'Course, dat's what you espect a' goblyns.

"Den I tought we ogres would stomp 'em, stomp 'em good. But dey wudn't fight fair, wudn't come out and let uz stomp 'em! Dey sat dere and shot wit' dem dang bolts, what poked out eyes and did all sorts a' nasties. We run at dem but dey hid—we din't know where dey went, 'till dey come up behind us and whomped us pretty good dat way too.

"Nope, sir, you kin tell me ta go but I ain't goin'—I ain't gonna fight no nomes no more!"

—from the battle diary of Barkan Delsuutor, Ogre veteran and brigade commander

Like halflings, gnomes are slow to anger and reluctant to wage war. However, also like their diminutive cousins, they become savage and tenacious fighters when fully motivated into battle.

Because of their small size, gnomes try to avoid combat situations that place them in open terrain where they must meet the head-on onslaught of much larger attackers. They prefer instead to fight in rough terrain, sheltered by rocks or trees, where their size can actually work to their advantage. In underground combat situations where they have sufficient time to prepare, gnomes like to excavate numerous low-ceilinged tunnels for mobility of attack and retreat.

They are not so adept with missiles as are halflings, but gnomish troops can nevertheless deliver a furious barrage of arrows and sling stones when such a tactic is needed. Firing in an undisciplined fusillade, they continue to pepper their targets with this painful attacks for as long as possible. They launch their arrows from sturdy shortbows or solid, albeit small, crossbows.

Though many of them wield spears, they prefer to use these as melee rather than missile weapons. Gnomes are adept (and very courageous) at setting these spears to meet the charge of much larger attackers. They will also use their quickness to strike from ambush, and when a force of gnomes can mingle among the troops of a larger enemy, their small size allows them to inflict a lot of damage. A favorite tactic, useable only when gnomes gain complete surprise (such as that provided by a *mass invisibility* spell), is to fearlessly dart among enemy horsemen, using their sharp daggers to cut the straps holding the riders' saddles onto their mounts. Such a tactic, when successful, can go a long way toward evening the odds of an unbalanced engagement.

When marching to battle, most gnomes will carry a missile weapon as well as a hammer, spear, or short sword, with a dagger reserved for the final line of defense.

Gnomes are also skilled at using deception, diversion, camouflage, and disguise as battle tactics. Their natural talents at illusionary magic help a great deal—gnomish illusionists will frequently create the appearance of the force in some unimportant area, while other spellcasters conceal the actual presence of the gnomes from enemy discovery. The sudden appearance of a gnomish force, virtually in

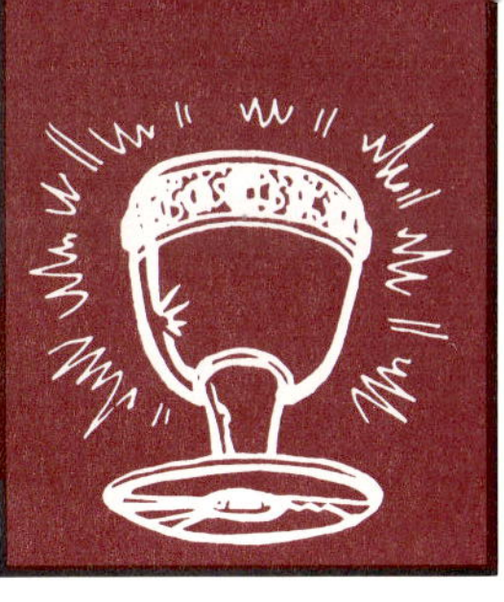

the midst of the enemy, can be enough to throw the most veteran army into confusion.

They are also good at using these spells to conceal the true nature of the battlefield—either to create the appearance of obstacles where there are none or to conceal the location of hazards such as ravines, thickets, bogs, and streams. Many a thunderous charge has been broken when the howling attackers suddenly find out that what looked like solid ground is actually intersected by a twenty-foot deep gully, its bottom lined with sharp stakes.

Other uses of illusionary magic have stretched the creative bounds of military imagination. In one famous battle, gnomish illusionists concealed the actual location of the sun and replace it with a duplicate, causing the enemies' reinforcements to march five miles to the east when they were supposed to be going west! They have also used images of dragons, giants, beholders, and other horrors to distract the attention of their foes and keep them guessing as to the true nature of their opponents.

Another asset that gnomes carry into battle is the lack of the hubris that can so often be the downfall of human or dwarven commanders. Gnomes show no hesitation when it comes to abandoning a lost cause; when things start to go bad, the gnomes will run away, preferring this pragmatic tactic to a doomed stand motivated mainly by pride. The retreating gnomes quickly scatter and (if possible) disappear down holes into the ground or vanish among the enclosing underbrush of a forest. Even if the victorious opponents pursue ruthlessly, they are unlikely to kill or capture more than a handful of the gnomish survivors. Of course, this scattering means that it takes longer to reassemble the force and prepare to fight again, but that is a drawback that any gnomish commander willingly accepts rather than see his or her forces annihilated.

Magic

The primary sorcery of the gnomes, of course, is illusionary magic. This is far more than a practical application of arcane powers, however—in gnome society, the casting of illusions affects all aspects of life from art to romance to celebration to war. A lover might woo his sweetheart with a message borne by a *whispering wind* spell, for example. For gnomes, illusionary magic is a way of life, not something they use just to make life easier.

Illusions are also constantly employed for practical jokes among these fun-loving folk. Of course, gnomes are more adept at recognizing illusions than are most other creatures, so those illusionary pranks targeted against them must be subtly crafted and strategically planned in order for them to succeed. *Invisibility*, *illusionary script*, and *wraithform* spells are popular choices for this purpose.

Illusionary magic is often used to complement the finest efforts of gnomish craftsmen. A fine piece of jewelry, for example, might be enhanced with a shower of light caused by a *phantasmal force*, or even a *hypnotic pattern*, in order to create a truly stunning work of art.

On the practical side, illusionary magic is not usually employed to screen the location or nature of a gnomish community. Though such arcane devices might prove effective at concealing them against mundane detection, the emanation of magical power actually serves as a beacon to those who use spells such as *detect magic*. The latter enemies are judged, rightly, to be far more dangerous to a gnomish community than the former.

However, on the battlefield or in other contests of might and skill, gnomes will pull out all the stops. *Hallucinatory terrain*, the various applications of *invisibility*, and *illusionary walls* will be used to disguise the true nature of the battlefield, while spells such as *phantasmal force*, *fear*, *phantasmal killer*, and *shadow monster* will be employed directly against the enemy troops.

Wandering

Unlike the other short folk, the halflings, gnomes are often possessed by a strong desire to wander. Their natural curiosity leads them to constantly wonder about what's beyond the next hill, or across that sea... or even down that dark hole in the mountainside.

A major compulsion for this wandering among all gnomes is the desire to find the perfect gem. Tales of rich veins of rubies, or a wealth of diamonds or emeralds, will often draw an entire party of gnomes onto a long and dangerous quest. Whether or not they've seen evidence of the find, their belief in its existence will be strong, even unshakable, and determined gnomes will brook no diversion in their pursuit of this ultimate treasure.

Despite their reticent nature and the care with which they conceal their communities' exact locations, gnomes are quite willing to make friends with those visitors who prove themselves worthy of that friendship. Many a wide-eyed gnomish youngster has listened to a human knight tell of great castles or a merchant describe the wonders of a large city market. These gnomes typically grow up with the desire to see these places, and no one thinks it odd when, after reaching adulthood, they pack up their belongings and head down the road.

Another strain of this honest friendliness is a deep-running loyalty to those the gnomes consider friends. The suggestion that one of these kindred spirits is in trouble will also prove a strong motivation to bring a gnome onto the adventuring road.

Finally, gnomes keep a close eye on their surroundings and are very familiar with the world in their general vicinity. If they notice things changing (for example, a village cropping up on what used to be a wilderness stream) they will be irresistibly drawn to the scene to find out what's going on.

CHAPTER 4

Gnome Character Kits

The kits introduced in this chapter allow players to define their characters with more detail and precision than are determined simply by race and character class. The gnome kits provide a selection of specialized PCs and NPCs, each designed for a specific character class or multi-class combination. Each kit has its own strengths and weaknesses, and each is tailored to illustrate some important aspect of gnomish life.

The kits are purely optional—no gnome *must* use one. They can be incorporated into characters already existing in the campaign, as long as the PC's background makes sense given the nature of the kit. Once a character has been assigned a kit, that selection remains for the life of the character.

These kits are specifically designed for gnomes and should not be employed by characters of other races. Gnomish characters who don't wish to use a kit from this book can select a kit from another handbook that is applicable to their character class: *The Complete Fighter's Handbook*, *The Complete Thief's Handbook*, *The Complete Priest's Handbook*, *The Complete Wizard's Handbook*, and *The Complete Bard's Handbook* all have kits that are available to gnomish characters of the appropriate class.

Gnomes can become clerics of up to 9th level, fighters of up to 11th level, thieves of up to 13th level, and illusionists of up to 15th level; exceptionally talented gnomes (those with high scores in their prime requisites) can exceed these maximums by up to 4 additional levels. Multi-class combinations are also allowed between any two classes available to gnomes, with illusionist/thief being a favorite. Priests are not terribly common among gnomes—the Svirfneblin have the most, Tinker Gnomes none at all—and multi-classed combinations including them are the rarest of all gnome character classes (and hence have no kits devoted to them).

Players and DMs may cooperate in the creation of original kits, as long as care is taken to balance the advantages and disadvantages with those presented here.

Structure of the Kits

Each kit begins with a general description of that character type, along with any background and ability score requirements that are necessary to qualify for the kit. Further information on the kits is broken down into these categories:

Role: The specific functions of this character type within gnomish society.

Secondary Skills: In campaigns using the secondary skills rules from the AD&D® 2nd Edition game, a character might be required to take a specific secondary skill.

Weapon Proficiencies: The character must take the proficiencies listed. Unless it is specifically stated otherwise, these required proficiencies do not increase the number of slots the character has available.

Bonus Nonweapon Proficiencies: A gnomish character using a kit gains these proficiencies for free—he or she is not required to spend a slot for any of them.

Recommended Nonweapon Proficiencies: These proficiencies are not required of the character, but they do match up well with the kit. They require a normal nonweapon proficiency slot(s) to be used for each one.

Thieving Skill Emphasis (thief, thief/illusionist, and thief/fighter classes only; there are no thief/priest kits): The AD&D® 2nd Edition rules allow considerable flexibility in a thief character's selection of thieving abilities. Characters wishing become Stalkers or Mouseburglars usually choose to specialize in stealth-related skills such as Move Silently and Hide in Shadows. A gnomish thief who needs to survive on city streets might prefer to focus on Pick Pockets and Open Locks. Each kit comes with suggested areas of skill concentration for that character type. These are not mandatory, nor do they grant any special bonuses or confer any penalties.

Equipment: Any special equipment needs of

the character are listed.

Special Benefits: These are things a character can do, or perhaps protections he or she gains, because of the kit.

Special Hindrances: These are requirements or limitations placed upon the character by the kit.

Fighter Kits

Breachgnome

This burly gnome takes a "heads up and face front" view to battle. Armed to the teeth and armored to the eyeballs, he or she hoists weapon, fully prepared to stand toe-to-toe with any attacker menacing home or ally. In some senses, this is the gnomish equivalent of the knight, mixed with a stubbornness and tenacity suggestive of the most determined dwarven heroes.

A Breachgnome devotes all his or her life to the fighter's art, from wrestling as a child to mastering an assortment of weapons as the character grows to adulthood. Often he or she will be taught by fighters of other races (human and dwarf, in particular) as well as accepting the tutelage of a gnomish master.

The Breachgnome must have a Strength of at least 16.

Role: This character is the one who steps out of the crowd of gnomes to confront the bullying ogre. Breachgnomes excel in defensive fighting; if his or her warren is invaded by enemies, the Breachgnome will stand in a corridor and hold the creatures at bay until the rest of the villagers can escape. Only after all have fled will the valiant defender (possibly) begin to think about his or her own safety.

The classic Breachgnome is an epic figure in gnomish battle lore. The tale of Maddi Gaddlroot is typical: Maddi supposedly held off a whole army of ogres for an entire day,

standing before a cave mouth between two trees, where only one of the enemy could get at her at a time. Behind her, her city of a thousand gnomes stood threatened, and during the course of that day the young and infirm (together with most of the treasure) were hustled through narrow tunnels into the depths of the earth.

Only after she had slain dozens of the brutes did Maddi fall before the superior might of her attackers. Then the ogres lunged into the lair, only to be met by a clever network of ambushes and illusionary traps—defenses which the Breachgnome's heroic sacrifice had given her fellow gnomes time to create. In the end, the attack was defeated, the city saved, and the hero elevated to legendary status among her people. Interestingly enough, virtually every gnome settlement considers itself to be the one Maddi Gaddlroot died defending and will often point out to visitors the site of her last stand!

Secondary Skills: The Armorer or Weaponsmith secondary skills are useful to the Breachgnome.

Weapon Proficiencies: The Breachgnome must have a proficiency in the use of the short sword and either the hammer or axe.

Bonus Nonweapon Proficiencies: None

Recommended Nonweapon Proficiencies: The Breachgnome should consider the Armorer, Weaponsmith, Endurance, and Blacksmithing proficiencies.

Equipment: The Breachgnome will typically carry at least two melee weapons, a shield, metal armor, and some type of missile weapon (crossbow and sling being preferred).

Special Benefits: Because of their short size and gusty determination, all Breachgnomes gain bonuses to their Armor Class when they can fight in a position with one or both flanks protected by solid objects such as trees, walls, or support beams. If the gnome has such an object within 3′ of either side, he or she receives a −1 bonus to AC; if both sides are protected, the bonus is −2. Assume the gnome is 2′ wide to determine if both sides are protected—i.e., the Breachgnome can gain the double bonus when standing between walls no more than 8′ apart. This bonus is cumulative with any applicable size and Dexterity bonuses.

Because of their single-mindedness in weapon training, Breachgnomes gain weapon proficiency slots at the rate of one every two levels (with the first extra proficiency slot becoming available at third level).

Special Hindrances: When faced with a battle that he or she *might* be able to win—but companions or common sense that urge a withdrawal—the Breachgnome must make a Wisdom check. He or she can repeat the check every round, but the character cannot retreat until it succeeds.

Goblinsticker

These gnomes are considered eccentric, if not downright mad, by their more normal kin—Goblinstickers actually seem to enjoy battle and will go so far as to seek out enemies for the purpose of wiping them out. The two most common foes of the Goblinsticker are, naturally, goblins and kobolds.

Often a Goblinsticker is propelled by some dark event or tragedy in his or her past—a wrong which cannot be righted but which he or she feels compelled to try and atone for or avenge for the rest of his or her days. A Goblinsticker is especially effective at fighting the particular foe which caused this tragedy (often, but not always, goblins), often forgoing treasure and other incentives to pursue his or her revenge. "Goblinsticker" is a generic term for this kit; there are also koboldstickers, skeletonstickers, ogrestickers, et cetera, who differ only in the focus of their animosity.

A character must have a Strength or Constitution score of at least 15 in order to choose this kit.

Role: Because they are virtually fearless, these characters form the shock troops of any gnomish assault against their chosen enemy.

They are likely to choose a life of adventure, one that will put them on a collision course with their hated foe.

Teams of Goblinstickers have been known to work together, for adventure or pay. In areas of monster infestation, Goblinstickers can frequently find employment as "exterminators"—especially in cases where the monsters are small, such as goblins or kobold, and live in dens where the size of human attackers would prove a drawback.

Secondary Skills: The Weaponsmith and Armorer are appropriate secondary skills for this character.

Weapon Proficiencies: The Goblinsticker must have a missile weapon proficiency and two melee weapon proficiencies.

Bonus Nonweapon Proficiencies: The Goblinsticker gains no bonus proficiencies.

Recommended Nonweapon Proficiencies: This character will find the Rope Use, Direction Sense, Blindfighting, Armorer, and Weaponsmith proficiencies useful.

Equipment: Together with his or her weapons and armor, the Goblinsticker traditionally carries the tools of the dungeon-crawler—i.e., ropes, hammer and spikes, oil, and several days' rations.

Special Benefits: At first level the Goblinsticker character must declare the hated foe of his or her life. When engaged in battle against this type of creature, the character receives a +1 bonus on all rolls to hit and to determine damage inflicted. This bonus applies to both melee and missile weapons and is cumulative with other gnome benefits, including the Rock Gnome's standard +1 attack bonus versus goblins and kobolds.

Special Hindrances: When confronted with an opportunity to attack or continue to fight his or her hated foe, the Goblinsticker must make a successful Wisdom check or be unable to decline the battle. The check can, however, be modified or ignored based on circumstances. For example, no Goblinsticker will break cover and blow an ambush to tromp on the first goblin to appear when he or she knows that a little patience will mean the chance to bop a lot more of them.

Thief Kits

Mouseburglar

These stealthy characters are consummate spies and sneak thieves who in some ways behave more like halflings than the average gnome thief. Striving to be as quiet as mice, they infiltrate lairs, mansions, or enemy camps. They rely upon secrecy, disguise, and silence in order to conceal their presence. Preferring very much to flee rather than fight, they consider a truly successful mission one which is concluded before the victim even learns that the gnome has been there.

A Mouseburglar must have both Dexterity and Intelligence scores of 13 or better.

Role: Mouseburglars, like other gnomish thieves, rarely prey upon victims of their same race. They will be much more inclined to look for targets among the settlements of clan enemies, especially humanoids, or in anonymous settings like large cities.

In addition to their larcenous activities, Mouseburglars also serve as scouts and spies, should there be a need for such reconnoissance. Their emphasis on stealth and concealment—together with their generally high Intelligence—makes them excellent eavesdroppers. Many a gnomish military campaign has been laid over the carefully gathered reports of a Mouseburglar.

These characters also find great application as adventurers, lending a lot of advantage to a party of mixed races and classes. Their small

size coupled with their skills (and the fact that most have infravision) allow them to get into places that larger thieves can't.

Secondary Skills: Any secondary skill can be appropriate to this kit.

Weapon Proficiencies: The Mouseburglar always chooses to specialize in weapons that can be wielded silently, preferring the sling or bow over the crossbow and the dagger or short sword over the hammer and axe.

Bonus Nonweapon Proficiencies: Mouseburglars receive either Disguise or Rope Use as a bonus nonweapon proficiency.

Recommended Nonweapon Proficiencies: This character can benefit by knowing additional languages (very important for one who intends to spy or eavesdrop!), as well as Forgery, Reading Lips, and Tightrope Walking.

Thief Skill Emphasis: The Mouseburglar is likely to find the Move Silently, Hide in Shadows, and Open Locks skills to be particularly useful. At first level he or she must divide the 60 discretionary points between these three abilities.

Equipment: The Mouseburglar will be sure to maintain a complete set of lockpicks. He or she prefers to wear dark clothes and soft boots when on a job and will often have the materials for one or two effective disguises concealed somewhere on his or her person.

Special Benefits: A Mouseburglar gains an additional 5% chance of success to both Open Locks and Move Silently at first level. For each additional level he or she advances, the character receives another 5% bonus that can be applied to any one of the following scores: Open Locks, Move Silently, Find/Remove Traps, or Read Languages.

Special Hindrances: The Mouseburglar so prefers stealth to combat that the character's fighting skills suffer as a result. Specifically, the Mouseburglar receives a −1 penalty on all attack rolls made in melee combat (except those delivered with the backstab benefit). This does not affect damage inflicted.

Tumbler

Tumblers employ size and energy as the main assets of a thieving career. Quick and nimble, they are able to use escape routes that larger and clumsier pursuers find quite unmanageable. Tumblers are part entertainer, part con artist, and part acrobat.

Coming from a variety of backgrounds, Tumblers usually have been exposed to a number of different races and often perfect their trade in some kind of urban environment. Often they will find work in a circus or carnival, moonlighting after show hours to augment their honest income.

The Tumbler must have a Dexterity score of at least 14.

Role: The Tumbler is a gnome who employs creative and vigorous means to get into places, meanwhile performing tricks and feats for the edification of his or her fellow villagers. Adept at climbing and falling, the Tumbler can walk a rope stretched between two high points, scale a sheer surface, and bob and evade his or her way through deadly combat—often rolling right between a larger opponent's legs!

Secondary Skills: Any of the secondary skills can be used by this character.

Weapon Proficiencies: The Tumbler is eligible to use any weapon available to gnomish thieves.

Bonus Nonweapon Proficiencies: The Tumbler character receives Tumbling as a free proficiency when first selecting this kit.

Recommended Nonweapon Proficiencies: The Tumbler must take Jumping, Juggling, and Tightrope Walking in order to practice his or her trade.

Thief Skill Emphasis: The Tumbler can find particular use in the Pick Pockets, Move Silently, and Climb Walls thieving skills. The kit places no restriction on how he or she allocates the discretionary points, however.

Equipment: The Tumbler will always be found with a coil of strong, lightweight rope—generally at least a 60' length.

Special Benefits: Gnomish Tumblers receive all the normal benefits of the Tumbling proficiency. Tumbling ability and small size combine to give Tumblers a −6 bonus to AC in rounds in which the Tumbler wins initiative and elects to forgo all other actions than evading enemy attacks.

Against larger than human-sized creatures, the gnomish Tumbler can try a special maneuver: rolling between the creature's legs. A successful Dexterity check means the Tumbler dives between the opponent's legs, rolls to safety, and bounces to his or her feet behind the enemy. If the Dexterity check fails, however, the gnome can be attacked with no special bonus to Armor Class. If the Tumbler successfully performs this maneuver and wins initiative on the next round, he or she can backstab that opponent.

At first level, Tumblers also receive a +10% bonus to their chances to successfully Climb Walls; this bonus increases by +2% per level thereafter.

Special Hindrances: Because of the boisterous nature of this specialty, Tumblers are limited in some of the other areas of thieving skills. Specifically, their base scores to Open Locks and Detect Noise begin at 0, not at the levels (10% and 15%, respectively) listed on Table 26 on page 39 of the *Player's Handbook*. The bonuses and penalties specified on Tables 27-29 are not affected by this provision.

Illusionist Kits

Imagemaker

This is the maestro of the gnomish world. His or her services are in demand at every gnomish festival; his or her skills known far and wide, sought by humans, dwarves, and others beyond the ken of gnome society. The Imagemaker is an artist in the art of illusion who can create spectacles and is capable of drawing audiences to the edge of awe and beyond with soaring images, thunderous sound effects, and realistic creations.

Any gnomish illusionist can elect to be an Imagemaker.

Role: The Imagemaker's role in gnomish society extends far beyond his or her ability to tell tales and create pictures. On the battlefield, Imagemakers are the primary source of the diversionary illusions that gnomish forces use so well to balance the odds against them. Since they specialize in the creation and manipulation of very realistic illusions, they can be very useful to adventuring parties—for example, by creating duplicate images of the party to distract a powerful enemy. And, of course, no gnomish ceremony would be complete without the sound and spectacle of the Imagemaker's art.

Secondary Skills: Any will work, though the Gambler and Scribe secondary skills can have particularly useful applications.

Bonus Nonweapon Proficiencies: The Imagemaker gains the Ventriloquism proficiency (normally available only to rogues) as a free proficiency as soon as this kit is selected.

Recommended Nonweapon Proficiencies: Artistic Ability is a useful accompaniment to the Imagemaker's skill, as are proficiencies in Ancient History, Astrology, and Singing.

Equipment: An Imagemaker likes to have several mechanical tools available to augment his or her spellwork, including smokepots, flashballs, and probably a musical instrument. Smokepots must be lit by a fuse, which can be set for 1-10 rounds; upon igniting they belch out a 10' diameter cloud of colored smoke, blocking all visibility. The cloud disperses in one round out of doors or in a large enclosed space; in more constricting quarters it lasts for 2-5 rounds. Flashballs erupt with a bright flash of flame when they are thrown (or dropped) and strike a solid object such as stone or metal. When used in darkness they will effectively *blind* (for 1-6 rounds) a character who witnesses the flash.

Special Benefits: The Imagemaker has perfected the use of specific kinds of illusions—

specifically, those that create the image of something from nothing. The various *phantasmal force* spells, *minor creation*, the *shadow monster* spells, *programmed illusion*, and *shades* are examples of spells that fall within this specialty; *invisibility*, *vacancy*, and *seeming* are spells that do not.

The pictures, sounds, and smells created by the Imagemaker are especially realistic. Therefore, any player attempting *disbelieve* them does so with a −2 penalty. In addition, *all* creatures—even those not normally susceptible to illusion—can be taken in by the creations of the Imagemaker. However, creatures that would not normally be fooled by illusions do not suffer the −2 penalty when they attempt to disbelieve.

In addition, the Imagemaker's skill is such that the images he or she creates last longer than those cast by a non-specializing illusionist. Illusions that do not require concentration have their duration doubled when cast by an Imagemaker. Illusions requiring concentration last for 2-12 rounds after the caster ceases concentrating. In the latter case, of course, the object will not be able to respond to specific events, but it can continue to repeat movements or patterns established when the caster was concentrating.

Special Hindrances: Because of intense specialization, the Imagemaker suffers additional restrictions on spells he or she can learn; specifically, Imagemakers cannot learn spells from the greater divination or conjuring/summoning schools of magic.

Vanisher

The Vanisher is an illusionist with the specialization of making things disappear—in that sense, he or she is the opposite of the Imagemaker. Invisibility is stock-in-trade, but the Vanisher is also adept at spells that alter and disguise the appearance of something, equally ready to replace the vanished object or creature with an alternate as to make it disappear entirely.

Any gnomish illusionist can elect to be a Vanisher.

Role: The Vanisher is the valued counterpart to the Imagemaker, whether on the battlefield or in a dungeon. By concealing the existence of a party he or she can insure them the advantage of surprise, which is always useful. His or her skills can also benefit reconnoissance or retrieval missions.

Secondary Skills: Any can be useful, though Scribe and Navigator skills preferred.

Weapon Proficiencies: The Vanisher has no restriction on weapon proficiencies.

Bonus Nonweapon Proficiencies: The Vanisher receives Reading/Writing skill without expending a slot.

Recommended Nonweapon Proficiencies: These include Spellcraft, Heraldry, Blindfighting, Direction Sense, Weather Sense, and Navigation.

Equipment: The Vanisher likes to keep a vial of *dust of disappearance* handy; see Special Benefits, below.

Special Benefits: The Vanisher gains extra skills with any spell involving *invisibility*, as well as other spells of the illusion/phantasm school that allow the caster to alter the appearance of a creature or object or to impair the sense of an observer. Some of the latter include *blindness* and *deafness* spells; spells which alter appearances include *blur*, *change self*, *fool's gold*, *illusionary script*, *Leomund's trap*, *Nystul's magic aura*, and *vacancy*.

When casting one of these specialty spells, the Vanisher gains several benefits. The duration of the spell is doubled. Saving throws against the effects of these spells suffer a −2 penalty. Characters or creatures that could normally see *invisible* objects must make a successful Intelligence check, with a −4 penalty to the roll, before they can see objects screened by a Vanisher.

Also, at the second level of experience the Vanisher gains the ability to make a simple form of *dust of disappearance* from flour and a modicum (100 gp worth) of crushed diamond. It takes the Vanisher a full hour and a successful Intelligence check to perform this task, which can be attempted once per day. This homemade *dust of disappearance* retains its potency for two weeks.

Special Hindrances: Like the Imagemaker, the Vanisher's devotion to mastering illusions is such that it precludes his or her learning any spells from the greater divination or conjuring/summoning schools of magic.

Multiclass Kits

Buffoon (Thief/Illusionist)

The name of this character kit is in no way a reflection on the intelligence of the character who plays the role. It does, however, reflect the way the non-gnomish world views him or her—it is a gentle deception that can consistently cause enemies and other NPCs to underestimate or even ignore the character. Indeed, the Buffoon carefully cultivates this role, often even to the point of concealing the fact that he or she possesses illusionist skills.

In order to use this kit, a character must have an Intelligence score of at least 15.

Role: Buffoons are travelers, entertainers, gossips, pranksters, and gadflies. They make friends everywhere they go and enjoy using their skills to aid those friends in a multitude of causes. Buffoons make themselves figures of fun and then use this as a means of making fun of others—usually with just the right element of sharpness in their wit. An empress, for example, will not be subjected to the ridicule that, say, a city guard might merit—at least not in her presence! Buffoons are alert and observant, quick to discern who are safe targets, currently out of favor with the powers that be; such unfortunates often become the butt of a Buffoon's jests.

Favorite Buffoon tactics include comical imitations of the character being lampooned and questions designed to trap the unfortunate victim in a no-win quandary—e.g., "Have you stopped overtaxing the peasants yet?" Every Buffoon is adept at keeping the crowd on his or her side, but it is said that every good Buffoon keeps one eye on the exit, ready to beat a hasty retreat should the mood of the onlookers suddenly turn nasty.

The Buffoon is an avaricious but capable adventurer, always on the lookout for gems of any shape, color, and size. He or she doesn't keep these in a horde, instead preferring to barter them for goods (or goodwill) whenever passing through a gnomish community. The Buffoon is quite likely to find good friends in any gnomish village along his or her trail and also among the gnomish citizens of larger cities and towns.

Secondary Skills: Jeweler is a popular secondary skill for the Buffoon, as are Navigator and Gambler.

Weapon Proficiencies: The Buffoon likes to keep several daggers concealed about his or her person and will be adept at using them both as missile weapons and hand-to-hand.

Bonus Nonweapon Proficiencies: All Buffoons gain a knowledge of Etiquette as a bonus proficiency—not that they practice it, but their natural sensitivity helps them judge what is and is not considered appropriate in a given situations (and tailor their barbs accordingly).

Recommended Nonweapon Proficiencies: History and Disguise, as well as Juggling, Lip Reading, Tumbling, and Ventriloquism are all useful complements to the Buffoon's art.

Thief Skill Emphasis: The Buffoon may wish to emphasize Hide in Shadows, Detect Noise, and Find/Remove Traps; the kit places no restrictions on his or her choices.

Equipment: The Buffoon generally travels with a variety of comical gimmicks, including horns and bells, whistles and juggling balls, and a full makeup kit that often includes wigs and false beards.

Special Benefits: The Buffoon benefits from an ability to distract and entertain. Often a Buffoon can break the concentration of a spellcaster with a rude jibe or irritating pun.

The gnomish character must speak a language in common with the spellcaster and must win initiative on the round. If both of these are met, he or she can say something (DMs are encouraged to require roleplaying of the remark) clever and distracting to the spellcaster. The caster is allowed a Wisdom check to ignore the distraction; failure means his or her concentration has broken and the spell is wasted. The DM may, at his or her option, allow the difference between the Buffoon's and spellcaster's levels to be used as a modifier (+ or −) to the Wisdom check.

The Buffoon also has two bard-like abilities: First, he or she can entertain NPCs with juggling, jibes, and buffoonery. This has the same effect as the bard's ability to *influence reactions* (explained on page 42 of the *Player's Handbook*). Second, he or she can counter the effects of songs and poetry used as magical attacks (see page 44 of the *Player's Handbook*).

Special Hindrances: He or she has to walk around looking ridiculous.

Stalker (Fighter/Thief)

Whether in woodland meadow or dungeon pit, the Stalker is a specialist in quiet movement and stealthy pursuit followed by sharp and deadly combat—on whatever terms the foe demands.

The Stalker must have Strength and Dexterity scores of at least 13.

Role: The Stalker is adept at hunting and tracking, both above and below ground. He or she is a skilled fighter but prefers to reach his or her objectives by quickness and stealth wherever possible. Stalkers wear light, quiet armor and have a keen eye with a missile weapon but don't shirk from a toe-to-toe sword fight when circumstances require.

Secondary Skills: Any.

Weapon Proficiencies: The Stalker must be proficient in both a missile and a melee weapon.

Bonus Nonweapon Proficiencies: Because of a lifelong interest in wild places, the Stalker gains a bonus proficiency in either Tracking or Set Snares (not both).

Recommended Nonweapon Proficiencies: Useful proficiencies for this character include Fire Building, Fishing, Hunting, Survival, and Disguise.

Thief Skill Emphasis: Move Silently and Detect Noise are the two skills which receive most of the Stalker's emphasis; at first level he or she must divide his or her discretionary points between these two.

Equipment: In addition to his or her weapons, the Stalker prefers leather armor and disdains the use of a shield. Most Stalkers possess a climbing rope; some carry a set of thief's lockpicks.

Special Benefits: When using a missile weapon, the Stalker gains a +1 on all attack and damage rolls.

In addition, the Stalker can blend into

underbrush, disappearing as effectively as a halfling when out of doors. In an underground setting, nonSvirfneblin Stalkers can *freeze in place* exactly like Svirfneblin (see page 25); a Deep Gnome stalker's chance of success with this tactic is 80% (not 60%).

Special Hindrances: The Stalker cannot use a shield or wear any type of metal armor (not even elven chain).

Priest Kits

Rocktender

This underground-dwelling gnomish priest is a specialist in understanding and relating to the fundamental powers of stone and rock. Most Rocktenders are Svirfneblin; a few may be found among Rock Gnomes. They venerate not the deities of earth and stone but the very rock itself, which they conceive of as a beneficent, living entity. Rocktenders are not averse to mining and excavation but strive to ensure that such activities are carried out with appropriate reverence.

Role: The Rocktender is a priest literally in touch with the world around him or her. While active in the community, a Rocktender spends much of his or her time alone, inspecting, studying, and meditating upon the strong bedrock of the world. He or she is keenly in tune with that rock, even to the point of being able to predict earthquakes and volcanic eruptions, and becomes a master at the working of stone into useful or beautiful shapes.

Secondary Skills: Mason or Miner are appropriate.

Weapon Proficiencies: The Rocktender will never use metallic weapons, preferring hammers and clubs with stone heads, slings with stone bullets, and spears or arrows with flint or obsidian tips.

Bonus Nonweapon Proficiencies: None.

Equipment: The Rocktender will only bear weapons of stone. He or she can use a wooden shield and leather or padded armor but will not wear metal armor nor carry a metallic shield.

Special Benefits: The Rocktender can detect underground features with perfect accuracy (sloping passages, faulty stonework, and the like) in most cases. Where the flaws or features are very subtle, the DM can allow up to a 1 in 10 chance of failure, but no greater.

Because of his or her intuitive link with the surrounding stone, a Rocktender can become aware of impending rock-based convulsions before they occur. These include rockfalls, earthquakes, and volcanic eruptions. The character is allowed a Wisdom check to see if premonitions of the disaster force their way into his or her consciousness; success will provide 1-12 hours of warning for quakes and eruptions or 1-6 hours of warning before a rockslide or collapse of stonework.

In addition, these characters have a special affinity to creatures from the elemental plane of earth. If a Rocktender summons an earth elemental, he or she will always get the largest possible type, and the elemental will be exceptionally loyal to the Rocktender.

Special Hindrances: A Rocktender can only cast spells or use one of his or her special abilities when he or she is in direct contact with unhewn rock.

Treetender

Dwelling in the woods, often knowing each stump and mossy bole with careful precision, the Treetender declines the companionship of his or her fellow gnomes in favor of a nearly hermit-like existence in the woods.

Role: Although they rarely interact with other gnomes on a daily basis, these nature priests are highly respected for helping to preserve the environment in which their fellows live. Like the druid of humankind, the Treetender takes a fierce interest in his or her domain and will vigorously strive to protect it against all threats. He or she is not a complete recluse, however, and will usually make it to a local village for all the major festivals, as well as helping gnomes (and, sometimes, halflings) who pass through his or her woods.

Secondary Skills: Forester is the secondary skill of choice; Navigator is also good.

Weapon Proficiencies: Treetenders specialize in weapons made of wood, though they are not averse to using stone heads on long wooden shafts. Unlike most priests, Treetenders can use bows.

Bonus Nonweapon Proficiencies: The Treetender gains an innate Set Snares skill.

Recommended Nonweapon Proficiencies: Fire Building, Weather Sense, Direction Sense, and Healing are all useful skills in woodland environments.

Equipment: In addition to weapons, a Treetender carries a selection of herbs and roots which he or she can use to make a *potion of healing*. Making the potion requires 6-12 turns, and it must be consumed immediately.

Special Benefits: All Treetenders have the abilities to identify plants, animals, and pure water and to pass through overgrown areas without leaving a trace. At third level he or she gains immunity to *charm* spells cast by woodland creatures. Also starting at third level, the Treetender gains one additional woodland language per level (i.e., one a 3rd level, two at 4th level, three at 5th, &c).

Special Hindrances: The Treetender cannot wear metal armor or wield weapons where more than 10% of the weight is metal.

CHAPTER 5

Granitehome—A Typical Gnomish Village

Located among a series of heavily forested ridges, this community of some three hundred and fifty gnomes is organized into seven clans, each with its own large underground warren. Though it is typical of a Rock Gnome abode, a Forest Gnome community would be very similar (although much more spread out and less densely populated)—and if it was much farther underground, the general layout is not unlike a portion of a Deep Gnome city.

On the surface, nothing of the community is visible—even the entrances leading into the warrens are well-camouflaged, screened by brush, disguised in the trunks of large trees, or hidden beneath flat boulders hinged from below.

1. High Warren

This series of excavated chambers serves as a gathering place for the community. Several stone-walled inns and gemshops line the walls of a vast cavern. The central chamber—a popular setting for festivals—is bowl-shaped, with rings of seats that can hold nearly a thousand gnomes. Atop the knoll, through an entrance reached by a high, spiraling stair, is a large clearing where the gnomes hold out-of-doors gatherings.

2. Kappelkourt Clanhold

These chambers are the homes and workshops of the major gemcutting clan in the town. The clan has some thirty members.

3. Lafftalligon Clanhold

This clan specializes in stonecarving; it has some forty members.

4. Astrolacyll Clanhold

The seventy-five members of this family do a great deal of foodgathering and patrolling of the forest. Traditionally, most of the village's priests have been from this clan.

5. Mines

These connecting tunnels and caverns hold the currently-worked veins of gemstones in the Granitehome area. The entrance to the tunnel is hidden in an innocuous room with a secret door to help conceal the mines from any intruders into the village.

6. Pipwhistlion Clanhold

These family of eighty provides the bulk of the community's miners.

7. Kwilliticutti Clanhold

This prosperous clan specializes in hunting and herding; they tend a small herd of sheep and rothe in their caverns. There are some sixty well-fed, plump Kwilliticuttis.

8. Mastacalatl Clanhold

The twenty-five members of this small but wealthy clan specialize in fishing. This family has also produced the most famous adventurers in village history, several of whom have come home to retire.

9. Barackathal Clanhold

This clan of forty souls have small noses (for gnomes) but great courage; they are responsible for defense of the warren.

10. Warehouse and Secret Exit

These chambers, concealed by secret doors and many traps, are kept stocked with plentiful supplies of food and drink; in a desperate situation, they will serve as a last bastion of the village's defense.

Granitehome—A Typical Gnomish Village

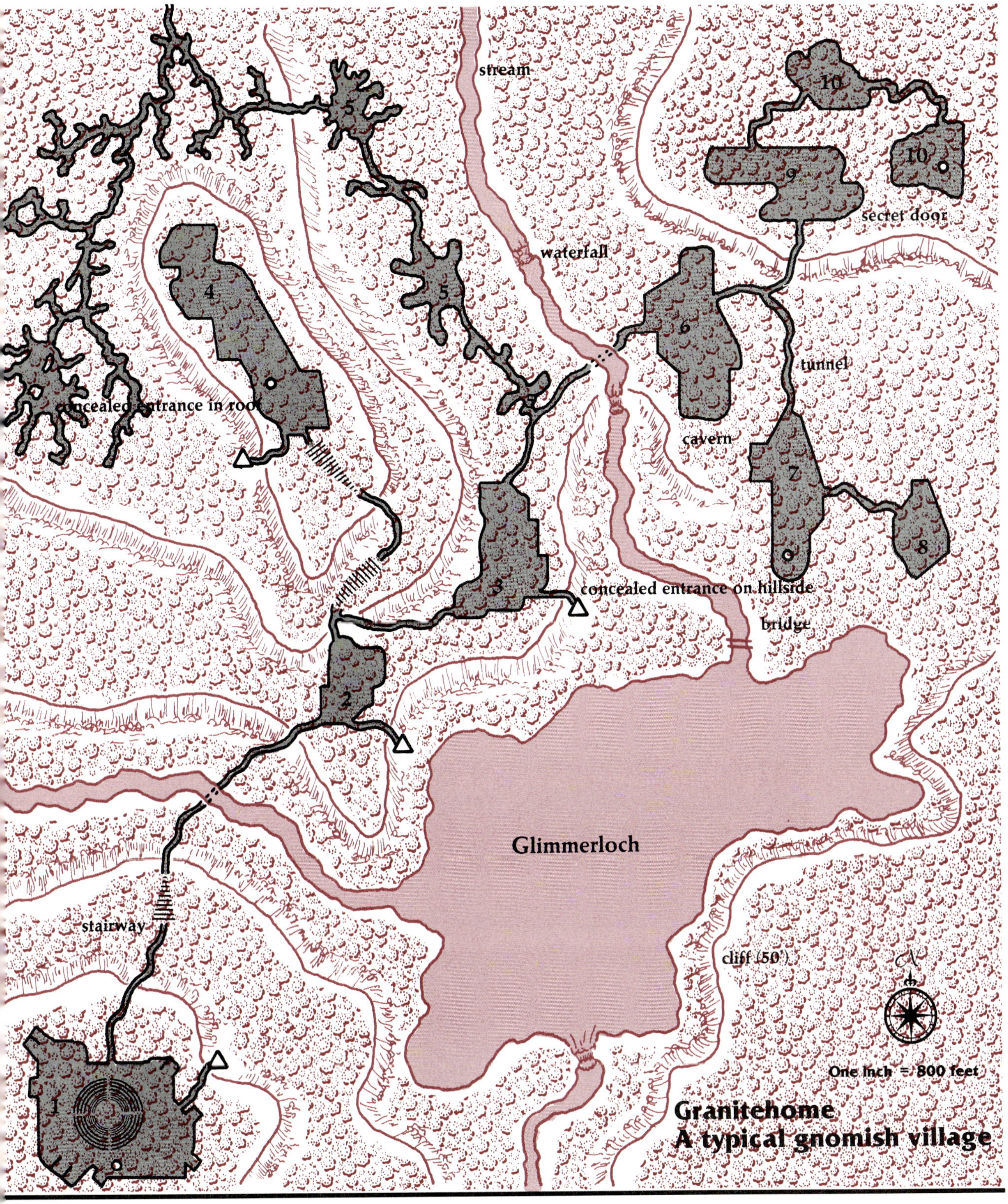

Halflings

"Sit with me for a while, young sprouts, while these coals soothe my aged bones."

"Your bones aren't old, Grandmother!" piped up the youngest of the brood—Kepli, a tiny cherub not two feet tall. He glared at his mother's mother's mother, as if challenging the venerable halfling to dispute her scion's faith.

"Oh, you're right about that, Little Kep—I could still dance a step or two! Why, I remember the night of the Twenty Year Festival, a dozen years back..."

"Tell us, Grandmother—please!" implored a chorus of voices.

But instead, the oldster held up her hand and shook her white head, hair tied in a neat bun at the back of her neck. Ample jowls jostled amiably as she chuckled at the youngsters' enthusiasm. "Another time, sprouts... you'll hear about that, all right. But tonight, you'll have a different tale."

The old halfling settled into her soft chair, adjusting her well-padded form amid the worn cushions, pulling back the comforter on her left, where she faced the fire.

"You see, the story I'll tell you now is one I had from my own grandmother, when I was not much older than Pedderee here." She ruffled the coppery curls of a beaming little girl. Pedderee turned proudly to her siblings and cousins, but their attention remained riveted on the seated figure of the matriarch.

"And it's my true hope," she continued, "that when one of you sits in this chair here—many, many years from now—you'll remember, and share it with your own little sprouts."

"We will, Grandmother! We promise!" Eyes wide, faces serious, the young halflings pledged their attention. They already understood that, tonight, it was no ordinary story they would hear.

The diminutive halfling has become as archetypical a character in heroic fantasy as the stalwart knight in shining armor or the robed wizard fumbling with his spellbooks. Perhaps it is because, in stature and appearance, halflings is so *un*heroic that they have won their way into our hearts and our adventuring consciousness.

Of course, for most halflings, the life of adventure seems a slightly mad choice of lifestyle—a road one takes out of dire necessity or because of profound misfortune. Sometimes simple eccentricity or mental imbalance is attributed as the reason for a friend or relative's leaving his or her hearth behind, with the townsfolk quietly clucking their tongues and sympathetically agreeing that the adventurer was "never quite right in the head, that one."

The halfling race, by and large, cherishes a pastoral existence full of comfort. As a people, they are remarkably lacking in ambition, content to dwell in a snug, well-furnished burrow, enjoying a pipe of rich tobacco and a filling, multi-course meal at dinner. The typical halfling would look askance at the meager trail fare of the average party of adventurers. Our well-padded Stout or Tallfellow, likewise, would be horrified by the rude, chill, and drafty sleeping accomodations available on a rocky forest floor or in the sheltered recesses of dim caverns and dungeons!

Yet, for a wide variety of reasons, a few members of this quiet race do choose to embark on the path of danger, adventure, and possible wealth. Indeed, it is the latter consideration that brings many halflings onto the adventure road—the comforts of life that make living so enjoyable are not always cheap or easily attained! Also, halflings all have a strong sense of duty, and a just cause in the name of a friend will often pry a reluctant halfling from his or her burrow when nothing else would.

Despite their short stature, halflings who choose the life of adventure can be splendid assets to a party. For one thing, the generally cheerful outlook of halflings, together with their ability to make friends with members of a wide variety of different races, can be powerful, if intangible, assets to the group's morale. Faithful and trustworthy to their friends, one of the Small Folk can often provide a focal point of trust and even leadership within a party of much larger characters.

On the more practical side, halflings' nimble fingers are famed for a dexterity that is the envy of many a human thief—and don't make the mistake of confusing small size with physical frailty or weakness. Though they admittedly weigh much less than most of their likely opponents, halflings have found that their speed and their wits are more than ample replacements for brute size. An unaggressive race, halflings have never been known to war with others of their kind, and they resort to organized warfare against other races only in cases of dire need. At such times, their tactics lean toward ambuscade and the use of screening terrain, rather than frontal clashes where the greater weight of any opponent's troops would likely prove decisive; given the choice, they would rather drive a foe away than slaughter it.

The small size of the halfling has proven to be a lifesaver on more than one occasion. Indeed, a party consisting entirely of halflings can investigate dens, caverns, and burrows where humans, elves, and dwarves would be fatally constricted by space.

Halfling society, too, is a flexible and forgiving structure, easily capable of allowing individuality and freedom. A halfling who leaves his or her home in search of fortune and fame will almost certainly be sure of a warm welcome on that perhaps distant day when he or she at last returns. At the very least, such a traveler is likely to return with interesting stories....

But to all halflings, travelers and homebodies alike, there is something compelling and desirable about the solid stone hearth of his or her own burrow. Even the most well-traveled halflings are likely to eventually return to the place of their birth when they are ready to settle down and remember.

Halflings in AD&D® 2nd Edition

Halflings are briefly described in the ADVANCED DUNGEONS & DRAGONS® 2nd Edition *Player's Handbook*. The three most common subraces (Hairfoot, Tallfellow, and Stout) are detailed in the *Monstrous Compendium*, Volume One, while the feral halflings of Athas are described in the DARK SUN® Rule Book as well as in the DARK SUN MONSTROUS COMPENDIUM appendix (MC12). Finally, players of campaigns set in the DRAGONLANCE® world of Krynn will find that the ubiquitous Kender has finally been ranked (for better or worse) among the official halfling subraces.

New Stuff About Halflings

The following chapters provide much greater detail on halflings than any previously published rulebook. This information is intended for players who enjoy running halfling PCs and for DMs who wish to create more interesting NPCs to employ in their campaigns.

The primary halfling character in a typical AD&D campaign is the Hairfoot; this book includes additional detail on not just the Hairfeet but all the halfling subraces—including a nearly unknown variety, the Furchin (hitherto featured only in a single SPELLJAMMER® adventure). Each subrace is differentiated not just by background but by special abilities and characteristics. Halfling society, too, is detailed in all its facets. A variety of halfling character kits are included to allow players to tailor their individual halfling PCs into specialists, each with its own strengths and weaknesses. A typical halfling village, suitable for any AD&D® campaign world, is given in some detail to provide a starting place for an all-halfling campaign, and the Appendix contains several adventure suggestions aimed at halfling PCs.

CHAPTER 1

Myths of the Halflings

Halflings can be found on almost all the worlds inhabited by demihumans and humankind—and, in at least one case, have settled a world without any human or elven inhabitants. Though they resemble their larger human cousins in physical characteristics as well as geographic locale, the halfling race differs significantly in the common tale of its origin.

Whereas humans throughout the known worlds have countless legends, tales, and myths to explain their arrival and presence there, halfling cultures all share a common story: the Story of Littleman. Of course, the common tale is inevitably flavored with local custom—for example, the role of the goddess Yondalla varies depending on who's telling the story. Yet its core is always the same: the story of a small person wandering in the midst of chaotic, populous lands, facing a thousand difficulties and triumphing over them all through luck, courage, wits, and persistence.

The Story of Littleman

"There, Petrilly—be a dear child and fill my teacup. Surely thanks. Oh, and just a wee splash from the bottle to give it some character. Well done, lass."

"The story, Grandmother—tell us the story!" Eyes wide, the youngsters waited impatiently until the old halfling's tea was properly mixed. She sipped, and smacked her lips, and then began.

"Yes... the story of Littleman. But it's not just a story of the first halfling—it's a story of the gods, as well. The gods of the Big Folk and the Bad Folk, humans and goblins, who dwell up in the Seven Heavens and look out over the worlds and watch out for their followers."

"And Yondalla, Grandmother? She's there too, isn't she?"

"Mercy, child! Where else would she be? All you little ones know she's the great Protector of all halflings. Of course she lives there! In fact, the tale's not just about Littleman, but about Yondalla as well. But in those days, when our story begins, she was not yet our protector. Indeed, back then Yondalla was held by most of her fellows to be an unimportant goddess and was little heeded by the great lords of Human and Elf, Dwarf and Monster.

"Not that she was weak, or meek, mind you—quite the contrary. Yondalla was bold and brave, and quick to speak her mind when the gods met together in one of their great councils. But alas, since she had no faithful worshippers, her wise words were often ignored by the other gods, deities who boasted of their multitude of followers like peacocks showing off their pretty tailfeathers. Then, too, there was the matter of her size—gods are like too many people I could mention and are quicker to give respect to the huge and awesome than the small and clever, and Yondalla barely reached to the knee of many of the mightier lords."

"But, but, Grandmother...?" Kepli spoke tentatively. "Yondalla's a mighty goddess—isn't she?"

"Aye, Sprout—that she is. But even in those days, many other gods already had the weight of worshipping legions to support them and cause others to listen to their words. Yondalla had none, and thus many of the greater lords ignored her, especially after she was banned from their councils for a time...."

"But why would they do that to someone as nice as Yondalla?" Petrilly wanted to know.

"Simple, lass. She'd often heard various of the gods boast that they were the wisest, or strongest, or most popular deity of them all. One time when all the gods were gathered in council, she asked 'Which of you is the greatest?' Quickly the responses grew heated, and the argument that followed lasted for a long, long time; by the time it was over just about everybody was mad at just about everybody else. And they decided to blame it all on poor Yondalla for bringing it up in the first place—isn't that just like Big Folks?

"But it wasn't just that; her questions had gotten her in the soup before, and not listening to the big gods making long speeches and

trying to impress one another was hardly punishment in her mind. I think it was more that she was tired of being ignored. It seemed to her that even those gods and goddesses who were her friends often treated her with condescension, as if her size meant she had no more sense than a child! Humph!

"Also, Yondalla is a kind and tolerant goddess. She admires kindness and generosity—not traits that the other gods held in abundance. But remember, my little ones, Yondalla is also a clever god. She saw the power that followers gave to the other gods, and she determined that she would have followers of her own. Finally, the goddess decided there was nothing for it but to find some worshippers of her own."

"Kepli, the fire needs another log—Ah! there's a good lad.

"Yondalla left the Seven Heavens and came to the Worlds Below, where she searched for a long time, looking for the perfect worshipper. But it was a long, hard search: most of the folks she came across already had gods of their own. She could have tried to steal away the other gods' worshippers, of course, but that would have meant trouble, and it was never Yondalla's way to stir up trouble when there was an easy way of avoiding it. Other folk had no gods, but watching them Yondalla saw that they were cruel and savage, hurting one another for no reason. She wanted followers she wouldn't have to scold every ten minutes, and decided to continue her search.

"I don't know how long she searched—my old grandmother used to say it was 'a day and a year and a year and a day'—but surely it was a long weary time. Then one day she saw Littleman sitting on a riverbank, fishing, and at that moment her search was over."

The old matriarch stopped. There was a long, thoughtful pause as her audience considered the story. Unnoticed, Pedderee refilled the venerable halfling's empty cup. Finally Kepli broke the silence: "Grandmother? Where did Littleman come from? What was he doing before Yondalla found him?"

"Ah, child, who knows? Remember, this was in the Bad Old Days, before our folk had farms, and villages, and shires of our own. Back then we were scattered like mice when the owls are out. Each family kept to itself and had its own hidden burrow. It was a hard life: sneaking, and hiding, and getting by on gleanings and scraps, always listening for enemies at the door.

"But Littleman, he wasn't afraid like the rest. He used to boast there wasn't a monster in the whole forest he couldn't outsmart, and he proved time and again that his quick wits were more than a match for brute strength by leading enemies into trap after trap as they chased him, until finally they'd given up and decided to leave him alone. Thanks to his carrying on so, his folk were safer than they had been in a long day, for none of the Bad Folk wanted to mess with any halfling they came across, in case it turned out to be Littleman.

"Yondalla watched Littleman for a long time and decided she liked what she saw. Here was a potential worshipper who was clever, brave, kind-hearted, and full of mischief. Best of all, he was just the right size. So one day she revealed herself to him and made him a bargain: if Littleman would gather all his scattered people into villages and communities, in return for their worship Yondalla would protect them from all their many enemies and give them a life of plenty and peace.

"Now, Littleman thought this over and decided it sounded fair, so he said 'Done!' And from that day to this, Yondalla has watched over our folk and guarded our prosperity, and we have been her people."

"And Littleman, Grandmother? What became of him?" Pedderee asked.

"Why, child, she sent him on his wanderings, to all the worlds where any of the small folk lived," chuckled the white-haired matriarch. "But that's a tale for another night."

A General History of the Halfling Race

The myth of Littleman is repeated in virtually all halfling cultures of the mortal realms. However, the details of the story differ with every teller. In some versions of the tale, Yondalla creates Littleman out of essences she has stolen from the humans, gnomes, dwarves, and elves. In others, she said to have created halflings long before Littleman's time but then left them alone for an age to see how they'd turn out, like a farmer who plants seeds and then leaves them be until the young plants have sprouted. Others give no explanation of how halflings came into the world but simply start with Yondalla's meeting with Littleman.

All versions agree, however, that before recorded history began, halflings were a shy and fugitive people living as hunter-gatherers on the edges of civilization, hiding in isolated burrows from the humanoids and monsters that preyed upon them. The civilized races—elves, humans, dwarves, and gnomes—took little if any notice of them, while to the humanoids they were merely tasty, if elusive, meals. Then, for reasons which these races have never fully understood, the small folk suddenly came out of hiding, gathered together, and created small agricultural settlements for themselves across the face of the known worlds (the halflings themselves attribute the impetus to their mythical cultural hero, Littleman, and the goddess Yondalla). At any rate, it is clear that halflings arrived on the scene after humans and well behind the longer-lived dwarves, elves, and gnomes. The halflings seem to have made a point of not competing with the brawnier neighbors, instead selecting regions of lowland or dense thicket which they industriously drained and cleared, forming the pastoral shires inherited by their descendants.

Halfling societies have developed among most of the lands that have seen significant human settlement. Sometimes the small folk live among the humans, sharing their cities (though many will be gathered in a well-defined "Halfling Quarter") or farming beside their larger cousins. More often, however, halflings will live in small enclaves on the fringes of human realms. As a rule, halflings do not display the urge to expand their frontiers that so characterizes humanity; they are on the whole an easy-going and unambitious people. Once every dozen generations or so some restless halfling will gather a group of like-minded souls and forge into wilderness to clear new lands, but like their ancestors they will avoid areas already inhabited by others (whether human, demihuman, or humanoid). There is no record of halflings ever invading an area for the purpose of driving its inhabitants out and settling there themselves, although they are adept at mingling with whatever inhabitants they find already there.

Halflings strive to form the most neighborly of societies wherever they live. The race has a gift for getting along with dwarves, elves, humans, and gnomes in all climes and environments. Lack of prejudice is a noted halfling characteristic—one which allows them to welcome all types of strangers into their communities and to mingle comfortably in the cities and towns of larger races. Typically, halflings will cooperate with their neighbors for the defense of a larger area. Thus they gain an alliance with larger troops, and the ally welcomes companies of superb missile troops.

The Gods of the Halflings

Like the universal story of Littleman, halflings have a common pantheon which undergoes a great deal of local variation. Community individualism runs rampant among halfling populations; thus, every village will honor the same gods but probably call them by a different name. Among the halflings of the Moonshae Islands in the Forgotten Realms, for example, Yondalla is known as Perissa and is held to have made Littleman on one of those faerie isles. Those halflings who live along the Sword Coast to the south of Waterdeep (not terribly far from the Moonshaes) refer to Yondalla as Dallillia and hold that her origins are as the village goddess

of a small woodland community. The halflings of Lurien far to the south insist in turn that their land is Littleman's original home. And of course each halfling pictures Yondalla as belonging to his or her own subrace (unlike Littleman, who is conceived of as sharing characteristics of all the subraces rather than belonging to any single one).

It's important to remember that this distinction extends farther than simply among the subraces. Halfling villages scarcely two dozen miles apart might each have a different name for Yondalla, and the citizens of each might believe that this goddess is a local deity, concerned far more with the single village than with the race of halflings as a whole.

This reflects an important fact of halfling mentality: the only really important things are those that happen close to home. They're far more interested in worshipping an immediate and beneficent deity—one whose responsibilities are to *them*, and no one else—rather than an abstract goddess who is presumed to overlook the entire race. The remoteness of most human deities bewilders many halflings, as does the deference human worshippers show to their deities. It's not that halflings are irreligious; it's just that while they treat Yondalla and her companions with respect, they're far less in awe of her than is the norm between god or goddess and follower.

As halflings see it, they have a bargain with the gods: in return for their worship, the gods promised to take care of them. Halfling clerics exist to see that both sides of the bargain are kept—to remind halflings to give the gods their due and to remind the gods that they are responsible for the safety and comfort of their loyal followers. Although this sounds like a cold-blooded business arrangement, it is not: stories of the "Bad Old Days" remind all halflings of how much they owe Yondalla, and the average halfling feels both gratitude and affection toward her for her gifts.

In addition, halflings will worship a vast number of very specialized minor deities, variously called "the small gods" and "the thousand home gods." Each house commonly has a protector of its own hearth, often inspired by some matriarch or patriarch in the clan's history. The Homesteader who starts a small community might well be accorded a similar status in later years—that is, his or her spirit might be invoked on matters relating to the health and prosperity of the village. Littleman is widely viewed (by nonhalflings) as a composite of a multitude of these forgotten cultural heroes into one archetypical figure.

Halflings are inclined to see evidence of these small local gods in many aspects of their surroundings. A patron deity of baking might be credited for the way a particularly good batch of bread comes out, for example; if the game is plentiful, the god of the neighboring woods (often pictured as a hare or fox) will be thanked with small offerings. Halflings who fish commonly revere venerable river denizens, such as an ancient and battle-scarred trout. In the latter case, a halfling who hooks or nets the great one will almost certainly let him go—you don't see mounted fish or animal heads on the wall of a halfling burrow!

A full detailing of the most common halfling pantheon is detailed in DMGR4, *Monster Mythology*. The listing here is intended as an introduction, summary, and quick reference.

The small folk have a very matriarchal view of religion: all their primary deities are female. The goddesses are all concerned with the most important aspects of halfling life; the male gods are viewed almost as sidekicks, ruling over peripheral (if necessary) aspects of life.

The avatar listed for each deity is a temporary incarnation, the form in which that goddess or god is most likely to be encountered during play. Of course, these avatars are not intended as NPCs to be commonly encountered by the player characters—rather, they can be used as beings of more or less normal appearance but great, almost unlimited, power. Perhaps they appear to offer the PCs a warning or to suggest a course of action. Lit-

tleman has no avatar, being not a god but a legendary (and possibly mythical) folk hero.

The following are the great halfling gods, universal to the race (though under many guises and names). The real force of daily worship, however, is much more likely to be directed to one of the "small gods," a locally famous deity who can influence the success or failure of mundane tasks and simple, creature comforts.

Yondalla the Provider (Greater Goddess)

Yondalla is a goddess of nature, plants, and growth. She is viewed as the chief matriarch in the halfling pantheon, responsible for the race's creation and for blessing them with peace, comfort, and plenty. She is also viewed as the race's chief protector; although benign and gentle in most of her incarnations, with a wave of her hand she can age or *wither* any who have wronged her faithful children. Her symbol is a shield bearing a cornucopia, representing her dual roles as Provider and Protector.

Avatar: Yondalla appears as a proud, vibrantly attractive halfling with long golden hair, a skirt of forest green, and a stout wooden shield.

Sheela Peryroyl (Intermediate Goddess)

The goddess of agriculture, nature, and weather, the image of Sheela is often mixed, almost interchangeably, with Yondalla herself; some hold that Sheela and Yondalla are different aspects of the same goddess. Just as concerned with preserving wilderness as tilling fields, she guards the balance between the two. Sheela is also held responsible for feasting and celebration and, perhaps most importantly, romance; her major festivals are held at harvest time.

Avatar: Appearing as a pretty young halfling maiden with brilliant flowers in her hair, Sheela is usually laughing and just generally delighted by life. Though she appears naive, even simple, she can wield great powers of nature magic.

Cyrrollalee (Intermediate Goddess)

This goddess is the overseer of many of the mundane and day-to-day aspects of halfling life, chiefly concerned with the burrow and the hearth; again, some believe her to be a persona of Yondalla rather than a separate entity. Friendship among her worshippers is considered the highest praise one can raise to her name; she is most displeased with those who fail to display proper hospitality and good fellowship.

Avatar: Cyrrollalee often takes the form of a stooped halfling of indeterminate years, worn by poverty and work into a frail shell. In this guise, she often visits halfling burrows to see if the inhabitants are truly hospitable; woe to the family that turns her away!

Arvoreen the Defender (Intermediate God)

A god of stern defense and aggressive watchfulness, Arvoreen is the patron of watchful diligence, not war. He is more serious than the typical halfling (or halfling deity) and serves as a reminder that the safety they currently enjoy was hard-won and can be easily lost.

Avatar: Arvoreen appears as a handsome young halfling warrior, muscular of build and generally very lightly clothed. He commonly carries a short sword and often a gleaming metal shield.

Brandobaris (Lesser God)

This is the god of adventure (and misadventure), a favorite among halfling adventurers (especially thieves). He has a bawdy sense of humor and little sense of propriety. Brandobaris is always ready with a joke or a jug, yet he is such a friendly rapscallion that he rarely makes an enemy. He is a good friend of Garl Glittergold and Baervan Wildwanderer.

Avatar: In avatar form Brandobaris appears as a plump and jolly halfling. He's always very well-dressed and ready with a smart reply to any attempt at conversation.

CHAPTER 2
Halfling Subraces

Three halfling subraces—the Hairfoot, the Stout, and the Tallfellow—are introduced in the *Player's Handbook* and detailed in MONSTROUS COMPENDIUM® Volume One; additional information on all three is included here. These three subraces exist almost everywhere halflings are found, frequently in mixed communities. Hairfeet are by far the most numerous of these three subraces, making up about 75% of most worlds' halfling population, with Stouts about 15% and Tallfellows only about 10%. Rumor persists that the original stock from which these three derive still exists in remote deep forests, but no sighting has ever been reliably confirmed; if a few rare feral halfling clans do survive in odd corners, these "wild halflings" guard their privacy so carefully as to be virtually undetectable by members of any other race. In most cases, these so-called "wild halflings" are probably Hairfeet, Tallfellows, or Stouts whose homes have been destroyed by war or some other disaster and have reverted to a primitive ancestral lifestyle.

Three other subraces are less common; each originated on a single world and is found primarily only on its home planet. The Kender are native to Krynn and have been featured in numerous DRAGONLANCE® products, including *Tales of the Lance* and the DRAGONLANCE MC appendix (MC4). Originally found only on Krynn, their insatiable curiosity has led many to stow away aboard spelljamming ships, spreading individuals to many odd places. The information here is for those players and DMs rash enough to allow them into their non-DRAGONLANCE® campaigns—or unfortunate enough to do so before they have a full grasp of the consequences!

The Athasian halfling from the DARK SUN® campaign world is described in the original DARK SUN boxed set and the DARK SUN MC appendix (MC12); so far as is known, no member of this subrace has ever been encountered anywhere besides Athas itself.

Finally, the extremely rare Polar Halflings, or Furchin, have spread beyond their desolate homeworld by spelljamming ships, albeit not by choice, and can now be found on the Rock of Bral and in many other places where spelljammers congregate.

All halflings, whatever their subrace, are highly resistant to magic and poisons; for every $3\frac{1}{2}$ points of Constitution, a halfling gains +1 to his or her saving throws vs. spells, rods, staves, wands, and poisons. Halflings also enjoy exceptional agility, gaining +1 to all their attack rolls involving missile weapons. Surefooted and stealthy, they are able to move very, very silently, giving them an excellent chance to surprise opponents (wearing metal armor naturally negates this ability). Finally, halflings are quick to pick up languages; in addition to their own language and the common tongue, most halflings will know at least a few words of gnome, elf, dwarf, goblin, and orc (the actual number of additional languages known being determined by the character's Intelligence, as described in the *Player's Handbook*, page 16).

The Wanderings of Littleman

"Now, Littleman set to work, and gathered his people together, and showed them how to outsmart their enemies, frightening most away and banding together to defeat the rest. Soon there was a small village along the riverbank. True to her word, Yondalla showered her blessings upon them and gave them a comfort and contentment they had never known before. There was enough to eat, and safe places to sleep; friends to visit, and a fire in every home.

"That was the greatest of all her gifts, the greatest treasure to show her love for her new people: the hearth you'll find today, my sprouts, in every halfling home, no matter how humble, no matter how small. Its fire kept the halflings warm, and cooked their food, and brightened their burrows, a constant reminder of Yondalla's gifts.

"So great was their love of their new life that most of Littleman's people wanted to remain always beside their hearths, till the Bad Old Days faded to a distant memory, a reminder to help them cherish their new way of life all the more."

The venerable ancestor coughed for a moment, and took another sip of her potent tea. Sighing contentedly, she leaned back in the soft chair. Kepli had climbed into her lap, and she patted the youngster's head absently.

"And what of Littleman, Grandmother? Did he settle down with the rest?" demanded Pedderee, sticking out her tongue at her privileged brother.

"Well, strange to say, all the changes that had come over his fellow halflings, changes he'd caused, didn't affect Littleman much. He was the same merry scamp he'd always been, and when he'd finished the task Yondalla had set him would have gone back to his old carefree ways, had she not had other plans for him.

"Yondalla was well pleased with her Littleman, and wanted him to do the same for halflings everywhere as he'd done for those of the Green Fields. And Littleman, he was full of wanderlust, and agreed, thinking it'd be a fine thing to travel the world and see all there was to see. So he set out on his travels, and for years he went from forest to forest, anywhere there were any of our people, and showed them how to put their fear aside and make places for themselves in the world alongside the Big Folk. And when he was done with that, Yondalla showed him how to travel the paths to other worlds, paths known only to the gods.

"So Littleman went on his way, traveling to all the worlds that were, looking for the scattered homes of our people. He noticed how people are more apt to like those who have a lot in common with them, so when he found

some of our folk living nearby settlements of the Big People, he taught them how to adopt some of the Big People's ways. If he found some of the small people living in a deep forest ruled by elves, by the time he left a village of Tallfellows prospered in a nearby forest glen. Where a few families had been driven into the hills not far from a dwarven underground city, a homestead of Stouts sprang up.

"And everywhere he went, Littleman found humans. It seemed that humans could live anywhere. Even in those days their numbers were far greater than those of the dwarves or elves. He watched the humans carefully, for of all the Big Folk they seemed the closest to the small folk in nature. He saw them in many guises, in many places. Whereas the elves kept to their forests and the dwarves their mountains, humankind dwelt in temperate plains, amid lofty mountains and forbidding glaciers—even in steaming jungles and parched desert. Most of the places Littleman found any of our people dwelling, their nearest neighbors were human farmers or pioneers. Hence the Hairfeet came into being, and the long friendship between our folk and the Big Folk begun."

"And Littleman, Grandmother? Surely Yondalla rewarded him for all his work?" wondered Calkin.

"Aye, lad, that she did—but in her own way, and her own time. For a very long time Littleman traveled the worlds, meeting new people and seeing strange and wonderful sights, marvels beyond belief. Many of the folk in the villages he founded invited him to stay with them, but always he refused and set out again to see what lay beyond the next bend in the road.

"Then one day he climbed a hill and looked down into a valley, and it seemed to him that he'd never seen a fairer sight. A shady river wound its way along through well-tended fields surrounded by friendly forest. It was a small village of our folk, and just as Littleman was thinking how he'd like to sit along that riverbank and fish, he saw that it was the very river he used to fish in all those years ago! He found his old burrow, kept clean and snug all the time he'd been away by his neighbors, and sat down contentedly by his own hearth once again. He'd come back to his own home at the end of all his wanderings, and if he's not gone away I 'spect he's there still."

Silence settled over the room, and the children wondered if the old halfling had fallen asleep—so comfortable did she seem, sunk in her chair by the fire. This time it was Pedderee who dared to ask the question.

"Grandmother... is it true that you yourself traveled the Wide Sea once... and even into the skies, and beyond?"

A twinkle of firelight reflected from a half-opened eye—an eye that gleamed with delightful memories.

"Aye, child... that I did. And a fine time I had of it, too! But that's a story that'll have to wait for another time."

Hairfoot

This most common of halflings is found throughout lands that have been settled by humans (with the notable exception of Krynn, where this role is filled by the Kender). They live much as humans do but prefer rural settings and villages to towns and cities. Their crafts tend toward the ordinary and practical—farmers, millers, innkeepers, weavers, brewers, tailors, bakers, and merchants are common in Hairfoot society.

Averaging about 3′ in height, Hairfeet are slightly stockier in build than is typical for humankind. Their complexions run the gamut from pale to very dark, with hair color correspondingly blond to black and eyes that are brown or hazel. They rarely wear shoes (only in bad weather and bitter cold) and can be easily distinguished by the thick patches of hair growing atop each foot. They have no facial hair (besides eyebrows and eyelashes, of course). They wear brightly-colored, comfortable clothes, such as trousers and shirts or dresses, with a vest, jacket, hat, sash, or bonnet added as a flourish. Their faces are round and very expressive, often appearing childlike to humans.

Hairfeet are slightly longer-lived than humans, averaging 100 years—though a few patriarch and matriarchs have reached ages of 140 and beyond. Full adulthood is generally recognized at about 25 years of age.

Hairfeet are only moderately industrious, but they tend to make up in talent for what they lack in drive. A Hairfoot farmer may tend a small plot in the morning, for example, and spend the afternoon lying in the shade—yet his or her irrigation ditch will be so cleverly aligned that his or her field yields a crop equal to that of a much larger human-tended farm. A Hairfoot-woven tunic will have a finer weave and be less scratchy than a similar human product, thus fetching a considerably higher price.

Hairfeet are the halflings most closely integrated into human society. They will work for human employers or hire human laborers, and many a Hairfoot merchant has made his or her fortune by appealing to the human elite of a city's population. While they will dwell in buildings in human neighborhoods, Hairfeet do prefer to live among others of their own race (though not necessarily their own subrace) when this is possible.

A Hairfoot's preferred type of house is the combined above and below ground burrow. The upper portion is almost always wood-framed, with several doors and windows and a bright, airy feel—though the ceilings are typically no more than 5′ above the floors. The lower portion will contain the fireplace and several small, cozy rooms.

Lacking the time, property, or means to build a traditional home, however, a Hairfoot will cheerfully occupy a human house, a sheltered cave, or even a shack or tent. Wherever he or she lives, a Hairfoot will find a place to have a fire and gather for social conversation.

Table 5: Hairfoot Ability Scores

Ability	Minimum	Maximum
Strength	3	17
Dexterity	8	19
Constitution	10	18
Intelligence	6	18
Wisdom	3	18
Charisma	7	18

Ability Score Adjustments: −1 to Strength, +1 to Dexterity

Languages: Any one human language in addition to normal halfling tongues.

Infravision: No

Special Features: Hairfeet are very good at getting along with humans; this translates into a +2 bonus to all their Reaction Rolls involving human NPCs.

Stout

Stouts are not as common as their cousins, the Hairfeet, but they are nonetheless a populous and widespread subrace. They are about the same height as Hairfeet, averaging an inch or two below 3′, but much stockier—indeed, a typical Stout weighs half again as much as the average Hairfoot! This girth is not all fat, however—Stouts are more muscular than any other halfling and tend to regularly best their kin in the wrestling contest that are a favorite Stoutish entertainment.

Ruddier in complexion than the other subraces, Stouts tend to blush easily when pleased or embarrassed and flush bright red when angry. Their hair color tends to be on the light side, with blonds and sandy reds predominating; their eyes are blue, grey, and green. Unlike Hairfeet and Tallfellows, male Stouts can grow some facial hair, although not full beards; usually it takes the form of unusually thick sideburns or muttonchops. Moustaches are rare, and the few able to grow them are often inordinately proud of their accomplishment.

Stouts favor sturdy garb, commonly made of well-cured leather. They prefer practicality to appearance, and thus the members of a community tend to dress with an almost drab sameness. However, a Stout will try to make a point of having a brightly colored outfit of exotic material (such as cotton, wool, or, rarely, silk), for use on special occasions. They often wear boots, which are really more like thick moccasins that offer good protection from the rocky or marshy ground typically under Stoutish feet.

These halflings tend to segregate themselves from human society more than do Hairfeet, preferring the company of dwarves. Stouts and dwarves mix very readily, and their communities will often be located near to each other. Military and defensive alliances between the two races are common, and prosperous trading is also the norm.

Stoutish villages will generally be in hilly or rocky regions near good fishing waters and well-watered fields. They are the only halflings with any affinity to mining, but they are quite good at it and will often develop a bustling business from the excavation of minerals. Stouts can also be skilled jewelers, stone-masons, builders, smiths, boatmen, and carvers. They are lackluster farmers at best, except where mushrooms are concerned, and as merchants they excel primarily at selling the products of the above trades.

Preferring underground habitation more than any other halfling subrace, a Stout will typically live in a fully-excavated burrow. He or she will have several round, shuttered windows placed in a few walls to let in light and air, but the overall place will be cooler, darker, and somewhat damper than a Hairfoot home.

The most industrious of halflings, a Stout can accomplish a great deal of work in a short time. They make doughty soldiers, and their infravision (60′ range) gives them a great advantage in night-fighting. They are skilled swimmers and boatmen and have used small, slender canoes with great effect in night attacks against larger vessels.

With a typical life expectancy of more than 130 years, Stouts are not considered adults until they reach 30 years of age. The eldest of the race have been known to exceed two centuries in age.

Table 6: Stout Ability Scores

Ability	Minimum	Maximum
Strength	5	17
Dexterity	8	19
Constitution	10	19
Intelligence	6	18
Wisdom	3	18
Charisma	5	18

Ability Score Adjustments: −1 to Strength; +1 to either Dexterity or Constitution

Languages: Any dwarven tongue in addition to the normal starting languages for halflings.

Infravision: Yes (60′)

Special Features: Stouts have a 75% chance to detect sloping passageways and a 50% chance of determining direction when underground.

Tallfellow

This subrace of halflings is not so common as the Stout or Hairfoot but exists in significant numbers in many areas of temperate woodland. Averaging a little over 4′ in height, Tallfellows are slender and light-boned, weighing little more than the average Hairfoot. They wear their hair long, often topped by a small brightly-colored cap.

The longest-lived of all halfling subraces, Tallfellows have an average life expectancy of 180 years, with the eldest exceeding 250 years. Like Hairfeet, Tallfellows shun footwear. Their characteristic foot-fur is somewhat sparser and finer than that of their cousins.

Tallfellows favor woodland shades of brown, yellow, and green and have developed several vibrant shades of the latter color through unique dyes. They enjoy the company of elves, and most Tallfellow villages will be found nearby populations of that sylvan folk, with a flourishing trade between the two peoples.

Preferring to live above ground, Tallfellows often dwell in spacious houses of wood, with many windows. Indeed, the ceiling of a Tallfellow house will typically be nearly 6′ above the floor! Though the house will often have a cellar, this will be used primarily for storage. However, during days of hot summer Tallfellows will often retire to their underground chambers for a long evening's conversation and sleep.

Tallfellows display the greatest affinity toward working with wood of any halfling. They make splendid carpenters (often building boats or wagons for human customers), as well as loggers, carvers, pipesmiths, musicians, shepherds, liverymen, dairymen, cheese-makers, hunters, and scouts. They are better farmers than Stouts (although not as good as Hairfeet) and more adept than any other subrace at harvesting natural bounties of berries, nuts, roots, and wild grains.

The only halflings who enjoy much proficiency at riding, Tallfellows favor small ponies. Indeed, many unique breeds of diminutive horse have been bred among Tallfellow clans: fast, shaggy-maned, nimble mounts with great endurance. In a charge, of course, they lack the impact of a human-mounted warhorse; nonetheless, Tallfellow companies have served admirably as light lancers and horsearchers during many a hard-fought campaign.

On foot, Tallfellows wield spears with rare skill. They are adept at forming bristling 'porcupine' formations with these weapons, creating such a menacing array that horses and footmen alike are deterred from attacking. This is one of the few halfling formations capable of standing toe-to-toe with a larger opponent in the open field.

Table 7: Tallfellow Ability Scores

Ability	Minimum	Maximum
Strength	3	17
Dexterity	8	19
Constitution	10	18
Intelligence	6	18
Wisdom	7	19
Charisma	5	18

Ability Score Adjustments: −1 to Strength; +1 to either Dexterity or Wisdom
Languages: Any one elven language in addition to the normal halfling starting languages.
Infravision: No
Special Features: Like elves, a Tallfellow can recognize a secret door on a roll of 1 on a d6. All Tallfellows receive a +2 bonus to surprise rolls when in forest or wooded terrain.

Kender

The fabled Kender is a curious example of convergent evolution. Their native world of Krynn is one of the few with no true halflings of its own, yet this "ecological niche" is filled by another race which, though unrelated, is similar in size, appearance, and culture: the Kender. Hairfeet, Stouts, and Tallfellows who have been to Krynn or have met Kender wanderers on other worlds have adopted them as honorary cousins, despite misgivings about the Kender's complete lack of the prized halfling virtue of common sense.

An extensive description of the Kender is provided in the *DRAGONLANCE® Adventures* hardcover rulebook and in the *Tales of the Lance* boxed set. The information given here focuses on playing Kender in a general AD&D® campaign—i.e., Kender who have strayed from the DRAGONLANCE® game setting into other worlds. It should be noted that it is entirely up to a DM whether he or she wishes to allow Kender into his or her own campaign—and he or she is encouraged to consider very carefully before agreeing!

Kender are somewhat taller than an average Hairfoot or Stout, averaging 3′7″. They are much more slender than true halflings, and they tend to show their age more—a fifty year old Kender will look like a forty year old human, whereas a Hairfoot will probably retain his or her youthful looks even into old age. Kender complexions are light, but they tan easily. They tend to wear their hair very long, with a characteristic topknot and long, trailing tail. They wear shoes most of the time, since unlike true halflings, they completely lack foot-fur.

Kender are the most curious of all halfling-kin, the most willing to depart from their hearth and home to embark on a life of adventure. Most Kender are infused with wanderlust about the time they reach adulthood (in their early twenties) and are likely to spend several decades in an exploration of the world around them, only to feel an equally compelling urge to return home and settle down as they begin to age (mid-fifties to early sixties). Kender are absolutely and utterly fearless—even to the point of immunity to magically induced fear—and as a result are willing to travel literally anywhere and try almost anything.

The life expectancy of a Kender is similar to Hairfoot's (about a century) but it must be noted that, due to their curiosity and fearlessness, Kender are far more likely than any other halfling subrace to meet with a sudden and violent demise. They are not suicidal, but they do get carried away.

Table 8: Kender Ability Scores

Ability	Minimum	Maximum
Strength	6	16
Dexterity	8	19
Constitution	10	18
Intelligence	6	18
Wisdom	3	16
Charisma	6	18

Ability Score Adjustments: +2 to Dexterity (to a maximum of 19); −1 to Strength.
Languages: Kender, Krynn Common, and any other(s) allowed by Intelligence.
Infravision: Yes (30′)
Special Features: Kender who are not thieves have a base 5% chance to perform any thieving skill except Read Languages (no chance) and Climb Walls (40% chance). Dexterity modifiers do apply, but these abilities never

increase as the Kender goes up in level.

Kender are totally immune to the effects of both magical and nonmagical *fear*, whether caused by monsters like the mummy or lich or by spells such as *scare* and *symbol of fear*.

The Taunt: Kender are adept at the art of taunting an enemy until that foe loses all ability for rational thought or restraint and is goaded into an uncontrolled attack. If the victim can understand the Kender's speech, he, she, or it must make a saving throw versus spells (Wisdom bonuses apply). If it fails, the victim will attack the Kender wildly for 1d10 rounds, suffering a −2 penalty to all attack rolls and a +2 penalty to Armor Class.

Athasian Halfling

This subrace of halflings is encountered only on the world of Athas, beneath the Dark Sun. Its members primarily inhabit the jungles along the ridgeline of the Ringing Mountains, the most well-watered terrain on all of Athas. They establish their villages in the dense tangle of the rain forest and jealously guard their territory against intrusion.

The Athasian halfling is by far the least social of all halfling subraces: clannish, suspicious, and distrustful of strangers. Their habit of eating intruders who venture into their territory makes them a danger to all unwary travelers. The Athasian halfling is unique among halfling cultures in this horrifying dietary trait (significantly, they do not consider themselves cannibals, since they don't eat each other, only members of other races).

The villages of these essentially nomadic folk are each centered around a great stone pyramid, with a scattering of small stone buildings around it. The village is the residence of a chief and a few of his or her followers. The rest of the halflings roam a well-defined patch of forest-land, though all the clans will gather at the village once every hundred days.

Athasian halflings average about 3'3" in height. Their skin color varies widely in tone, though even the paler shades tend to be well-bronzed by the sun—since this is a subrace that, as a rule, shuns clothing. Both males and females wear their hair in long, unkempt manes, aside from priests, who usually shave their heads; otherwise, their bodies are completely hairless.

Adept at negotiating all types of forested terrain, including dense swamps, thorny thickets, mangroves, and so on, Athasian halflings utilize this natural cover to screen their villages from larger folk. A network of pathways, each less than 4' high, will pass throughout the huge, densely verdant forest.

Athasian halflings thrive in terrain where other societies might have a hard time surviving. In part, this is because they are so self-sufficient, sharing many skills among the members of a single clan. Woodcarving, weaving, hunting and snaring, tanning, pottery, herbal medicine, alchemy (including the preparation of deadly or paralyzing poisons), farming and herding, jewelry, and featherwork are all common proficiencies among the Athasian halflings.

Though they will cautiously open trading arrangements with nearby cultures, whatever their race, these halflings tend to conduct all transactions in a neutral location or in the other party's community—foreign traders are not allowed into their villages. This arrangement is satisfactory to the other races as well, since these traders realize that they're taking their lives in their hands by venturing into the halflings' jungles—even large, well-armed parties are subject to raids and thievery by these halflings.

Halflings of Athas will treat members of their own subrace from other tribes with respect, generosity, and friendship—even if those halflings are accompanying enemies of the clan (a few renegade clans, however, refuse to recognize the common kinship, and traveling halflings are advised to avoid falling into their clutches).

As with all halfling subraces, a few Athasian halflings are very curious about the customs and traits of other cultures outside the boundaries of their own jungles and will become wary wanderers. While they find it hard to overcome suspicions that the folk they meet on their travels are only waiting for their guard to drop before trying to kill and eat them, these bold wanderers will experiment with different types of behavior and show great openness in trying new forms of food, entertainment, and other experiences.

The only halfling subrace to show any inclination for climbing trees, some halflings of Athas even make their homes in the branches of particular types of forest giants. The homes of such a village are connected by hanging bridges, often leading down spiraling ladders to additional buildings on the forest floor. A more typical camp is located in a clearing beside a steady supply of clean water. A thorny barrier, grown like a hedge to a height of 10′ or more, protects the entire village except for a single, endlessly-guarded gate.

In combat, halflings of Athas prefer short bows, slings, and daggers. Since there is little metal on Athas, most of their weaponry is made of wood and bone. The subrace is also adept at the use of a very accurate blowgun which can silently fire darts up to 60′. These darts are typically coated with one of the virulent toxins or fast-acting paralytics distilled by the tribe's alchemists.

Table 9: Athasian Halfling Ability Scores

Ability	Minimum	Maximum
Strength	3	18
Dexterity	12	20
Constitution	5	20
Intelligence	5	20
Wisdom	7	20
Charisma	5	20

Ability Score Adjustments: +2 to Dexterity; +2 to Wisdom; −2 to Strength; −1 to Constitution; −1 to Charisma

Languages: The halflings of Athas have a language of their own based upon the sounds of forest animals (hoots, howls, chirps, whistles, and the like). Most halflings speak this language and no other. However, a tribe's chiefs will usually know the languages of their neighbors as well in order to handle trade. Wanderers can pick up any language allowed by the individual's Intelligence score.

Infravision: No

Special Features: In addition to the usual priest, fighter, and thief classes, Athasian halflings can be druids, gladiators, rangers, illusionists, and psionicists (all in their DARK SUN® setting variations).

Also, in keeping with the world of Athas campaign, these halflings begin play as 3rd (not 1st) level characters.

Furchin (Polar Halfling)

This rarest subrace of halflings originated on Falakyr (which simply means "the World" in the Furchin tongue), a frigid world of ice, mountain, and glacier. The Furchin are the dominant intelligent race there, though dwarves also inhabit some of Falakyr's underground regions; humans, elves, and gnomes are not found on Falakyr.

The Furchin would probably still exist in blissful isolation, had not an evil spelljamming wizard come across their world in his travels and decided these bearded halflings would make good slaves. Consequently, many were captured and taken to different worlds by the wizard's ships. Some escaped in various ports and eluded recapture until their ship had departed; thus, while they are extremely rare, Furchin can conceivably be met with in any campaign setting.

The most distinguishing feature of this subrace is the full, long beard that sprouts from the chin of the mature males. These beards are a matter of great pride, and in older Furchin often extend as far as the waist. The race favors warm clothing, woven of animal hair or lined with fur. They regularly wear snowshoes and boots.

Furchin halflings resemble Stouts in both height and girth, though their average life expectancy (80 years) is considerably shorter, no doubt due to their harsher native environment. Hair and skin color vary widely, but tend to be pale, though eyes are usually dark. Those few Furchin born with green eyes are accorded much status—they are believed to be emissaries of the gods and are treated to a life of near-royal privilege.

In their own environment, the Polar Halflings are primarily nomadic, ranging across icy glaciers and barren tundra, following great herds of migrating animals. They have become adept at surviving in these very harshest of conditions.

The Furchin dwell in small clans, usually no more than thirty individuals in a community. In summer they live in tents of leather; in winter they make small, domed shelters of ice. Their clothing is made of fur, their equipment from leather, bone, and ivory; wood is almost unknown on Falakyr. Tribal leaders often wield metal weapons and tools acquired through trading with the dwarves inhabiting Falakyr's interior.

Having developed a number of specialized skills, the Furchin halflings are among the most adept demihumans in existence at surviving in their grueling environment—and seemingly having a good time while they're doing it! In general, the Furchin are a good-humored people who enjoy practical jokes, funny stories, and bawdy songs. Both parents care for the young with great tolerance and tenderness, teaching their children early on the secrets of surviving in their harsh clime.

Strangers—especially those who bring gifts, objects for trade, or interesting stories to tell—will be welcomed by the Furchin with warm hospitality. Although their lives are hard, they are an unselfish people and will treat visitors with kindness and generosity (unless given reason to do otherwise).

Members of this subrace are very proficient in specialized skills suited to their environment, some of which will carry over quite effectively into other locations. They are among the most patient trappers in the known worlds and skilled hunters, tanners, and leatherworkers as well. Their characteristic boat is a miniature kayak, a virtually water-tight shell of leather covering a sturdy bone frame. While only one of their skilled boatwrights can craft these vessels, virtually all adult Furchin are adept at piloting them.

When hunting, the Furchin use leather slings for small game and long, barbed spears for more formidable foes; a strong line can be attached to the spear to allow it (and whatever it has impaled) to be drawn back toward the launcher. In melee combat (which they avoid if at all possible), the Furchin use short handled axes and daggers. Because of their small numbers and an absence of potential foes, the members of this subrace are unused to war and have developed no tactics for fighting an organized formation of soldiers.

In the realm of hunting and stalking, however, the Furchin are second to none. Occasionally, a few Furchin led by an experienced warrior will embark on an mission to slay some dangerous threat to the tribe—such as a band of yetis or a frost giant. Through clever use of terrain and diversion, as well as patiently planned and executed ambush, these halflings have been known to vanquish foes many times their own size. In this respect, obviously, they are not so different from their cousins who live in warmer climes.

Table 10: Furchin Ability Scores

Ability	Minimum	Maximum
Strength	3	17
Dexterity	8	19
Constitution	10	19
Intelligence	6	18
Wisdom	3	17
Charisma	7	18

Ability Score Adjustments:
+1 to Constitution; +1 to Dexterity;
−1 to Strength; −1 to Wisdom
Languages: Furchin and Dwarven
Infravision: No
Special Features: All Furchin automatically receive a proficiency in Cold-Weather Survival. In addition, they enjoy a +4 bonus to all saving throws versus cold-based attacks, whether magical or nonmagical, in addition to any other bonuses due to Constitution.

Because of their nimbleness at evasion, all Furchin receive a −4 bonus to Armor Class when fighting giant-class creatures and a −2 bonus to Armor Class against attacks from man-sized creatures. The two bonuses are not cumulative.

CHAPTER 3

Halfling Culture

A culture of harmony and peace, a warm emotional attachment to family and friends—including a willingness to look beyond physical differences to the common bond beneath—and an appreciation of the finer things in life... these are the hallmarks of halfling existence. Whereas Chapter 2 looked at the differences between the halfling subraces, this chapter focuses instead on the things all halflings have in common—their gregarious nature, trustworthy character, and delight in whatever physical comforts their surroundings provide.

No culture has displayed such a willingness, even enthusiasm, in mingling with members of other races. And halflings, with their generally cheerful demeanor, more or less honest approach to life, and helpful ingenuity, have been sincerely welcomed into communities of humans, elves, dwarves, gnomes, and even treants, giants, and (rarely) goblinoids.

But despite this willingness to diversify—or, perhaps, *because* of it—halflings of all cultures feel a strong identity with their extended families; the company of other halflings is important to members of this small race. Families remain close, however large they grow in size, and many adult halflings will consult with their brothers, sisters, grown children, or parents concerning important decisions; if no kinfolk are about, they will turn to friends and even mere acquaintances, so long as they are fellow halflings. Even if advice is not taken, halflings feel a sense of comfort in knowing that other small folk have been privy to the decision.

The Name "Halflings"

It should be noted that, so far as halflings themselves are concerned, the name "halfling" is a misnomer. They don't consider themselves half the size of anything; in their opinion, it's everybody else who's oversized. Their own name for their race translates simply as 'the folk' or 'the small folk' (a term which sometimes includes gnomes as well); humans, elves, and dwarves are collectively referred to as 'the Big Folk.' The halflings also have a slang term they use to refer to humans which translates as 'too-talls.'

The Hearth and the Burrow

"See the fire, there, sprouts... how he settles in his bed, snug and warm. He has no flame for us now—but we don't need it. If anything, his coals are even warmer."

"Warm enough for a story, Grandmother?" inquired Pedderee, quickly taking the coveted lap position while her sister Petrilly as well as Kepli, Calkin, and the others settled around the stone hearth, snuggling into thick fur rugs.

"You know me too well, Little Kitten. Tonight, you pick; what story do you want to hear?"

"Well... last time you told us about how Littleman came home again after all his wanderings. What was his burrow like?"

"Ah, but that's a question you could answer for yourself if you thought for a minute, Little One. You see, when Littleman returned to Green Fields, Yondalla was determined to see that he would never leave again. Before he'd left, his burrow had just been a place to sleep, or a refuge to hide from enemies in. She decided to make it a place that would draw him like the sun draws the dew from the grass, a home so perfect that no place in all the worlds could lure him away. Now, children... what things would she look for?"

"Water!" squeaked Kepli. "A flowing stream to chuckle in the night and soothe him with its song."

"Good, lad—very good. And water deep and clean enough for a cool bath, wide enough to shelter plump trout. Also, a small waterfall, beautiful to watch and hear."

"Flowers too?" asked Pedderee, tentatively. "Or a hillside of soft grass or clover to lie on in the sunny afternoons?"

"Both, lass—and bushes and trees as well. Littleman loved growing things, and wild things as well, so outside his windows Yondalla

placed a perfect meadow. His burrow was on a hillside, facing the south so that it warmed to the sun in autumn and winter—with an overhanging fringe of grass to shade the doors and windows in summertime when the sun was high. Flowers blazed in the meadow from spring to fall, and tall trees surrounded it—hardwoods, with broad, shady boughs, and tall pines, green for all the year 'round."

"And the burrow, Grandmother—surely it had a fireplace?"

"Aye, Calkin, you've put your finger on it there. You see, sprouts, the hearth is the heart of any burrow—it's the place where you should dream now of where you'll go and what you'll do when you grow up... and then, in later years, the place where you'll sit and savor your memories...."

The old halfling stared into the fire, a faraway look in her half-closed eyes. For a moment the children wondered if she was drifting off to sleep—but she merely took a brief stroll down the paths of her own memories.

To the halfling the primary symbol of the importance of home, family, and community is the burrow and its ever-present hearth. No halfling dwelling will be without some sort of fireplace, and even halflings who live aboveground tend to refer to their dwelling as a 'burrow,' even if it's only a room in a inn.

While burrows will naturally vary somewhat depending on the climate and terrain—a Furchin's icehouse will, for example, differ significantly from an Athasian halfling's tree house—all halfling dwellings have some features in common. If at all possible, there will be windows, which will be open during all but the chilliest of days—halflings never confuse 'snug' with 'stuffy.' Tallfellows carry this fondness for fresh air the farthest, positioning their homes to take advantage of whatever gentle breezes waft through the area, while Stouts represent the opposite extreme and might well have only a few small port windows.

Although well-ventilated, the burrow will be shielded against drafts by shutters of wood or leather that can be tightly closed and sealed against gusts and storms. Unlike dwarves, halflings keep their homes brightly lit, with lamps in every room, yet shutters and doors will be so well-set in their frames that not a glimmer of illumination will show on the outside when the burrow is locked up tight.

The fireplace will be built with as much stone as possible, given materials at hand, and capped with a large wooden mantle. It will have a wide mouth and a well-designed chimney to draw smoke up and out of the room. In colder climates, elaborate fireplaces are sometimes constructed with their own air-inlet ducts connecting to the outside of the burrow, allowing the house can be snugly sealed without suffocating the fire, while other ducts channel the heated air away. Conversely, in very warm locales halflings enjoy gathering around communal outdoor fires for an evening's conversation and fellowship—yet even so, each individual burrow will always have its own homefire as well.

It is not uncommon in a halfling burrow for a single fire to last for years, even decades or generations, without a second kindling. Even in very warm climes where it is allowed to die down to coals during the daylight hours, the embers are coaxed back to life at nightfall. Well-seasoned hardwoods are a favorite fuel, but wherever they live, halflings will quickly learn the best fuels for producing a warm, steady heat. Halflings are adept at using different local firewoods (hickory, mesquite, applewood, &c) to "sweeten the air" or season the food they cook.

A halfling fireplace usually has several racks beside it, so that a variety of cauldrons and kettles can be swung over the coals. In this way dinners are cooked, milk curdled into cheese, and clay pottery fired by the steady heat. Often a large oven nestles in one corner of the coal bed, for use in baking the bread that forms the centerpiece of the halfling diet.

A lazy man sits in his old chair all day enjoying the sunshine, while an industrious man labors to earn the money to buy a fine new chair he may sit in someday. I ask you, who is the fool?

—Hairfoot Philosophy

Halflings have been called connoisseurs of comfort, and the interior of a burrow will be furnished as cozily as the inhabitant(s) can afford. The floor will boast several rugs, mats, or carpets. Every halfling, however poor, has a table and a few stools, and at least one well-padded comfy chair. The bed will be small but snug, its mattress filled with clean straw or sometimes down, with several soft pillows.

The mantlepiece will feature a variety of decorations—most practical, like dishes and candlesticks, a few ornamental or exotic. The latter will often be among their owner's prized possessions, even if he or she hasn't a clue as to what the things are, provided they look interesting enough. Paintings and statuary are rare, as halflings generally prefer their treasures to be useful as well as pretty to look at.

The Family

"Pedderee, when your mother was a little girl she had those same curls dangling by her cheeks—she was my first granddaughter, you know, and I couldn't have been prouder! And you, Calkin—your dad was my second nephew on my brother Theadric's side. He had Theadric's stubborn jaw, and—if you don't mind me saying so—I see that same firm set of the chin in you!"

A single burrow will be occupied by members of one family. Depending on the size of both burrow and family, the dwelling could have as many as twenty-five residents or as few as one. A populous burrow will have a patriarch or matriarch (occasionally both) who presides over the brood with genial authority. Four generations of a family living in a burrow is not at all uncommon, although sometimes a just-married couple will decide they want a burrow of their own. Occasionally an older halfling will decide that he or she would like a private burrow, but such individuals are viewed as eccentrics by their families and neighbors—it is hard for most of these gregarious folk to imagine anyone *wanting* to be alone.

Halflings respect experience and wisdom and defer to their elders out of affection and trust. Aside from the venerable head of a family, adult halflings of different generations (even parents and children) view each other as equals. Only the youngest halflings, not yet adults, are subject to rules and restraints imposed by authority; all grown halflings living in the burrow will be there because they want to be.

Parenting duties are shared by all the adult members of the family; fathers, mothers, aunts, uncles, grandparents, and older siblings all share in the upbringing of youngsters. It is a rare halfling who grows up as the only child in a household; it is more common to be one of a number of brothers and sisters and cousins who play and explore together.

Though family bonds are felt warmly, they are not a cause of exclusivity. Feuds between clans are rare, since most disputes are blamed on the disputers themselves, not their families. For example, a halfling who gets into a fight (a rare, but not unheard of, occurrence) is likely to be criticized soundly by his or her own family for his or her lack of self-control—there's no "Let's go and whup them guys what beat on my brudder!" mentality.

Although disagreements are naturally inevitable in these crowded living conditions, halflings rarely engage in outright bickering or argument. For one thing, the presence of two people arguing in a burrow several dozen people call home is considered a major intrusion into the privacy of the others and hence a severe breach of etiquette by those engaged in the fracas.

Many of the traditional causes of such fights among humans are removed by the halfling's communal outlook on life. Supper is prepared by everyone who has a free hand, and those who didn't cook will pitch in the cleaning up or help entertain the youngsters after the meal. Only when all the chores are done is an individual member free to go about his or her own business. Because of their ready-to-help nature, tasks like cooking and cleaning up don't take very long, so this still leaves family members with plenty of time to get their feet up and their eyelids down.

In cases of deeper disputes, such as a couple's disagreement on whether to move out and find a place of their own, the discussion will generally be waged quietly, over a period of months or even years. One member might make a friendly remark, after a crowded dinner around a small table, how pleasant it would be to have enough room to stretch out his elbows at the table. A week later his spouse might reply, in an equally pleasant tone, how nice it is that there was such an interesting conversation—"so *many* points of view"—around that same table on a different evening. Naturally, it takes a long time to resolve an issue like this—but when it's resolved, the decision is far more likely to have been mutually arrived at than it would have been among a human couple.

Growing Up

Offspring are a source of great pride and joy to their parents. Halflings enter the world as helpless as human infants, requiring similar care for the early part of their lives.

For the first ten years, a halfling's relative growth pretty well parallels a human's—i.e., a ten year old human and halfling will look much the same age, although not in size, and will have about the same level of maturity. Children of both sexes and many different ages commonly play together, following rules created by the older youths that still allow the youngest a measure of freedom and decision-making in the game.

It is during these formative years that young halflings practice those traits that will form some of their basic skills when they grow up. Hide and Seek is a favorite game among halflings and is almost always played out of doors. Thus the youngsters become adept at concealing themselves in all sorts of natural cover—in patches of brush, behind tree-trunks, and even amid beds of flowers. Young halfling quickly develop the calm patience that allows them to remain still for long periods of time, since they learn over and over that it is the one who moves that is seen first.

Another favorite game is called Knock the Block, in which a small object such as a block of wood, or perhaps a tin pot or iron kettle, is placed some distance away, and the young halflings take turns throwing things at it, recording points for hits. The game is sometimes played with slings and stones (among older youths). For special tournaments and important matches, clay targets are used, with the winner determined by whoever's shot strikes hard enough to shatter the object. This common game is presumably one reason why so many halflings grow up to be so adept with missile weapons.

From the age of eleven or so on to adulthood, halfling development slows in comparison with the Big Folk. A halfling's adolescence lasts for about a decade and a half (more in the case of the longer-lived subraces). However, the period is characterized by a lot less angst than is typically felt by a human—perhaps because of the warm, supportive, noncompeting environment provided by family, burrow, and community.

Halfling artisans and craftsmen do not follow a formal apprenticeship program—indeed, adolescents are encouraged to experiment with a wide variety of pursuits. The cheesemaker, for example, will be helped by virtually every village youth over the course of several years. Those who find that they enjoy the work will spend more and

more time with the 'master,' until by adulthood the youth has learned everything the cheesemaker can teach about the trade.

Another reason, perhaps, for the relaxed adolescence of the typical halfling is that male-female friendships are as common as friendships between members of the same sex, often lasting from childhood through adulthood. Many of these lifelong friendships culminate in marriage.

Sustenance, and More

In another moment the old matriarch's eyes flashed open, and she grinned at the eager faces around the hearth.

"What else, Grandmother?" inquired Kepli. "How did Yondalla keep Littleman home in his burrow?"

"She kept him there with the other things he loved... with bread hot from the oven, and fresh butter and cheese. With the tangy scent of meat cooked just right, and good drink to nourish the meal along—wines sweet and dry, and cold milk, and even colder beer. She made stout and mead for him, to help the fires of his hearth keep him warm."

Halflings enjoy eating and drinking in plentiful quantities—indeed, despite the difference in size, the typical halfling will eat as much if not more than a human twice his or her size; this is because halflings have a very high metabolism. Most halflings eat three large meals a day, interspersed with three sizable snacks: breakfast, brunch, lunch, teatime, supper, and bedtime snack. Although they enjoy an occasional meal of meat, especially poultry or wildfowl (roast pheasant is considered a great delicacy), the short folk rely extensively on bread, fruit, and cheese.

Halfling bakers are famed for their abilities with dough, making all types of sweet or salty, light or heavy breads. Cheesemaking is another skill in which many halflings are proficient, and here, too, variety is a prime hallmark—each individual cheesemaker will typically specialize in one kind of cheese, no two of which will be alike, allowing a halfling community to offer a variety of sharp and mild, hard and soft cheeses.

Halflings are born gardeners, far exceeding any other race in their knack for growing foodstuffs. Any halfling with access to a plot of ground will usually maintain a garden, wherein he or she will carefully nurture fruits and vegetables of all types appropriate to the climate. Even in a small garden, a halfling will generally plant at many different times during the spring, assuring a continuing harvest from early summer through late autumn. Halflings do not favor a lot of spice in their foods, however, so few raise peppers or other strongly-flavored crops unless a nearby ready market for them exists. Onions are a notable exception—many halflings love them and have even been known to munch them raw, much as a human might eat an apple.

Halfling brewers are well-known and their products popular with humans as well as other halflings. As with cheesemaking, a brewer will specialize in a single beverage. These can vary from heavy stout (halflings often jokingly hand a first-time human drinker a knife and fork with the glass) to light and creamy ales. Fruit wines are also popular, with halfling vintners specializing in using whatever fruit is near to hand.

It should be noted that, though halflings favor many sorts of wines and ales, they rarely get drunk, due no doubt to their high metabolism. Rather, the alcohol tends to make them pleasantly drowsy, and a group of halflings that share a bottle of potent stuff will typically become quite relaxed, quiet, and contented as the evening wears on.

The Village

The key to the village is the halfling's desire for the maximum of comfort with the minimum of effort. These pragmatic folk long ago learned that, though one halfling might learn to grow and cook and sew and build and so forth, specialization in these tasks creates a much higher level of quality all around. Thus, we see the cooperative roots of the halfling's picture of community.

Indeed, this cooperation extends to all aspects of life. The breadmaker will give his or her loaves to the other villagers, as will the cheesemaker with his or her cheese and the brewer with his or her beverage. Perhaps the baker's family gets the best loaf from a particular batch, but everyone gets a fair share.

Burrow excavation and house-building operates under the same pattern—the most experienced builder in the town will supervise a legion of workers, so that the initial portions of the task can be accomplished in a few days. As to the furnishing of the burrow, the occupants see to that themselves.

Though halflings mingle well with human society, this does not mean they have departed from the concept of the village—rather, it is an indication of their broad vision, for nowhere is it written that the villagers must be fellow halflings. A halfling who dwells in a city will treat his or her neighbors as fellow villagers—this is what makes halflings such good neighbors. They are quick to recognize when their generosity is not reciprocated, however, and thus will soon narrow their circle of 'villagers' to those who feel a similar sense of cooperation and friendship.

Crafts, Labor, and Products

Halflings are adept at utilizing local resources in their labors. Although only the Stouts are very effective at mining, all subraces will be intimately familiar with the surface features of their surroundings. If they live in an area with a lot of trees, carvers will know everything about each variety of wood available. If the environment is rocky, experienced stone-masons will predominate. The most dramatic evidence, perhaps, of this adaptability is the fact that the Furchin have developed a high level of skill at working the raw materials in their nearly woodless and stoneless environment: they make everything from their homes to their tools, weapons and clothing out of leather, bone, and ice. The specific skills likely to be found in a halfling community vary by subrace (see Chapter 2).

The quality of halfling work is very consistent. While rarely the equal of the greatest artisans in the world—dwarves make better axeblades, elves better wine—on the average it is better than the average available elsewhere.

Areas where halfling craftsmen truly excel include many tasks involving dexterity and great detail. The small folk make splendid jewelers, engravers, locksmiths, woodcarvers—indeed, artists of all types. They love colors, and once again the propensity for detail allows a halfling painter to bring a scene to bright and vivid life. If clocks are known to a world (e.g., if its technology is sufficiently advanced), then it is likely that the finest clockmakers will be halflings.

Also, because of their proclivity for entertaining gossip and news of all kinds, halflings make great storytellers. Some of them have a gift for music, and halfling musicians and storytellers are in great demand at any village feast or festival.

Halflings are ill-suited for jobs requiring size and strength, such as blacksmithing, ocean sailing, or cargo hauling. Though a halfling village will usually have a smith who makes nails and horseshoes, his or her work will not be up to the level of most human smiths and will probably be for local consumption only; the same is true of halfling teamsters.

Trade

"They cleaned me out! What's even more amazing, they made me feel like I was having a good time while they did it!

"Now, I've taken my wagon of goods into many a village before, and always I came away with a little more than I took in. This trip I had it all: bright copper kettles, some jeweled necklaces and bracelets—trinkets, really—and an assortment of good hammers and knives.

"I'd no sooner rolled into town than I smelled bread baking. I think that was the start of it—I didn't realize how hungry I was. The baker came out and gave me a piece—free! Best crust I ever tasted, too.

"Then there was the innkeeper, who brought me over a mug of sweet ale. Why, before I knew it they were givin' me a bit of this and a taste of that, and I just sort of started doing the same thing back.

"Fact is, though, you can't make it in this business if you trade a steel knife for a glass of beer, or a copper kettle for a loaf of bread. Why, the liveryman took such good care of my horses—they positively gleamed in the morning!—that I paid his bill with a smile.

"Gave him one gold for each horse, I did. You know, I can't even remember when I've forked over that much to put myself *up for the night!"*

—Grantancrous Jute, Human Tinker and Tradesman

Barter is a way of life to the halfling—though in more cases than not it is the unspoken, unrecorded barter of village life. However, halflings also trade among themselves on a more formal basis and are skilled at interacting with human suppliers and customers. They have a keen eye for detail and are generally quick to spot counterfeit or low-quality goods, all the while proclaiming the good points of whatever they are offering in return.

Most trade between halfling villages, and between halflings and other folk, is carried on by professional halfling merchants called Traders (see Chapter 4: Character Kits). These halfling merchants transport surplus goods from one village to trade for the products of another. While halfling merchants will certainly take gold and other coinage as payment, they are also willing (more so than human or dwarven traders, certainly) to accept goods in return for goods. Pragmatic here as elsewhere, however, Traders generally don't take goods unless they feel that they will be able to sell or barter those same goods at one of their next few stops.

Since they enjoy the give-and-take of a good bartering session, a typical halfling merchant will offer far less for the goods he or she desires than they are actually worth, while at the same time asking an exorbitant price for his or her own. The small folk view bartering as something of a game and sometimes forget how much better they are at it than most of the Big Folk. However, a halfling who belatedly discovers that he or she has unwittingly talked a human into buying goods at considerably more than their value will often salve his or her conscience by throwing in a 'bonus' once the deal is closed to compensate the poor bargainer.

Society Norms and Taboos

"As pleasant as his burrow was, Littleman often felt there was something missing as he sat alone by his hearth. It wasn't long before he realized that he was lonely, and it wasn't long after that till he knew he'd found the perfect person to cure his loneliness—Melindy, the fairest maiden among all his neighbors, she of the plump, red cheeks, bouncing curls, and smoothest downy fur on the tops of her feet. But, as luck would have it, she was already being courted by another—stolid Genrill, a farmer and herdsman of good wealth and solid standing in the community.

"Naturally, Genrill objected to his new-

found rival but—alas for him—Melindy's heart was swept away by the dashing Littleman, with his tales of travel and adventure, his ready laugh, and his warm smile."

"But Grandmother—did Genrill not fight for his love? Didn't he bash Littleman over the head... or something?" wondered Kepli.

"Posh, child—you talk like a human! Of course he didn't. Melindy made known her choice, and she became Littleman's bride. Genrill himself provided the roast beast for the wedding feast!"

Though they have no lack of courage, halflings shun violent or aggressive behavior in social settings. They are slow to anger and always ready to seek a negotiated solution to any dispute.

A halfling feels no sense of shame if he or she chooses to leave the presence of some obnoxious bully rather than getting involved in a fight—even a fight the halfling thinks he or she can win. Fortunately, because of their communal village upbringing, few halflings are this rude, and such situations mainly arise when the halfling mixes company with humans, dwarves, or goblinoids.

Personal insults delivered to a fellow villager are considered low class, reflecting more poorly on the one who makes the insult than the target. Politeness is much admired, and one who shows tolerance to a neighbor who has wronged him is considered to be the epitome of a class act.

Parties among halflings are common and will be given for a variety of reasons. Birthdays are always cause for celebration, and with so many family members living together it's rare for a month to go by without several birthdays in it. Each community will also have many annual holidays. These vary by culture—there are no such holidays observed by halflings everywhere. Often the Small Folk will celebrate whatever festivals are popular among their human and demihuman neighbors, soon giving these observances a character all their own.

The hosts of a party are expected to provide food and drink—but much of this will be contributed by neighbors prior to the event. Thus, none of the guests show up with anything to contribute, but they've all provided a bottle, a wedge of cheese, loaf of bread, or the like beforehand. Indeed, this is one way halflings get invited to parties—if you find out that your neighbor is celebrating his birthday, for example, take over a small jug of ale in the morning and he can hardly turn you away when the festivities commence in the afternoon!

There is little sense of social status among the halflings in a village, aside from the amused tolerance shown by adults to children and the general respect for the elderly. Wealthy halflings are expected to throw bigger parties and to generally show generosity to those less fortunate—yet they are not accorded any 'upper class' standing because of this. The villagers may well elect a sheriff, mayor, or constable and give this individual nominal authority to arrest troublemakers. Rambunctious behavior is rare among halflings themselves, however, so the sheriff's main concern will be to control the behavior of humans, dwarves, and other possible troublemakers who come through the community.

Joy and Humor

Halflings are a folk who can derive pleasure from many simple things and are not afraid to show it—a halfling who is happy laughs; one who feels affection or love will express himself or herself with words or deeds.

The small folk love to tell and hear stories and will generally be attentive and silent when anyone spins a tale. Not surprisingly, they especially love stories in which the small and clever triumph over those who are physically larger and stronger but clumsier and less quick-witted.

Halflings also have a frank appreciation for bawdy humor and practical jokes. They have the ability to laugh at themselves, though one prank often leads to another in retaliation, and so on. Such good-natured exchanges have been known to continue, reciprocated back and forth, for decade after decade.

Sorrow and Anger

"There came a time of troubles to the Green Fields. In the first year, bitter winds blasted from the highlands, drying out the fields and leaving no grain and no fruit to harvest in the fall.

"But Littleman turned to his bride, Melindy, and he said—'we've still got our sheep, and our pony, and our plow. We'll have a good crop next year!' And she smiled at him, and they waited.

"Then, when spring came, it brought the rains in a flood, and with them came a sickness of flies across the land. They bit the animals, and the sheep and the ponies all got the evil sickness. They wasted away and died, even before the crop got in the ground.

"So Littleman turned to Melindy and he said—'be happy, my wife. We still have our stream, and our flowers.' And again she smiled at him, and they waited for the flies to go.

"Which they did, but only when the frosts came to freeze everything across the land. The stream dried away, caught in the highlands in a grip of ice, and all the flowers and even the grass withered away and died.

"This time Littleman turned to his wife and he soothed her fears: 'Don't worry, my dear—we have our hearth, and our burrow to shelter us.

"But next came the storms, with such wind, such power, that the very roof was torn from the burrow, and the stones of the hearth fell down into a great pile, nearly crushing the two of them before they could flee from the broken wreckage of their home. At last they stood outside, shivering and desolate, with no food, no animals, and not even a shelter over their heads."

"Then what, Grandmother?" asked Kepli, wide-eyed and sorrowful. "Then did Littleman know sorrow and grief?"

"You might think so, Sprout—but you'd be wrong. For even then, with all of his life in ruins around him, he turned to Melindy, and he said: 'Be happy, my love—all we have lost we shall regain, in years to come. And for now, we still have each other.'"

The small folk know the same griefs as humankind—death and illness, partings, natural disasters, and other tragedies. Though they, as a people, are deeply affected by such misfortune, halflings tend not to display their grief as openly as do humans. Halfling villagers who have just lost several neighbors and friends to marauding bandits will shuffle around as if they are in shock—there will be few tears, little wailing or crying.

Even more surprising, there will be few expressions of outright anger or hostility. Revenge is not a great drive to most halflings, though occasionally a wrong will be judged so heinous, so unforgivable, that retribution is required (deliberate murder is a prime example). Loss of possessions, however—whether due to accident or the malicious acts of others—tends to be greeted with a more relaxed attitude of 'easy come, easy go.'

In their day-to-day lives, halflings are remarkably impervious to frustration and depression. Members of the small folk show a remarkable ability to adapt to the circumstances of their surroundings. If the crops fail and food is short, they derive that much more pleasure from the meager fare that they eat. If the roof caves in and the family has no place to sleep, they will remark how fortunate they were that no one was seriously hurt—and they'll mean it!

Riddles

"Did you ever try to get a straight answer out o' one of the little maggots? I know I have, and I ain't succeeded yet! Why, they'll answer

a question with another question sure as the sun goes down at night! Most irritatin' thing I ever done was ask a halfling for directions!

"'Where can I find the mayor?' I said, straightforward-like.

"'Which mayor is that?' says the little runt.

"'The mayor o' this town, o' course,' I told the dummy, nice as you please.

"'Why, do you want to see her?' says the dang fool.

"'Course I do!' I said, trying to resist the urge to wring his scrawny neck. 'Why else would I be askin'?'

"'Don't you know?' he has the gall to ask me!

"I tell you friend, if the mayor hadn't come walkin' down the street that very moment, I think that scene might have ended in bloodshed!"

—Dwarven wayfarer, describing his unwitting participation in the Question Game.

A favorite form of contest among halflings of all subraces is the exchange of riddles. These can vary from simple questions and answers to complex puzzles involving clues vague and obtuse. It's not uncommon for a halfling to spend an hour or more pondering such a problem in silence punctuated only by his or her frequent admonitions: "don't tell me the answer!"

Even more baffling to nonhalflings is the Question Game, a contest in which each participant must answer a question with another question. Each response must be a complete sentence, relevant to the one that preceded it, and delivered within ten seconds, or the player loses a point. Experienced players can continue the game for hours; one legendary brother-and-sister team are rumored to have carried a game on every time they met for the last twenty years of their lives. Some halfling enthusiasts of the game will treat every question addressed to them as an invitation to play, with sometimes regrettable results

Villages and Shires

Halfling settlements for the most part tend to remain small—they will live in towns and shires scattered throughout a human empire, for example, or they might occupy several small villages in a forest ruled by an elven king. In a few cases, halfling holdings have expanded to the size of a kingdom—both the Forgotten Realms and Krynn boast nations populated and ruled entirely by halflings. But even here, they have labored to maintain peaceable relations with the realms that share their borders.

Warfare

Though they abhor war, halflings nevertheless have proven to be tenacious fighters in defense of their homes or in the service of an alliance. The following letter, written by General Krastarian of Keltar upon the event of his defeat at the hands of an outnumbered halfling militia, perhaps best describes their tactics:

The little devils stayed out of the open country—undoubtably they knew that our horsemen would have trampled them like rabbits! They gave us their towns and farms in the plain, while they fell back to the accursed wood. And there I, the conqueror, would follow with my footmen—though in truth I knew there to be ten of them to every one of my own men.

My companies vanished in the tangle, breaking ranks and thrashing blindly ahead. And then, across the length of the front, came a murderous shower—a thousand deadly arrows piercing the flesh of my men, while the vermin archers remained invisible.

I swear, Your Majesty, they swarmed through the brush like mosquitoes! Thousands of them, on all sides! Everywhere we turned, little figures skulked—arrows flew with uncanny accuracy, piercing eyes and

necks, dropping even armored men in their tracks! We charged and they scattered, vanishing into the thicket as if they had never been—only the bodies of my men told otherwise.

At last I determined to fire the wood—the wind favored our advance—and gave orders to do so. The blazes took hold with great effect, but again that hellish place betrayed the logic of war. The brush exploded like tinder, and the blaze swept not only with the wind—but back into our faces!

Many fine men perished in that inferno—a blaze I believe to have been sorcerously altered by the enemy. Minutes after my own very narrow escape, my scouts reported the bulk of the enemy force slipping from the brush while we fled the blaze.

I request, Excellency, that we return to Lurien with sufficient forces to deal with this pestilent threat—perhaps two legions, and a full column of horse. I realize that this will stretch the defense of your borders in a tenuous manner, but I believe there to be no other way for the forces of Keltar to prevail against this pervasive foe.

It makes an interesting historical footnote to add that the general commanded some eighteen hundred men, including companies of elite guards, longbowmen, and light lancers. Never did the halfling force opposing him number even a thousand! He was subsequently removed from command through the simple expedient of removing his head from his shoulders; the halflings of Lurien were left alone for many decades to follow.

Though this is an heroic incident in the annals of halfling military history (and admittedly, a more patient and imaginative commander may well have found the human force sufficient for the conquest), it is illustrative of the tactical finesse and courage displayed by the small folk when they are motivated for battle.

Another feature has also contributed to the halflings' fine reputation as allies: the small folk traditionally have demonstrated a willingness to honor the terms of a longstanding alliance. They will provide the troops they promised, when and where they are required—and those troops display almost as much determination in supporting an alliance as they would in defense of their own burrows. However, they must have some strong motivation before resorting to violence to solve a dispute. Almost always this motivation is defensive in nature—either the halflings or their friends are attacked by some aggressor. Occasionally the small folk might participate in an offensive campaign, but only when it is a preemptory strike against a foe who has already committed enough bloody acts to warrant retribution **and** is currently gathering forces for an attack on the halflings or their allies.

However, when the need is clear, halflings are speedy and resolute to answer the call to arms. Indeed, this trait is one that makes halfling/human treaties attractive to the rulers of the latter. Also, the deadly accuracy of halfling bowmen and slingers is known to all who have faced them—and few of those desire to do so again!

Tactics

As already noted, halflings prefer to avoid war if at all possible. A community of the small folk will be willing to negotiate extensively, and even yield to a certain amount of extortion, in order to avoid bloodshed.

However, when pressed to the point of no return, halfling troops make determined fighters with a number of effective tactics at their command. In most cases, only about half the adults will fight, the remainder remaining behind to protect the elderly and children. In cases of dire need—where the very survival of the community is at stake—every able-bodied adult may well be drafted into the cause.

Halflings have a reputation for being easygoing and somewhat lazy, but this does not mean they cannot fight effectively if they need to—the legends of the Bad Old Days remind every halfling of what life was like before they had villages and lands of their own, and they will fight with surprising tenacity, even ferocity, to keep from slipping back into that fugitive existence. Thus each halfling has something that can be used as a weapon in his or her burrow, no matter how peaceful the area. If the village has had to fight in the recent past, then each resident might have a short sword and shield as well as a bow and arrows or a sling and bullets. Even if battle is rare or virtually nonexistant, villagers will be able to arm themselves with a missile weapon apiece (bow, sling, or perhaps darts) and at least a long knife or spear for melee combat—a fact invaders expecting to find them easy prey have discovered time and again, to their surprise and regret.

Halfling companies are almost always irregular—i.e., they don't fight in neat ranks and lines. They will be quite capable of firing volleys of missile fire upon command, and they will advance and withdraw on the orders of their captains—but they would have a hard time facing, for example, a tight rank of armored human infantry or orcish swords.

Instead, the halflings favor battles in wooded or otherwise obstructed terrain. Their scattered formation is ideal for each fighter finding his or her own source of cover, though they are far more adept than humans at holding their company's unity even in thickets where visibility and mobility are severely limited. The fabled ability of halflings to virtually disappear in underbrush is never more useful than at moments like this.

A favored tactic of a halfling force, when fighting in this type of concealing terrain, is to create a loud diversion. A few veteran warriors will thrash through the brush, firing many arrows, giving the impression that they number scores of times more than they actually do. Then, if the opponent's force turns to face this imaginary onslaught, the real halfling company screened by the woods attacks the enemy's flank.

If a halfling force is attacked in unfavorable (i.e., open) terrain by a force of large creatures, the small folk might try to stand off the attack if they feel they have a chance of success. If they are attacked by horsemen or are out-numbered by well-armored infantry, however, the entire formation will usually scatter, joining up again at a place offering more concealment and protection.

Halflings rarely fight mounted, though Tallfellows are a notable exception, occasionally riding into battle on small ponies or, very rarely, beasts such as dire wolves. When halflings fight as members of an alliance, they are often used as missile troops. Well-screened behind formations of human or dwarven foot-soldiers, halfling archers and slingers can shower the enemy with a deadly rain of arrows and bullets.

Another common specialty of halfling troops is tunneling and underground operations. They are not particularly adept at digging such passages—that task is better left to dwarves—but halfling troops can negotiate much smaller passages than can most of their allies. Thus, if combat is expected in close quarters or beneath a low ceiling, halfling troops are often selected to lead the way.

Magic

"I could tell that they feared me when I came into their village and demanded a place to sleep for the night. Gave me a nice room, they did, too.

"But when I woke up, everything I had in my pockets, my pouches—even my wand and the rings from my fingers—all were gone! Only my spellbook was left—though how they knew about the runes I'd put on it to fry anyone who touched it besides me I'll never know.

"I spent the whole morning negotiating for most of my equipment back. Then, when I would have turned to whole nest of them into

an anthill, something made me think the better of it. A couple of them might have stuck me with arrows before I could finish the spell—not a pleasant prospect.

"So I left, and brother, let me tell you it'll be a long time before I subject myself to halfling hospitality again!"

—Parzemon the Mighty, Wizard of Thay

Sorcery is one area of power where halfling skills are lacking. Their inherent resistance to magic protects them against many of the power-crazed spellcasters in the world, but it also prevents them from mastering those forces for themselves: no halfling has learned much about the wielding of arcane power (although comic tales about bumbling but well-intentioned halfling apprentices are popular in many places). Unlike many humans and dwarves, they do not regard magic as particularly threatening; trust in their innate resistance enables halflings to extend to spellcasters the typically friendly greeting they give to all strangers—a fact which no doubt explains the fondness some wizards have for the race.

Why Most Halflings Are Homebodies

Almost all halflings suffer to some degree from feelings which resembles the condition humans call agoraphobia—a fear of unknown or open places. It's not that halflings are literally *afraid*, merely that they become very uncomfortable whenever they're too far away from their villages and burrows or in unfamiliar places. Whether this is one of Yondalla's 'gifts,' designed to keep them close to home and hearth, or a holdover from the Bad Old Days when enemies lurked behind every tree and bush, none can say. But it has been observed that the symptoms increase with age—halfling children freely range far and wide, while the very old rarely step outside their burrows. Not that the halflings see this as a bad thing: to them, it's simply the way things are and ought to be—youth is the time to gadabout, age the time for rest and reflection.

Why Some Halflings Pursue Adventure

If his or her burrow and its attendant company and comforts are the most important features of a halfling's life, why then would any halfling leave this perfection for a life of short rations, crude lodging, exposure to bad weather, danger, and possible violence?

That's the question asked by most of the rest of a village when a young halfling packs his or her tote bag and waves goodbye to his or her parents. His or her neighbors will often gather to see the would-be adventurer off, watching the already small form grow smaller in the distance, knowing there's a good chance that they'll never see their friend again.

There are nearly as many answers to this question as there are halflings who have walked down that road. Some do so reluctantly, out of a sense of duty. Others find the temptations of excitement, adventure, and treasure too great to ignore. One thing almost all of them share in common, however, is that they lack the characteristic halfling dread of faraway places.

For reasons which once again are unknown—halflings call it 'the legacy of Littleman'—a few rare halflings are born entirely free of the condition which keeps their fellows tied to their homes. Instead, they are filled with an endless curiosity to see new places, new people, and new things. Usually this wanderlust fades later in life and the homing instinct reasserts itself, but a few halflings remain wanderers for the rest of their days (see the Traveler kit in the next chapter). These restless individuals are considered 'eccentric' by their fellow halflings, but their exploits are often admired just the same.

Some examples of the specific callings of halflings who leave their villages behind are discussed in the next chapter.

CHAPTER

4 Halfling Character Kits

Despite the fact that halflings are defined by their subrace and their character class, many players enjoy a little more distinction in their PCs. The halfling kits present a variety of different frameworks for playing a character of the small folk, each with its own strengths and weaknesses—but more importantly, each with a specific niche in his or her society.

Kits are optional—no halfling *must* follow one. They can be incorporated into characters already existing in a campaign, as long as the PC's background is consistent with the character type of the kit. However, a character who is assigned one kit can never exchange that kit for another.

The kits in this chapter are designed for halfling characters and should not be employed with PCs of other races. It should be noted that halflings can use many of the kits introduced in other rulebooks, including the *Complete Fighter's Handbook*, the *Complete Thief's Handbook*, the *Complete Priest's Handbook*, the *Complete Psionics Handbook*, and *The Complete Spacefarer's Handbook*. Indeed, one kit usable only by halflings, the Whistler, appears in *The Complete Bard's Handbook*.

Each of the four character classes available to halflings (fighter, thief, fighter/thief, and cleric) is given several kits. A character may only take a kit suited to his or her character class. All characters are limited to a single kit. Halflings may become clerics of up to 8th level, fighters of up to 9th level, thieves of up to 15th level, and fighter/thieves of up to 9th and 15th level, respectively. At the DM's option, exceptionally talented halflings (those with scores of 15 or above in their prime requisite) can exceed these maximums by up to 4 additional levels.

The Structure of the Kits

Each kit begins with a general description of the character type, including any background requirements that might be necessary. Following this, additional information is organized into these categories:

Roads to Adventure: This category, unique to the halfling kits, suggests several reasons why the character might be motivated to do such a rash thing as leave his or her hearth and burrow for a life on the road.

Role: The specific functions of this character within halfling society and beyond.

Secondary Skills: In a campaign that uses the secondary skills rules from the AD&D® Second Edition game, taking a particular kit might require the character to take a specific secondary skill.

Weapon Proficiencies: The listed proficiencies must be among those taken by a halfling character at first level. Unless the entry specifically states otherwise, they do *not* increase the number of proficiencies available but must be taken out of the standard allotment of slots.

Bonus Nonweapon Proficiencies: A halfling character using a kit gains these proficiencies free—the PC is not required to spend a slot for any of them.

Recommended Nonweapon Proficiencies: These proficiencies are not required of the character, but they do match up well with the kit. They require normal nonweapon proficiency slots be expended for each one.

Thieving Skill Emphasis: (For thief and fighter/thief characters only.) The AD&D® Second Edition thief rules allow considerable flexibility in a character's selection of thieving abilities. A character may wish to specialize in the stealth-related skills such as Move Silently and Hide in Shadows if he or she is a spy or cat burglar. A thief who needs to survive on city streets might prefer improved scores in Pick Pockets and Open Locks. This entry lists appropriate skills for each kit. They are not mandatory, nor do they grant any bonuses or confer any penalties beyond what they would grant any thief character.

Equipment: Any special equipment needs of the character are detailed here.

Special Benefits: These are things a character can do (or protections he or she gains) because of the kit.

Special Hindrances: These are limitations placed upon the character by the kit.

Fighter Kits

The Archer

An Archer is a halfling warrior who devotes nearly all of his or her time and energy to the development of skill with a missile weapon. "Archer" is the generic name for this kit: a "slinger" version of the kit also exists and is nearly as popular as the Archer itself, while halflings who live in jungle regions (like the wild halflings of Athas) have developed a blowgun variant. In those rare campaigns where firearms are allowed, this kit can be used to create a halfling sharpshooter (assuming the firearms are small enough for a halfling to wield; i.e., muskets rather than arquebuses).

An Archer must have a Dexterity score of at least 15.

Often an Archer comes from a background as a hunter, though membership in the local militia is another possible avenue into the kit.

Roads to Adventure: Archers are likely to be drawn into adventure for several reasons. The challenge of competition is strong—the best Archer in the village will naturally be tempted to test his or her skill against small folk, other demihumans, and human archers. Because their skill is so easily measurable, halfling Archers are particularly susceptible to this urge to go out and test their abilities against the toughest competition they can find. Alternately, a halfling Archer may be vigorously recruited by other adventurers who recognize the value of a skilled bowman.

Also, the Archer's skill helps to make him or her an accomplished hunter, and many an adventure can begin during a long stalk through the trackless forest. At the same time, his or her likely status as a prominent member of the village's defense militia makes the archer a likely candidate for any rescue party or guard duty that might develop.

Role: The Archer is a respected figure among a race where missile skill is the norm—he or she is the best of the best. In a small village he or she will be one of the primary hunters. Archers work well with Forestwalkers; it is often the Archer's task to bring down the game the Forestwalker has tracked.

The Archer also forms a staunch pillar of the community defense force—often, a skilled Archer will be placed in command of a company of halfling bowmen.

Secondary Skills: An Archer should have the Bowyer/Fletcher secondary skill.

Weapon Proficiencies: Three of the Archer's initial weapons proficiency slots must be used for missile weapons. If the weapons specialization optional rules are used, the Archer can specialize in one chosen missile weapon by expending two (not three, as is the norm) slots

for the weapon of specialization.

Bonus Non-Weapon Proficiencies: All Archers automatically receive the Bowyer/Fletcher proficiency.

Recommended Non-Weapon Proficiencies: The character should consider taking Hunting, Firebuilding, Tracking, and Weather Sense.

Equipment: The Archer's most essential piece of equipment is his or her bow or sling. At the start of his or her career this is likely to be a non-magical (although well-made) weapon, but throughout his or her adventures the character will continually search for the perfect bow. All Archers carry a plentiful supply of ammunition—usually at least twice the usual quiverfull of arrows.

As often as not, halflings with this kit will collect a variety of special missile types for use in special situations. For example, an Archer might have a few blunt-headed arrows (for stunning, rather than killing, targets), barbed arrows with thin lines attached (enabling him or her to retrieve small game simply by reeling in the string after a hit) and fire arrows (extra-long arrows with rags wrapped around their heads; when soaked with oil and ignited, these missiles fly half the distance of regular arrows but have an excellent chance to ignite any flammable substance that they strike). A slinger will likewise have a selection of special sling bullets—some spiked, others hollow and filled with skunk oil, sleeping gas, or a number of other noxious substances.

Special Benefits: The Archer can choose to make a *called shot*, earning additional bonuses on his or her missile attacks in certain circumstances. By electing to take careful aim, he or she gains a +2 bonus on his or her attack roll for that arrow. However, this requires that he or she forgo initiative (i.e., the shot must be the *last* act of a melee round). Also, the Archer must concentrate on the shot, meaning he or she can only make one shot that round. Finally, any successful attack against the Archer will naturally break his or her concentration and cause the benefit to be lost, although in this case the shot still has a normal chance to hit. The +2 bonus is in addition to any other attack bonuses the character might have due to Dexterity, weapon specialization, *bless* spells, or magical weaponry.

In outdoor melee, the same procedure (single shot; last act in the round) can be used to increase the range of the shot instead of gaining the attack bonus (i.e., the Archer can choose to make a called shot with increased accuracy **or** extended range, but not both at the same time). The extra range is equal to the weapon's medium range added to the long range; the attack is modified with the long range penalty to hit.

Special Hindrances: The Archer can gain normal proficiency in only one melee weapon. He or she can spend proficiency slots on others but will always wield them with a −1 penalty on all attack rolls. For example, suppose Willem the Archer learns to use a short sword as well as his bow, sling, and throwing knives. If he later decides to use a proficiency for hand-to-hand knife-fighting, he can do so (assuming he has the proficiency slot to spare) but he will suffer a −1 penalty on his melee attack rolls with the knife.

Forestwalker

The Forestwalker is the halfling version of the Scout, adept at moving through the woodlands, tracking prey and trespassers. Forestwalkers are very protective of their woods and tend to be loners, although they are far from being hermits. Indeed, a Forest-walker is happy to share his or her campfire with guests and will often come to the aid of travelers who treat the woods with due respect; many are the tales of adventuring parties lost in the woods rescued by a friendly Forestwalker.

Whereas most halflings consider a single burrow or building their home, for the Forestwalker the whole forest in which he or she lives is "home." The Forestwalker is likely to maintain several shelters in the particular woods he or she has claimed for his or her own. These might range from cramped niches in hollow tree stumps, providing little more than bare shelter from the elements, to elaborate burrows in small caves or earthen holes excavated beneath a sheltered bank. Though the halfling cannot be said to live in any single one of these, he or she is likely to keep them all well-stocked with food, fuel, candles, blankets or furs, and perhaps a jug or two. If at all possible, each shelter will have some kind of fireplace—in some cases, a simple circle of stones; in others, a well-built hearth complete with chimney or vent to carry the smoke away. Where no fireplace is possible, the Forestwalker will seek consolation in a pipe of tobacco.

The Forestwalker must have a Wisdom score of at least 13. Most, but not all, Forestwalkers are Tallfellows.

Roads to Adventure: The Forestwalker is extremely protective of his or her woods and will seek retribution against any force that hurts the forest; he or she will be willing to go to great lengths (and travel great distances) to see justice done in such a case. This retribution might be seen as exceeding the typical halfling nonchalance regarding revenge. It's not, though—the Forestwalker thinks of his or her wood as a living being, not a thing. Consequently, any affront against the forest is treated like an attack on a friend, not like the theft of a possession.

The curiosity that lies latent in so many halflings bubbles near the surface of the Forestwalker—a simple love of exploring will often draw him or her away on long expeditions. He or she delights in following the course of streams and rivers and in analyzing the various drainage patterns in a watershed. The opportunity to encounter new types of trees and map out hitherto unknown regions of forest and woodland is often enough to tempt a Forestwalker into joining an adventuring party on a short-term basis, but he or she will always return to his or her home forest eventually.

Role: The Forestwalker is the protector of the woods: the guardian of game, fire marshal, and an important scout against enemy incursion into a halfling realm. He or she is a respected figure in the village and is more likely than not to have a family and comfortable burrow amid the dwellings of his or her neighbors. However, between a sense of duty and sheer wanderlust, a typical Forestwalker will rarely spend more than one day in ten with spouse and offspring, a situation his or her family respect and accept.

The Forestwalker also tends to be one of the more skillful hunters of a halfling community. Thus, when he or she does come in to town, it is often with a large cache of fresh meat—a trait which further endears him or her to these feast-loving folk. Often the Forestwalker can barter for all the other essentials of life, simply through knowing how to gain the bounty of the woods.

Besides hunting, Forestwalkers are also adept at finding nuts, edible berries and other fruits, herbs, roots, and—best of all, from a halfling's point of view—mushrooms. Many are fine cooks, able to serve up savory soups and rich stews that would be the envy of any fine restaurant.

Secondary Skills: The Hunter and either the Trapper/Furrier or Fisher secondary skills fit in well with this character's lifestyle.

Weapon Proficiencies: The Forestwalker must spend an initial proficiency slot on a missile weapon, and another on a weapon that can be made from wood, such as a club or a small quarterstaff.

Bonus Nonweapon Proficiencies: The Forestwalker gains Survival (Woodland) and Tracking (the latter with a +2 to all proficiency checks made in woodland settings), plus any one of the following (player's choice): Firebuilding, Fishing, and Hunting.

Recommended Nonweapon Proficiencies: Whichever of the above not taken as bonus proficiencies are recommended; the Animal Lore, Set Snares, and Bowyer/Fletcher proficiencies can also be of daily use to the Forestwalker. Artistic Ability is also popular, as whittling and woodcarving are common pastimes among Forestwalkers.

Equipment: In addition to his or her weapons, the Forestwalker will rarely be found without flint and tinder for firemaking, a large waterskin, and a heavy cloak or blanket that can double as a bedroll. He or she will always have a knife, even if it is too small to properly be considered a weapon, for marking trails, skinning small game, and whittling.

Special Benefits: In addition to the normal halfling benefit of being hard to spot in natural terrain, the Forestwalker can move at his or her full movement rate through tangled undergrowth ("born and bred in the briar patch, Brer Fox!"). If he or she chooses to slow down to the normal movement rate, however, he or she can Move Silently through such terrain (no ability check necessary).

Forestwalkers are also adept at hiding tracks. By slowing his or her movement rate to half that allowed for the terrain type, a Forestwalker can conceal all trace of his or her passage and, if he or she is walking in the rear of a party, a number of companions as well. To determine if the trail of a large party is effectively concealed, the player must make a successful Tracking proficiency check with a −1 penalty for each non-Forestwalker in the party (−2 for each horse, mule, or other four-footed animals accompanying the party). If the proficiency check is successful, the track will be invisible even to a skilled tracker. Note that even though some characters may be riding instead of walking, this does not improve the Forestwalker's chances to cover their tracks, as the added weight makes the mount's trail more difficult to conceal. The halfling will know whether or not his or her efforts have met with success.

Special Hindrances: Forestwalkers may only wear leather armor, and many eschew armor altogether. Since metal makes so much noise in the woods, they will avoid carrying much of it on their person and will not use any metal weapon larger than an arrowhead, hatchet, or knife.

The Forestwalker is a bit of a loner and consequently may be a little slow to learn of big news that sweeps through the community and the realm. Also, Forestwalkers tend not to be terribly skilled in the social graces and suffer a −2 penalty to NPC Reaction rolls from non-halflings (−4 when the setting calls for good manners and/or elegant dress).

Homesteader

This is a doughty brand of halfling that, by his or her very nature, represents a departure from the halfling norm. Often a young and unattached individual, either male or female, the Homesteader is a halfling who sets out to found a new farmstead in a region of wilderness or abandoned land. Another common homesteading situation involves a young couple, recently married and previously living in a very crowded burrow. Such small folk, if adventurous enough in spirit, can find immediate rewards to homesteading.

Rarely will a Homesteader challenge an established authority over an area—if humans or orcs have laid claim to a fertile valley, for example, the Homesteader will probably look elsewhere for his or her plot.

Many halfling villages have grown around the individual plot of a brave Homesteader—and indeed, unlike many human frontiersmen, the halfling Homesteader welcomes the company of his or her fellows and will actively recruit other halflings to live nearby.

The Homesteader is a hardy halfling, willing to work harder than the average farmer and to accept a certain reduction in the comforts of his or her life—at least, temporarily. His or her ideal, however, is to have a comfortable burrow and cheerful batch of neighbors by the time he or she reaches old age.

The halfling Homesteader must have a Strength of at least 12 and an Intelligence or Wisdom of at least 12.

Roads to Adventure: The Homesteader's most common route to adventure is in the enacting of his or her goal: seeking out free land, clearing it, and defending it against any who might care to take it away. However, once the farm is established, the Homesteader is likely to embark on a long journey, visiting many farflung halfling communities in the attempt to recruit other settlers to come and join him or her. Indeed, this journey can involve several years of travel and often forms the seeds of an epic tale that becomes the cornerstone of the community's history—if the community survives, that is.

Also, the very trek involved in reaching the homestead can form a grand adventure for the brave halflings who seek unsettled land. By nature curious, the Homesteader might pass through a lot of different locales in the search for the perfect steading. The adventures and obstacles of such an epic journey can easily create the foundation of a great character history.

Role: Homesteaders are responsible for much of the expansion of the race across the known worlds. Most halfling villages can trace their history back to a hardy Homesteader couple, and these individuals tend to be revered by the generations who have followed in their footsteps. This matriarch or patriarch will be honored and feted in his or her old age and regarded as a prime source of interesting stories. This is regarded as nothing less than a just reward for one who took such risks and endured such hardships in order to bring another halfling community into being.

Commonly, a halfling that sets out on a homesteading adventure will take at least one stone from his or her family fireplace along on the journey. Then, when he or she finally builds his or her own place, this stone will be used as a key part of the new hearth.

Secondary Skills: Farming is the secondary skill most necessary to the homesteader.

Weapon Proficiencies: The Homesteader should be proficient in either the short bow or the sling and should also have a melee weapon proficiency with the knife or short sword.

Bonus Nonweapon Proficiencies: Agriculture or Animal Handling is a bonus proficiency to all characters who select the Homesteader kit. In addition, the character can select either Hunting or Fishing as an additional bonus proficiency.

Recommended Nonweapon Proficiencies: This character has need of a wide variety of skills; some of the more useful include Carpentry, Rope Use, Weather Sense, and Survival. Others can be tied to the type of farming the Homesteader intends to do: a shepherd can benefit from Weaving, a dairyman from Cheesemaking, any herdsman has a use for Leatherworking, and a grain-grower can

profit from a knowledge of Baking or Brewing, for example.

Equipment: There is no specific item of equipment universal to halfling Homesteaders. Many of them will have a handcart or small wagon, however, to carry their belongings on the quest for the perfect plot of land. Additionally, a beast of burden such as a pony or mule or animals that produce something useful (a few ducks, chickens, or geese; a dairy cow or goat; a few sheep) can be worth their weight in gold. Animals large and steady enough to pull the cart can prove of double value when the homestead is finally reached.

Special Benefits: The Homesteader who carefully selects his or her land, works hard at tending it, and then travels far and wide to recruit settlers is likely to end up a very wealthy halfling, having earned the respect of the new community and a place in the local histories. In effect, he or she exchanges a lot of hard work and difficulties at a young age for the chance to be treated very well when he or she grows old. Other intangible benefits can include such grandiose attainments as having a town named after you, or the simple satisfaction of seeing well-plowed fields and a thriving village where there was none before.

Special Hindrances: The primary hindrance to the hardy Homesteader is that he or she has to do just about everything on his or her own—he or she does not have a community of skilled neighbors to draw upon for help, barter, and advice.

Mercenary

The halfling Mercenary is a bit of a rare bird—one of the small folk proficient enough as a fighter to earn a place alongside warriors of larger and more aggressive races, and one who doesn't mind the difficulties of campaign life or the terror and confusion of battle. Note that this stops well short of saying: "A Mercenary loves to fight and kill."

A halfling Mercenary must have ability scores of at least 13 in two of these categories: Strength, Dexterity, and Constitution.

Roads to Adventure: It would be a rare halfling who would adopt the Mercenary lifestyle by choice. Mercenaries are almost always outcasts who for some reason or another have been disowned by their families and driven from their villages, forced into a life of violence and danger. Many of them are, not surprisingly, quite bitter about this involuntary exile. Whether or not the individual was actually guilty of the crime of which he or she is accused is irrelevant; the effect is the same in either case. Whatever misdeed or misfortune drove the halfling to become a Mercenary, it tends to be a private matter, jealously guarded.

Role: The Mercenary is an outcast from halfling society who is forced to mingle with humans, elves, dwarves, even goblinoids—and consequently, over time he or she will begin to acquire some of the characteristics of those races. Now and then in his or her wanderings, a Mercenary might enjoy an opportunity to visit a friendly burrow and sit by the hearth of a fellow halfling for the night or two, but soon he or she will be wanting to move on, perhaps propelled by the frowning looks of neighbors less open-minded than his or her host.

Secondary Skills: Since no halfling plans to grow up and become a Mercenary, he or she could have almost any secondary skill to represent his or her former profession.

Weapon Proficiencies: The halfling Mercenary must be proficient with at least one melee and one missile weapon. If the optional weapon specialization rules are used, the character must have a weapon specialization by the time he or she reaches second level of ability (see Special Benefits, below).

Bonus Nonweapon Proficiencies: None.

Recommended Nonweapon Proficiencies: Halfling Mercenaries have been known to find the following proficiencies useful: Carpentry, Riding, Armorer, Blindfighting, Bowyer/Fletcher, Tracking, and Weaponsmithing.

Equipment: The Mercenary will typically be offered decent weapons and armor by his or her employer—nothing special, but equal to the equipment of the rest of the company. Anything superior to this has to be provided by the Mercenary himself or herself.

Special Benefits: Due to his or her continual exposure to warriors—and typical Small Folk quick-wittedness—the halfling Mercenary receives two extra weapon proficiency slots upon reaching second level. The slots must be used to purchase a weapon specialization, if he or she does not already have one. Like the Archer, the halfling Mercenary can specialize in the bow or other missile weapon at a cost of only two proficiency slots (not three).

Special Hindrances: This is not generally considered a socially acceptable career for a halfling. Thus, a halfling Mercenary is likely to be given quite the hairy eyeball by others of his or her race—at least, those who know what the character does for a living. This translates into a −2 penalty on Reaction Rolls.

Sheriff

The halfling Sheriff is really more of a benign constable than a tough enforcer, but he or she does represent the long arm of the law (so to speak) among the villagers and visitors in his or her community. The position is, for the most part, an honorary one—since halflings don't have a lot of troublemakers among their own ranks and don't run the kind of establishments that tend to draw humans ruffians. Still, the post represents the faith and confidence of a good number of villagers, and the responsibility tends to be taken very seriously by the halfling who holds it.

A halfling Sheriff must have a Charisma of

at least 13 (most have Charismas which are much higher) and a Strength of at least 11.

Roads to Adventure: The solving of a complex crime can serve admirably to draw a halfling Sheriff into an adventure. Though his or her primary duty always lies with the halflings of his or her village or shire, the Sheriff is willing to range far and wide in pursuit of those who have wronged those neighbors. In keeping with halfling values, however, this dogged pursuit extends only to those who have caused bodily harm—the Sheriff is not likely to make a vigorous pursuit merely to recover lost property. Thus a Sheriff may turn a blind eye on the doings of Bandits and Smugglers in the area, but ruffians who beat up an elderly farmer will soon find the same Sheriff leading an angry posse in hot pursuit.

Role: Within the village, the halfling Sheriff has a small office—often a corner of his or her own burrow—where he or she can usually be found when not out "keeping an eye on things." Jails are not common in halfling villages, but if there is a lockup it will be nearby. It will, however, have its own separate entrance, secured by a stout door and lock.

Most of the Sheriff's time is spent in seeing that all goes as it should and in looking out for signs of trouble ("Odd that Old Mistress Elderberry didn't come to market this morning; she hardly ever misses a day"). Although he or she doesn't maintain a regular 'beat,' the Sheriff does spend a lot of time ambling through the village and will try to find an excuse to visit outlying farms and isolated families at least once a week to see that all is well with their inhabitants.

Often he or she is politely nosy, asking questions about things that have changed, displaying interest in everything going on in the community or canton. A Sheriff knows all the local citizens by name and is familiar enough with their normal habits to take note of any break in routine—such as the baker not firing up her oven in the morning, or the farmer leaving his irrigation gate closed. In these instances, the Sheriff would make a friendly check to make sure nothing is amiss.

Among halflings there are not a lot of laws that require the attention of law enforcement. Thievery is one, and so is violent assault and of course murder. None of these crimes are likely to be committed by one villager against another—in the rare case where this occurs and can be proven, a thief is forced to make restitution, while a halfling guilty of deliberately harming another is banished from the community for life (many of these become Mercenaries; see the preceding kit). More common are boundary disputes, complaints from halfling fathers about overzealous suitors who pursue their daughters, or charges of unfair trading. The Sheriff usually resolves all of these with calm diplomacy, and it is not uncommon for even the loser to come away from a settlement feeling that he or she has received very fair treatment.

The Sheriff also typically has the authority to call up the Small Folk in times of crisis, crying for a muster of all who can bear arms. The post does *not* necessarily entitle him or her to command of the company when it assembles; such leadership is more often a matter of past experience and age.

Being Sheriff of a halfling village, especially if it's a smaller community, is not necessarily a full time job, so it is quite likely that this character will run a small farm or practice some sort of trade as well. Running a small store is a common practice among Sheriffs, since it allows them to remain at their post most of the time and also provides interaction with the village citizenry.

Secondary Skills: Any.

Weapon Proficiencies: The Sheriff should be proficient in the use of the short sword, the club, and the knife.

Bonus Nonweapon Proficiencies: None.

Recommended Nonweapon Proficiencies: Tracking skill and knowledge of an extra language or two are proficiencies that can make a Sheriff's job a lot easier.

Equipment: A Sheriff's arms and armor usually come with the job, so the character doesn't have to purchase these. It is not unlikely that he or she will also have access to a pony, should the need for a mount arise.

Special Benefits: The authority of respectable halfling society is the primary benefit of the Sheriff. He or she receives a +2 bonus on all NPC Reaction Rolls made for halfling NPCs (as long as the other character knows of the Sheriff's rank).

Special Hindrances: All Sheriffs have a strong sense of duty and will respond at once when called upon—i.e., whenever anyone in the village has a need for his or her services. This can often entail long hours and rude interruptions in the Sheriff's enjoyment of life.

Squire

Halfling fighters have been known to form strong friendships with fighters, rangers, and paladins of other races—most notably human, but not disallowing dwarven, elven, and other more exotic folk (one chaotic evil halfling is said to have formed a partnership with a red dragon!). Since such adventuring pairs typically encounter most of their excitement in nonhalfling societies, the halfling partner is often regarded (by the members of that other society) as an apprentice, squire, or sidekick to the warrior of local origin. Such an assumption, naturally, is very far from the truth; the two are in fact full partners.

However, the halfling warrior does serve a number of useful functions that would prove difficult for the larger partner to accomplish on his or her own. Squires make marvelous scouts and spies, since they specialize in acting dumb and nonthreatening.

The size of the halfling, together with the ability to hide in bushes and undergrowth, makes him or her an exceptionally valuable companion when it comes to gathering information. It's even possible for a Squire to disguise himself or herself as a human child to gain access to places where adult adventurers fear to tread.

The Squire needs two minimum attribute score: a 10 for Strength and a 12 for Charisma.

Roads to Adventure: For the Squire, friendship is a strong enough inducement to draw him or her away from the typical halfling comforts. In this case, anything that compels the first member of the pair will draw the halfling character along as well.

The Squire is often motivated by genuine friendship for his or her partner, sometimes coupled with a sense of gratitude for something that has happened in the past, or a mutual goal (perhaps even a quest) that the pair have embarked upon together.

Role: When among strangers, the halfling Squire often plays the role of simpleminded servant; this increases his or her chances to eavesdrop and usually causes potential enemies to underestimate the danger he or she poses. All Squires are adept at observing nearly everything that goes on around them and often act as ambassadors to other races—particularly those who might be hostile to the Squire's partner.

It is important to realize that, in reality, the Squire and his partner are full equals—the halfling is not a squire in the traditional sense of apprentice or servant. Even if the two act out a false relationship for appearances' sake, the Squire and his partner remain together because of trust and affection; there is no room for one or the other to be the boss.

Secondary Skills: A Squire should have the Groom secondary skill.

Weapon Proficiencies: This character should have a proficiency in at least one melee and one missile weapon. A proficiency that matches his or her partner's can provide extra benefits (see Special Benefits, below).

Bonus Nonweapon Proficiencies: The Squire character receives either the Animal Handling or the Riding (Landbased) proficiency as a bonus. In addition, the halfling can

gain proficiencies known to his or her partners, simply through the progress of their cooperative adventures, as follows:

When the halfling goes up in level and at least half the necessary experience points to gain the new level were earned from tasks that the Squire performed with his or her partner, the halfling can add one proficiency slot, filling it with a proficiency that his or her partner holds and used during the course of the previous adventures.

Recommended Nonweapon Proficiencies: Heraldry and Foreign Languages are proficiencies that often prove useful in a Squire; also, the Armorer, Bowyer/Fletcher, and Weaponsmithing skills can be helpful.

Equipment: A Squire's companion will try to provide a suitable steed for his or her partner, as well as weapons and armor for the halfling, if he or she has the means.

Special Benefits: The Squire becomes very familiar with the habits and characteristics of his or her partner's race; thus, he or she gains a +2 bonus to NPC Reaction Rolls made for members of that race.

In addition, the Squire can advance to slightly higher levels than can other halfling warriors. The Squire can reach a total of two levels higher than he or she would otherwise be allowed (see page 92); however, he or she cannot pass the level of his or her partner by this means.

Special Hindrances: The loss is mostly intangible, but the halfling Squire is forced to do without the comforts of hearth and burrow that are so fundamental to his or her kind. In effect, he or she chooses to replace his or her family with the partner; a Squire who loses that partner to death or other mischance is a lonely halfling indeed.

Tunnelrat

This is a dirty-under-the fingernails halfling with an unusual amount of courage and a scrappy attitude toward dangerous and powerful foes. The cheerful, matter-of-fact, bloodthirsty attitude of these professionals usually comes as a great surprise to humans and others who think of all halflings as jolly farmer-types. The Tunnelrat specializes in underground search-and-destroy missions, especially in areas where constricted space or low ceilings would put larger warriors at a significant disadvantage.

The Tunnelrat must have a Strength score of at least 13 and a Constitution score of 11 or greater.

Roads to Adventure: Most Tunnelrats are drawn to this deadly calling by some dire event in the past—usually nothing less than a life-shattering trauma will suffice to drive a normally peaceful halfling into such gritty and dangerous work, as when a halfling who has lost loved ones to the depredations of goblins or kobolds becomes an implacable enemy to those evil creatures. Occasionally, of

course, the drive is not due to such dark causes—the lure of easy money, simple talent, or mental instability might propel a sturdy halfling into a career as a Tunnelrat. After all, this is one of the few areas (perhaps the *only* one) where small size is not only not a liability but a basic prerequisite.

Role: The Tunnelrat specializes in rooting out smallish humanoid monsters who make their lairs underground. Goblins, Duergar and kobolds are the most common of these enemies, though many other types are possible—including lycanthropes, undead, and animal monsters like giant rats, giant weasels, and carrion crawlers.

Tunnelrats generally seek out the dens of their enemies, attacking them for whatever profit they can find there—and, more importantly, for the satisfaction of eliminating an enemy of their people. Tunnelrats sometimes work together as a team and will sometimes band together with gnomish Goblinstickers on a joint mission, especially if the two groups share the same foe. In the latter case, the gnomish presence provides a very useful complement to the halflings—without any increase in size. Tunnelrats will sometimes join forces with dwarves as well, but since a typical dwarf is significantly larger than a gnome or halfling, this severely restricts the size of tunnels that the party can investigate.

Secondary Skills: No particular secondary skill is required for the Tunnelrat.

Weapon Proficiencies: The Tunnelrat should be proficient in the use of the short sword, hand axe, or war hammer, as well as either the crossbow, short bow, blowgun, or darts. If weapon specialization is used in the campaign, the Tunnelrat must have a melee weapon specialization by the time he or she reaches third level.

Bonus Nonweapon Proficiencies: The Tunnelrat automatically receives Blindfighting in addition to any other proficiency. Also, he or she can select one of the following languages in addition to any the character would normally know: goblin, orc, kobold, and Duergar.

Recommended Nonweapon Proficiencies: Rope Use, Swimming, and Mountaineering (for scaling underground cliffs) are all useful to the Tunnelrat.

Equipment: The Tunnelrat is typically equipped with a generous coil of thin but strong rope, flasks of oil, flint and steel, at least one lantern, and metal climbing spikes. His or her weapons will be slung from belts and straps, readily reachable with either hand. Also, he or she will be sure to carry a plentiful supply of ammunition for his or her missile weapon.

Special Benefits: Tunnelrats who are not Stoutish will gradually develop an infravision-like ability to see in the dark. The range of this sight (which works exactly like infravision) is equal to 10′ per level of the Tunnelrat (to a maximum of 60′).

Special Hindrances: Tunnelrats are considered shockingly crude and more than a little mad by most other halflings—why would anyone *choose* to root around in dirty holes after dangerous monsters? Therefore, the Tunnelrat suffers a −2 penalty on Reaction Checks made for NPC halflings.

Thief Kits

Bandit

The halfling Bandit is a far cry from his or her human or orcish counterpart. While the basic approach to thievery is the same, he or she pulls off robberies with more panache. The target is confronted with a choice: hand over your goods or suffer bodily harm—yet the halfling Bandit always retains a certain amount of sympathy for his or her victims and will never bully someone simply for the pleasure of it.

Bandits tend to work in small groups, though not all thieves in the band need be members of this kit—or even halflings. They will have a headquarters in some remote location, almost always screened by forest (including forested swampland). Trails to the lair are well hidden, and if the entire band is composed of halflings it's likely that in many places these access paths will pass under low-hanging branches, through close and thorny thickets, and even under stone arches only 2′ to 3′ tall. Depending on the size of the Bandit band, one or two lookouts will probably be on duty at all times along the most-traveled of these obscure paths.

A Bandit PC should have a Charisma of at least 12 and a Strength or Constitution of at least 13.

Roads to Adventure: Some halflings become bandits because they want to put a healthy distance between themselves and the nearest authorities; others choose this profession for the fun of the thing. For example, a halfling who stands up to a local duke's rapacious tax collector and drives him out of the village will probably want to consider a very long vacation as soon as she calms down. Once she has fled to the woods, established a hideout, and made a reputation for herself by harassing more of the human lord's agents, other halflings may flock to her banner—some because they believe in her cause, some because the lifestyle appeals to them.

The Bandit has a curious standing in halfling society—officially he or she is disapproved of, and the local Sheriff will often send the area's ruler long reports lamenting his or her inability to stop the holdups. Privately, the same Sheriff might be a friend of the Bandit leader—indeed, he or she may have relatives belonging to the band—and remain content to leave them alone so long as they avoid violence and don't rob members of their own race. Most of their fellow halflings will regard them with amused tolerance, shading to frank envy and hero-worship by the young and young-at-heart. A local Bandit gang might trade occasionally with halfling villagers in the surrounding area. In this way, the Bandits can maintain most of the comforts of the hearth and burrow and also have the benefit of a job where they don't have to work too hard.

Consequently, young halflings from these neighboring villages become acquainted with the Bandits, and at least a few of them are drawn to that apparently idyllic forest life—and thus the ranks of the band are replenished. Others who have become fugitives through the same causes as the original Bandit can find safe haven and join the cause; many of them may choose to remain even after the original injustice is eventually rectified.

Sometimes an entire halfling community is driven to banditry—as when a human lord forces halflings from their homes to make way for human setters, or when wars and invasion sweep across the land. In such cases, Bandits have been known to become the backbone of the halfling defense, harassing enemies and supporting friends until the crisis passes. It's memories of times like these that explain the forgiving attitude of the typical halfling toward these carefree rogues.

Role: Bandits consider themselves equalizers of wealth. After all, a quick look around will show that some folks have just too much money—and the Bandit takes it upon himself or herself to correct this inequity.

Halfling Bandits will avoid violence, in so far as they can while still accomplishing their objectives. They will not use violent ambush (such as an arrow barrage) to halt a merchant party, for example—though nets and pit traps are popular tactics. Utilizing the halfling ability to conceal themselves in underbrush, Bandits delight in suddenly appearing around a daydreaming trader and his or her bodyguards. By the time the victims can react, it's usually too late. Often, one or more halflings skilled in Rope Use will lurk ahead and behind the ambush, ready to lasso any of the intended victims who might make an aggressive move or a break for freedom.

Those victims who have the good sense to quietly surrender will be politely relieved of

the better part of their wealth and allowed to go their way. Those who put up a fight will be subjected to a certain amount of indignity—the better to teach them to behave next time, according to the Bandit's admittedly convoluted version of justice. For example, Bandits traditionally will leave a victim his or her horses and wagons (if any) and enough of his or her goods or money to get started again in the next town. Indeed, a very believable tale of hardship ("What! *All* of you are orphans? Poor fellows!") might possibly succeed in causing the Bandit to let the poor unfortunate(s) pass unmolested!

However, a target who chooses to be "difficult" and is nonetheless captured will be treated much more severely. His or her mount will be taken, along with all his or her goods; the unfortunate victim will be left to make his or her way back to town on foot, probably having been relieved of even his or her outer garments!

Secondary Skills: Forester is a useful secondary skill to the Bandit; however, any secondary skill is acceptable.

Weapon Proficiencies: The Bandit should be proficient in the short bow or hand crossbow, as well as at least one melee weapon.

Bonus Nonweapon Proficiencies: The Bandit can claim one of the following as a bonus nonweapon proficiency: Direction Sense, Fishing, Rope Use, or Disguise.

Recommended Nonweapon Proficiencies: In addition to those listed above, Swimming, Weather Sense, Forgery, Set Snares, and Tightrope Walking can all prove useful to a bandit.

Thieving Skill Emphasis: Any.

Equipment: Bandits can equip themselves in whatever fashion they choose (within reason).

Special Benefits: The Bandit usually enjoys a considerable amount of support from the halflings in the local population ("local" being within about three or four days' travel of the bandit lair). This typically translates into advance warning of any attempt to seek out and destroy the lair by militia, men-at-arms, or hired parties of adventurers.

Special Hindrances: There's always the chance that the Bandits will pick on the wrong victim—a powerful wizard who only *looks* like a plump merchant, or an arrogant young lord or lady who determines to have revenge at all costs. In the latter case, the full weight of the local ruler, whether king, duchess, or baron, could well be thrown into an effort to root out the Bandit lair.

Bilker

The Bilker is a clever halfling thief who entertains his or her victims even as he or she steals from them—and, as often as not, the target of the crime doesn't even realize he or she has been robbed until the Bilker has traveled on to the next town. Bilkers are unusually larcenous for halflings, although it is only fair to point out that the Bilker tends to regard his or her activities as a grand game, and the profits thereof as a just fee for the entertainment he or she has provided. He or she is a diminutive con artist who likes to leave 'em laughing—but also to leave 'em far behind, and quickly.

A Bilker must have Charisma and Dexterity scores of 13 or higher.

Roads to Adventure: The Bilker is forced onto the road, you might say, because he or she tends to outlast his or her welcome rather quickly simply by practicing his or her trade. Like other halfling thieves, he or she will generally avoid victimizing fellow halflings. Unfortunately for all concerned, the Bilker's definition of "victimize" doesn't always match up with the victim's. For example, a Bilker will not consider it theft to gamble with the innkeeper for free drinks every night—the innkeeper, after losing for seven straight nights, may beg to differ.

Naturally, a fresh supply of targets is essential to the Bilker's activities. A Bilker who works smaller towns and villages must of necessity be prepared to stay on the move to keep one step ahead of his or her former customers. A Bilker who decides to exercise his or her talents in a large city might be able thrive for a considerable while, but eventually a gradual increase in the number of victims will inevitably pressure the halfling to move on. Obviously, a fine sense of timing is important for any Bilker who does not wish to end his or her career at the hands of an angry mob. Ever optimistic, he or she often tells friends about a wonderful opportunity that has just arisen to sample the life in some far distant locale—immediately before decamping with the goods!

Role: The Bilker is a curious fellow—undeniably a scoundrel, scallywag, and all-around rascal, yet also a thoroughly likeable person whose powers of persuasion can make him or her a valuable asset to any adventuring party. Many a Bilker has used his or her silver tongue to get friends out of a sticky situation, only to cheat them out of their pocket money the next night. Fellow halflings can almost always see through a Bilker's schemes and view the gullibility of Big Folk with amused disbelief.

A Bilker travels from town to town—usually by himself or herself, sometimes in the company of a group of companions. His or her tricks can range from simple gambling games intended to earn enough to pay for his or her room and board to complex schemes involving the exchange of valuable treasures. Sometimes these are even legitimate transactions in which the Bilker has somehow gotten involved and out of which he or she has engineered a percentage of the profits—perhaps from each party!—in return for his or her services. On other occasions, the transaction might be an out-and-out fraud, where the purchasers acquire something that has been counterfeited. Such complex schemes can involve property deeds, rare objects of art, bogus trea-

sure maps, or beautiful and valuable jewelry that will be recognized as stolen the first time the unwary buyer wears it in public.

Secondary Skills: Gambling is the secondary skill most appropriate to the bilker.

Weapon Proficiencies: The Bilker should be adept at the use of the knife. The hand crossbow, often concealed under a cloak or inside a hat, is a favored missile weapon of Bilkers everywhere.

Bonus Nonweapon Proficiencies: Gaming.

Recommended Nonweapon Proficiencies: A knowledge of Disguise, Local History, Appraising, and Ventriloquism can all prove useful to the enterprising Bilker.

Thieving Skill Emphasis: Manual dexterity is essential to the Bilker's sleight of hand games; hence, Pick Pockets is a favorite. Hear Noise also often comes in handy.

Equipment: The Bilker is a cautious soul; he or she usually appears unarmed in order to disarm suspicion, while carrying a weapon or two concealed somewhere on his or her person. Also, he or she will never be found without the tools of his or her trade—a pack of cards, some dice, a few shells, and knucklebones. After all, you never know when you might be able to get a friendly game together!

Special Benefits: The Bilker is adept at presenting an acquaintance (the "sucker" or "mark") with an interesting gaming opportunity. The game involves the acquaintance guessing about some apparently random chance—which shell is the pebble under, or what number will come up on the knucklebone? The sucker is usually allowed to win a round or two, but by the time the game is over, the Bilker ends up holding the coins.

Use the following procedure to resolve these attempts, once the Bilker has found an appropriate NPC mark:

The bet usually centers around a single coin—silver or gold, most likely, but varying by the standards of the surrounding establishment. The Bilker can automatically lose any round he or she chooses. A fair game can be played by rolling 1d10 for the Bilker and another for the NPC, with a tie going to the mark.

If the Bilker wants to rig the game, his or her Dexterity score is subtracted from the mark's Wisdom score (to a minimum Wisdom of 0). The victim must then roll that number or less on 1d20. If the check fails, the Bilker wins the bet. If it succeeds, the mark realizes he or she is being hoodwinked, and an intriguing roleplaying encounter may occur.

The Bilker can repeat the attempt as many times as he or she wants—however, for each attempt, the victim gains a +1 bonus to his or her roll. Thus, a wise Bilker knows when to call it a night.

Bilkers also have the additional ability which helps them sometimes talk their way out of trouble. When confronted by a potentially hostile person or persons, a Bilker may attempt to *smoothtalk* the other party (naturally, the attempt is only possible if both parties speak a common language, and the ability will not work if combat has already been joined). The Bilker's Charisma score is subtracted from the victim's Wisdom score, and the victim must then roll under the resulting number or he or she (or it) will find himself-herself-itself nodding in agreement with whatever the Bilker is proposing. Naturally, truly outrageous proposals will give the victim a hefty bonus (+1 to +5, depending on the nature of the suggestion). The victim also gains a cumulative +1 bonus for each previous time the Bilker has used this ability on him or her. Still, this ability is very useful to help get a Bilker and his or her friends out of a tight spot. Alas, the effect is temporary, lasting only a minute or two, so a Bilker soon learns to get while the getting is good.

A Bilker's larger schemes and scams should be are left to the player character to create and enact. The DM should take appropriate precautions for whatever NPC faces bilking.

Special Hindrances: The Bilker is a fun character to have around, but he or she usually leaves bad tempers behind when he or she departs. His or her opportunistic behavior makes it difficult for the halfling to make longterm friendships or keep allies, eventually leaving the character to face the woes of his or her own making alone. The longer a Bilker plies his or her trade, the more numerous his or her former victims become, making it almost inevitable that one day, when the Bilker least expects it, his or her path will cross that of an "old friend." Often, the previous victim is *very* glad to find the halfling thief who made him or her feel like a fool and walked off with a goodly amount of his or her money. The Bilker, naturally, might not be so delighted with the reunion.

Burglar

The halfling Burglar is a benign specialist at retrieving objects of value from those who have come by them wrongly—at least, that's the way the Burglar sees it (admittedly, the one who has been burgled tends to disagree). Adept at stealthy movement, lockpicking, recognizing traps, and removing them, the Burglar aspires to a life of comfort simply by virtue of his or her talents—the ultimate in halfling accomplishment.

A Burglar must have a Dexterity score of at least 15.

Roads To Adventure: Burgling involves skills that most halflings learn at a young age—children are forever sneaking into each other's rooms, borrowing each other's toys, and spying on their siblings. As the youngsters mature, a few of them begin to consider the potential profitability of their skills, turning their attention toward more lucrative and dangerous targets. As with many kinds of thievery, burglaring has a built-in inducement to travel—if the local authorities begin to grow suspicious, the life of a simple Burglar

can become very complicated indeed.

Other motivations can include the recovery of property that has been wrongfully taken from the Burglar or his or her friends. Naturally, the Burglar won't face certain death simply to recover stolen goods, but if the character thinks he or she can get away with it, he or she might derive a certain amount of satisfaction from setting matters right. Sometimes the simple challenge of slipping into a great fortress or burglaring a well-defended treasure is enough to draw a Burglar's interest—not so much for the value of the goods as for the test of skills involved.

Like the Archer, the Burglar is the best of the best, a halfling who has developed to perfection skills all halflings possess to some degree—stealth, nimbleness, and unobtrusive movement. As such, he or she is highly respected by the halfling community for his or her expertise. Whereas an accomplished human thief usually tries to hide his or her profession, a Burglar's trade will be well-known by his or her halfling neighbors and his or her accomplishments highly-regarded—indeed, it is a source of civic pride for a village to be home to a really first-class Burglar, something for the town as a whole to boast about. This acceptance works to the community's benefit, since most Burglars will be willing to help out in times of crisis by using their talents for spying or gathering information that might prove useful to the village as a whole.

Role: The burglar is the master of several thiefly arts, most notably Move Silently and Open Locks, though skill at finding and removing traps can be another lifesaving talent. Burglars can be found in all areas of halfling society, including the comfortably wealthy as well as the most destitute.

Most Burglars congregate in areas of larger communities, where they can mingle with members of other races. Like most halfling thieves, the Burglar tends to avoid halfling victims, preferring the treasures of humanoid monsters and humans above all others. Occasionally a Burglar will choose to use his or her skills to aid fellow halflings who have suffered injustices; such Burglars can rise to the status of folk hero.

Secondary Skills: Many Burglars have skills at Trading and Bartering.

Weapon Proficiencies: Burglars prefer weapons that can be wielded quickly and in relative silence. Daggers and short swords are preferred for melee, though some specialize in other weapons. The sling is a popular missile weapon for a Burglar, as are darts and, in areas where they are known or used, the blowgun and hand crossbow.

Bonus Nonweapon Proficiencies: The Burglar gains a nonweapon proficiency for Appraisal.

Recommended Nonweapon Proficiencies: Rope Use, Disguise, and Tightrope Walking are all useful to a Burglar.

Thieving Skill Emphasis: Move Silently;

Hide in Shadows; Open Locks; Find and Remove Traps.

Equipment: A rope and a set of lockpicks are the standard tools of the Burglar. He or she will often scorn the use of armor altogether, and in any case will wear nothing heavier than leather, delighting in dark, silent clothing.

Special Benefits: At first level the Burglar gains an additional 10% to Open Locks **or** Move Silently. Each time he or she gains a new level, the Burglar receives a +5% bonus that can be applied to either of the above two talents or to Find and Remove Traps.

Special Hindrances: The Burglar devotes so much of his or her time to developing the skills of stealth that he or she is at something of a disadvantage in face-to-face combat, suffering a −1 penalty on all attack rolls in melee. However, attacks made as a *backstab* are not affected by this penalty.

Smuggler

The Smuggler is a halfling thief who gives every appearance of being an honest trader. In fact, he or she would *prefer* to be a straightforward and upright merchant, but (generally speaking) the impossible situation created by taxes and tolls of intrusive humans, dwarves, and elves drives him or her to more underhanded dealings. Thus, he or she imports and exports many things from many places—most of which are not supposed to be leaving or arriving at these specific locations.

The reasons for smuggling goods vary considerably; the following are the most common among them:

Excessive Taxation. A local government may wish to retain a monopoly on a local product (wine from the duke's vineyard, for example) and so seizes or stamps a high tariff on any competing goods brought into the duchy.

Belligerent Status. Two rival states involved in a border dispute will often prohibit trade with the enemy. Local farmers and tradesmen, however, don't always grasp the wisdom of a policy that cuts them off from their customers—thus, the aid of a Smuggler can keep the economy alive.

Contraband. A particular commodity might be banned outright, with penalties of varying severity for those who violate the prohibition. If a rival religious sect, for example, values bloodstones in its rituals, the entrenched state religion might bar that stone from the realm, decreeing that anyone caught with a bloodstone be put to death. Whatever the nature of the contraband, chances are that it is very valuable to someone—and consequently, there's a great deal of profit incentive for the bold Smuggler.

A Smuggler must have a Charisma or Intelligence score of at least 13.

Roads to Adventure: Smugglers almost always begin as traders, transporting goods from one location to another, turning a small profit, and bringing something new back to the point of origin. Sooner or later, as he or she expands his or her routes and the world changes, such a trader runs afoul of one of the above prohibitions—and the pragmatic halfling doesn't see why such a minor detail should change the way he or she conducts business. Thus, the merchant continues to do what he or she has always done—but with a little more risk, and a little more profit.

Tied into the Smuggler's normal way of life can be any number of special missions—tasks which allow the Smuggler to employ his or her skills in the name of a higher cause. Rescue of a prisoner is one, or the delivery of a message or item of great importance. A Smuggler can function as a very effective spy, reporting back on the mood of the local people as well as more typical information on land features and defensive preparations.

Role: The Smuggler is a vital cog in the unofficial economy of virtually any region in a civilized world—for without him or her, a far greater proportion of the wealth would remain in the hands of those who hold the reins

of power. Many goods that would otherwise have no outlet find their way to customers thanks to the intrepid Smuggler. Whether he or she carts it down rural highways or barges it along placid streams, the Smuggler will, quietly and reliably, see that his or her cargo reaches its destination.

Smugglers build a network of loyal friends and companions (which is why high Charisma is such an asset) and treat these accomplices well in return for protection and help.

The value of the goods smuggled is dependent on two factors: the market for those goods at their destination (supply and demand) and the difficulties and dangers endured by the smuggler in transporting them. Something which is valuable to begin with that now carries the threat of death will bring many times its normal worth to the Smuggler.

Secondary Skills: Either the Trader/Barterer or Teamster/Freighter secondary skills are appropriate for the Smuggler.

Weapon Proficiencies: Any.

Bonus Nonweapon Proficiencies: All Smugglers gain the Local History proficiency for areas on their regular routes. Also, Smugglers pick up languages during their travels, gaining the ability to speak and understand an additional language every other level, starting at second level. Naturally, the new language must be one he or she has had contact with during the course of the previous two levels of experience.

Recommended Nonweapon Proficiencies: Riding, Appraising, Disguise, and Forgery can all help a Smuggler in his or her work.

Thieving Skill Emphasis: Move Silently helps a Smuggler avoid attracting unwanted attention, while Hear Noise often alerts him or her to unwanted company.

Equipment: Unless he or she transports very small quantities, the Smuggler needs some way to haul cargo. Wagons and carts are easy to trace, so Smugglers prefer either some form of boat (e.g., canoe, river raft, or small sailboat) or a pack animal (such as a mule, pony, donkey, or large hound). In general, a Smuggler will only use a wheeled vehicle when he or she has a very good road to follow and is certain his or her smuggling activities have gone unsuspected.

Special Benefits: A Smuggler who possesses the Local History proficiency for an area gains a +4 bonus to NPC reaction checks in that area. He or she will also have full knowledge of any hidden pathways or secret trails along his or her regular route.

Special Hindrances: The inherent risks of challenging authority, including threat of imprisonment or worse, are the primary drawbacks to the Smuggler's career.

Urchin

The Urchin is a specialized halfling thief who attempts to pass as a human child. Many an unsuspecting victim has tried to collar the annoying brat, only to learn that the apparently feeble child who robbed him or her is in fact an adult with all the skills of an accomplished thief.

Urchins are encountered almost exclusively in cities and large towns, where people don't know all their neighbors. Roaming the chaotic network of a city's streets and alleys, the Urchin blends in to the local population, keeping several escape routes and hiding holes ready to hand at all times. Living mostly on the street, the Urchin takes shelter where he or she can find it—as often as not among the poor and destitute of the community.

The Urchin must have a Charisma score of at least 11.

Roads to Adventure: The Urchin character is typically a kit chosen by necessity—a halfling comes to a city alone and finds no market for his or her skills. At the same time, he or she grows tired of sneering bullies, some of whom pick on the halfling merely because of his or her size. Finding it easier to escape unwanted attention by blending in than by flight, he or she finds welcome anonymity in a life of disguise.

Role: The Urchin typically works alone, though he or she may well be a member of a small group; urban thieves' guilds made up entirely of halflings have been known to exist, most of whose members will be either Urchins or Burglars. Sometimes a halfling Urchin becomes the leader of a gang of children, both human and demihuman. In this case the Urchin will take a very protective, almost parental care with his or her young charges.

Dressing in juvenile clothes, with a haircut similar to those of local children, the Urchin will wander about the city like any child with a free day. However, he or she is adept at picking pockets and always has several escape routes memorized, ready at any moment for a quick getaway.

Diversions and distractions are a part of the Urchin's typical routine. If he or she can topple—or better yet, get someone *else* to topple—a fruit vendor's cart, for example, the resulting confusion will result in a situation ripe with possibilities for profit.

Secondary Skills: Any or none.

Weapon Proficiencies: The Urchin's double life prevents the character from openly wearing weapons children would normally not carry ("Say—what's that kid over there doing with that crossbow?"). Hence Urchins tend toward easily-concealed or disguised weapons (dagger, darts, sling, quarterstaff).

Bonus Nonweapon Proficiencies: Because his or her very existence depends upon playing a role, the Urchin quickly develops a knack for disguise. At first level, the Urchin can effectively disguise himself or herself as a human. Upon reaching second level, the Urchin gains the Disguise proficiency in full.

Recommended Nonweapon Proficiencies: Forgery, Blindfighting, Tumbling, and Ventriloquism can all have their uses to the Urchin.

Thieving Skill Emphasis: Urchins are consummate pickpockets (see Special Benefits, below); Climb Walls and Hide in Shadows are helpful when it comes to getaways.

Equipment: Aside from weapons and perhaps a set of lockpicks, the Urchin needs no special equipment.

Special Benefits: With Urchins, picking pockets is both a hobby and a way of life. Because of constant practice, Urchins develop unusual skill in this particular aspect of thievery. This translates into a +5% bonus **per level** to their Pick Pockets rolls, starting at second level (i.e., +5% at 2nd level, +10% at 3rd level, &c.).

Special Hindrances: The local guardsmen and city officials can take a real dislike to the activities of an Urchin, causing no end of trouble for the poor player character.

Fighter/Thief Kits

Cartographer

This character is an explorer and mapmaker who sets out to see the world and wants to return with a good account of his or her adventures. Although such a calling is unusual among halflings (except among Kender, many of whom believe themselves to have great talent along these lines), the Cartographer exists among all halfling subraces, however rare he or she may be. Indeed, his or her exploits form the great part of many popular legends among the small folk.

Cartographers are, by their nature, very interested in the land and its features. They are inclined to take little note of the occupants of those lands, unless forced to do so. To a Cartographer, a city's setting on a high riverside bluff will seem far more profound than the fact that the guards of that same community have just arrested him or her under suspicion of being a spy or just generally being a stranger.

A Cartographer must have an Intelligence score of at least 13.

Roads to Adventure: The Cartographer is drawn to the road for no other purpose than curiosity of what lies over the next hill—though many a Cartographer has become entangled in events along the way that resulted

in fame and fortune.

If the Cartographer enjoys exploring and adventuring for its own sake, he or she also enjoys keeping records of his or her experiences (to reminisce over in his or her old age, assuming the character survives to have one)—primarily by mapping out everywhere he or she goes. He or she has a great interest in new places and will often journey far out of his or her way simply to investigate some unique feature he or she has heard about. Cartographers tend to ignore obstacles created by an area's inhabitants (hence, Cartographers have a high mortality rate) but will be well aware of the difficulties involved in crossing certain geographic challenges, such as deserts, mountain ranges, seas, and swamps.

Role: The Cartographer is a happy wanderer, as comfortable under the encircling limbs of a thick pine as in a goosedown bed. The weariness of the trail may weigh down his or her feet, but curiosity will still propel the traveler over one more hill, around another bend.

The Cartographer doesn't go looking for trouble (i.e., adventure), but it seems to have a way of finding him or her, due no doubt to his or her inexhaustible curiosity. Often a halfling Cartographer will be found mapping a trade route through a war zone or tracing the path followed by an ancient expedition through a forgotten dungeon, oblivious to the arrows flying around him or her!

Cartographer rarely hold any sort of official positions as court mapmakers, with the ironic result that many a trackless land lies virtually unknown to its human or dwarven overlord while some retired halfling Cartographer has a perfectly good map of the place tacked up above his or her hearth. Fortunately Cartographers are often willing—even eager—to show others their maps; adventurers willing to listen patiently to the halfling tell at length of his or her journeys will often gain much valuable information for their trouble.

Unfortunately, it must also be noted that just because a map was drawn by a halfling Cartographer, there's no reason to assume that a map is entirely accurate. Any feature the Cartographer has seen for his or her self will be just as it is drawn; however, some Cartographers are trusting souls and will incorporate features into their maps that they have only heard about second- hand. In such cases, the second-hand information is only as reliable as the source. Kender maps are notoriously unreliable, because a Kender Cartographer will exaggerate what he or she sees in order to make a more interesting map: mountains become taller, rivers wider, distances farther apart, and the like. Thus Kender maps are entertaining but relatively useless; a grain of truth will lie behind them, but it may be somewhat difficult to extract.

Secondary Skills: Any (player's choice).

Weapon Proficiencies: The Cartographer is a well-rounded character, proficient in at least one missile and one melee weapon. Short bows and short swords are the most popular, though the sling-staff is another favorite. Kender Cartographers will of course specialize in their national weapon, the hoopak.

Bonus Nonweapon Proficiencies: Cartographers gain Direction Sense as a bonus proficiency when the character is created.

Upon reaching second level, halflings using this kit gain a unique proficiency: Cartography. The Cartography proficiency allows a character to accurately render on paper or parchment the distances and directions of features that he or she has personally seen. If a Cartographer sails along a coastline, for example, he or she will be able to chart its bays, points, reefs, and inlets, as well as give a general impression of the shoreline—is it forest or meadow, mountain or plain? However, he or she will not know the shape of inland features such as valleys or the course of rivers and streams.

Cartographers who spend time chatting with local folk will be able to learn about more than the places they see themselves. Such second-hand maps, however, are only as accurate as their source—and even then they will lack a level of detail that the Cartographer can add from the scenery before his or her own eyes. Thus, secondhand maps tend to have more imaginary or inaccurately-described features.

Recommended Nonweapon Proficiencies: A character desiring to be a Cartographer *must* take the Navigation proficiency. In addition, Modern Language can prove very useful in asking directions, while Weather Sense and Survival can help keep the Cartographer alive in the wild.

Thieving Skill Emphasis: Read Languages skills enable a Cartographer to research old maps and help plan his or her journeys; Climb Walls can help overcome obstacles on the way.

Equipment: The Cartographer feels lost without his or her mapmaking kit: paper or parchment, quills, and ink. He or she will improvise in a pinch, using virtually any material that comes to hand (leather, bark, driftwood, &c.), but will transfer such crude maps to more permanent form as soon as the chance presents itself.

Special Benefits: Cartographers almost never get lost, even in places they have never been before, above ground or below. If confronted with a question like "Which way back to town?" or "Which of these corridors leads toward the surface?" a Cartographer can make an Intelligence check; success means that he or she know the answer and failure means that he or she doesn't know and realizes the fact. Optionally, the DM can rule that on a fumble (a result of 20 on 1d20) the Cartographer *thinks* he or she knows the way but starts out in the wrong direction.

Special Hindrances: None to speak of.

Trader

The halfling Trader is a legitimate version of the Smuggler—an honest merchant who spends more time in legal activities and has a little more fighting ability with which to protect his or her cargo (and, incidentally, his or her self as well). Traders generally stake out a territory and a regular route and don't range too far afield; only a chance to dramatically increase his or her profits will tempt a typical Trader into deviating from the established routine. A Trader is very likely to have a burrow in a local community, and though he or she may be absent for several days at a time he or she is always glad to return home again.

A Trader must have a Charisma score of at least 11.

Roads to Adventure: The Trader is a natural target for thieves; fortunately, his or her combination of character classes makes this hardworking halfling merchant well equipped to vigorously defend his or her cargo.

By the nature of his or her business, the Trader has the chance to make many friends and become acquainted with the problems in

many different areas. Motivated by a strong sense of right and wrong, together with the strength of his or her influence, the Trader will often take a leadership role in situations that call for dramatic and decisive action.

Role: Trading among halflings begins as a very simple, need-based process. The Trader finds some high quality commodity, usually from his or her own village, which is in large supply. Typical goods, especially for starting Traders, include cheese, produce, wine and beer, pottery or cloth, shellwork, unique spices or flavorings, and woodcarvings. Often, in fact, the local source of these goods will 'front' the Trader for his or her first cargo, in anticipation of much increased business. This is only done, however, if the young Trader is a local lad or lass known to be a sober and responsible individual.

Next the Trader determines another area, where he or she anticipates a demand for those goods and decides what he or she will trade for in return. The Trader typically starts small, with a limited and regular route upon which he or she tries to establish a professional reputation. If the enterprise prospers, he or she might show a (generally conservative) tendency to expand business; since he or she is a halfling, any new stops along the route usually means the Trader will be making new friends there as well.

Secondary Skills: The Trader/Barterer is the typical secondary skill of this kit.

Weapon Proficiencies: Any.

Bonus Nonweapon Proficiencies: The Trader can select either Appraising or Local History as a bonus proficiency at the onset of his or her career.

Recommended Nonweapon Proficiencies: Direction Sense, Animal Handling, and Weather Sense are all useful proficiencies for anyone who spends a lot of time on the road.

Thieving Skill Emphasis: Detect Noise helps the Trader anticipate ambushes, while Read Languages is useful for bookkeeping.

Equipment: The Trader will typically have a cart or wagon to haul his or her goods and some beast of burden—a pony, donkey, draft horse, or ox. River-based Traders will have a small, easily-managed boat with plenty of cargo space. Unlike Smugglers, Traders keep to well-traveled (and well-guarded) highways and hence prefer wagons to pack animals.

Special Benefits: The Trader is a well-known and popular character, privy to the local news all along his or her trade routes, often the first to bring news and gossip from village to village. He or she is quick to learn of new and interesting discoveries and to determine what goods and commodities are in demand in various locales. Additionally, he or she has a marvelous opportunity to get rich.

Special Hindrances: In a word, thieves.

Traveler

This popular character is the halfling equivalent of the bard, a musician and storyteller traveling about out of curiosity and a general love of life. His or her wanderings give the character grist for the tales and legends by which he or she earns a living. Like the Cartographer, he or she is curious about the wide world, but it is people, not places, that draw a Traveler's attention. Nothing makes a Traveler happier than meeting people from a wide variety of cultures, and this enthusiasm translates into a remarkable ability to understand and adapt to local customs.

A Traveler must have a Charisma score of at least 15.

Roads to Adventure: The Traveler is another of those rare (some would say 'mad') halflings for whom the comforts of hearth and burrow are simply not enough. It begins almost always in childhood with the feeling that the fair in the *next* village must be just a little grander than the one at home. Accomplished Travelers can become the confidants of kings and queens, the emissaries of earls, the entertainers of nobles and sages.

Role: The Traveler does much the same work as a bard but takes himself or herself far less seriously. He or she is an accomplished wordsmith, capable of spinning a yarn on the spur of the moment that can reduce an audience to tears or helpless laughter. All Travelers play a musical instrument, but it will always be a simple, homey instrument like a banjo, harmonica, or fiddle rather than one of the more sophisticated instruments favored by bards. Travelers are also fond of entertaining children with simple sleight-of-hand tricks, and one will often put on a special show just for children when he or she comes to town.

A Traveler's performances are almost always informal, homespun affairs—swapping stories and sharing a jug with the old folks around a hearthfire, playing the fiddler and being the caller for courting couples at the local hoedown and square dance, thrilling youngsters with monster stories enlivened by special sound effects. Travelers are masters of the Question Game and enjoy matching their skill against that of the local champs. Because of their genuine enjoyment of people, Travelers are quick to make friends. As a rule, they are welcomed nearly everywhere they go and remembered fondly when they depart.

Secondary Skills: Most Travelers will avoid secondary skills on principle.

Weapon Proficiencies: The Traveler can use any weapon; usually he or she will try to select something unique. Travelers are particularly fond of weapons that don't look like weapons—for example, a walking stick which is actually a swordstick, or wooden juggling balls that can be used as missile weapons.

Bonus Nonweapon Proficiencies: The Traveler receives Musical Instrument as a bonus proficiency.

Recommended Nonweapon Proficiencies: Dance, Disguise, Etiquette, Juggling, Tumbling, and Ventriloquism are all useful proficiencies for a Traveler.

Thieving Skill Emphasis: Travelers do very little actual stealing, as a rule, but the Pick Pockets skill comes in handy in their sleight-of-hand shows.

Equipment: Aside from his or her musical instrument, weapons, and the clothes he or she wears, a Traveler will have few possessions, no more than he or she can easily carry. Gold has a tendency to tie a body down, in his or her opinion, and the character is likely to leave any excess wealth that comes his or her way on the door of some worthy widow or orphan as he or she leaves town, light of heart and empty of pocket.

Special Benefits: The Traveler has several bard-like abilities: he or she receives a +2 to all Reaction Rolls due to the character's innate goodwill to all and friendly demeanor. A Traveler who has time to tell friends and allies an inspiring story before they enter a combat gives them the same attack and saving throw bonuses as a *bless* spell. Finally, his or her music offers immunity to song-based *charm* attacks (for example, a harpy's singing) to all within earshot, but only so long as the Traveler can keep playing non-stop.

Special Hindrances: As noted above, all Travelers are poor, by choice. It has been said that a Traveler has a million friends and no home, and this is true; while his or her folksy manner and homespun ways win the character a welcome everywhere he or she goes, he or she has no family or burrow to return to. Travelers are essentially sociable loners who dread the day when old age will force them to stop their wandering at last.

Cleric Kits

Healer

The Healer is the community physician, counselor, and spiritual adviser for his or her fellow halflings (though not every village or town is fortunate enough to have one). Healers must have an alignment of good or neutral and specialize in the benign arts of tending injuries, curing diseases, midwifery, and general public health.

The Healer must have a Wisdom score of at least 12.

Roads to Adventure: Typically, the Healer gets drawn into adventure not because of any all-consuming drive to see the world or to gain fame and fortune, but because he or she feels that he or she will genuinely be able to help his or her friends—who for some reason the healer cannot fathom *are* seeking fame, fortune, and excitement.

Healers are very confident in their abilities and those of their friends and are thus comforting to have around. They tend to be righteous, even a tad stodgy, in their beliefs, but loyal to a fault (even to those who might not feel a similar loyalty in return) and very determined when in pursuit of a worthy goal.

Role: The Healer is fond of reminding his or her companions that he or she is "just a simple country doctor," a phrase which rarely does this highly competent cleric justice. He or she has very little aptitude for combat, preferring instead to let more vigorous allies handle the tasks of violence. Naturally enough, the Healer specializes at repairing the damage inflicted by such battles after they are over—or, sometimes, while they rage around him or her.

Healers also often function as "the voice of reason" in a party; they give advice freely, whether it is asked for or not, and are not afraid of speaking their minds—whether to defend an underdog, praise an unpopular decision, or criticize an evil warlord to his or her face.

Secondary Skills: The Healer's calling is a full-time job in itself, leaving no time for any secondary occupation.

Weapon Proficiencies: The Healer only receives *one* weapon proficiency slot at first level; he or she can select any weapon eligible for a cleric.

Bonus Nonweapon Proficiencies: The Healer automatically receives the Healing proficiency, without any penalty to his or her proficiency checks.

Recommended Nonweapon Proficiencies: The Healer can benefit from a knowledge of Agriculture, Herbalism, and Reading/Writing.

Equipment: A Healer will never be without his or her bag, which contains scalpels, bandages, ah-sticks, and various herbs, barks, and roots useful in the event he or she needs to whip up a quick poultice or ointment.

Special Benefits: The Healer gains a +1 hit point bonus per die rolled to all *cure wounds* spells he or she casts.

Special Hindrances: Healers refuse to wear armor in all but the most dire circumstances. A Healer's famed lack of tact can also cause problems in some situations.

Leaftender

The Leaftender is similar in many ways to the druid—he or she is a priest who lives in and watches over the wild places that are so important to the halfling race. Despite the fact that his or her home and burrow is located deep in the woods, the Leaftender is not antisocial—halfling visitors will always find a warm welcome and be invited in to share a cup of a tea, a bit of conversation, and a warm fire. Nonhalflings will meet with a similar reception once the Leaftender has ascertained that they offer no threat to his or her treasured domain.

Unlike the Forestwalker, who is devoted to keeping the forest the way it is, and the Homesteader, who wishes to turn it into farmland or pasture, the Leaftender works to slowly tame a forest without destroying it. He or she will plant nut trees and berry bushes to provide more food for the local wildlife, tend sick trees, and generally make the woods he or she dwells in a healthier, friendlier place.

Roads to Adventure: The Leaftender is like a wilderness gardener. Anything that threatens to undo his or her work by endangering the peace or health of the trees, water, or animal life in his or her woods will draw the ire of the Leaftender—and compel him or her to take steps to counter that threat.

Role: The Leaftender is more integrated into his or her society than is the druid—he or she is not a hermit, even though he or she may live some distance away from the community. Since the wild and beautiful places are so important to halflings as a whole, the community tends to be very supportive of this cleric's activities.

When a Leaftender visits nearby halfling communities (which he or she will do far more often than would, say, a druid) he or she will bring gifts of the woods' bounty—berries, mushrooms, and herbs—to add variety and spice to the village menus. Alone of all halflings, Leaftenders are vegetarians and eat no animal products.

Secondary Skills: Agriculture is a possible, though not a necessary, secondary skill for a Leaftender.

Weapon Proficiencies: The Leaftender is limited to the following weapon types (listed in order of preference): sling, sickle, spear, scythe, dagger, staff, club, and dart.

Bonus Nonweapon Proficiencies: The Leaftender receives Herbalism and Survival (Woodlands) as bonus proficiencies.

Recommended Nonweapon Proficiencies: Weather Sense and Direction Sense can prove very useful, as well as Animal Lore, Swimming, and Firebuilding.

Equipment: The Leaftender will assemble whatever materials he or she needs to carry out his or her work of tending the forest.

Special Benefits: As they advance in level, Leaftenders become increasingly attuned to their environment, granting them the following abilities:

At 2nd level, the Leaftender can pass through overgrown areas at his or her normal movement rate without leaving a trail.

At 3rd level, he or she can identify plants, animals, and pure water with perfect accuracy.

At 5th level, he or she becomes immune to *charm* spells cast by woodland creatures such as dryads and nixies.

Special Hindrances: Leaftenders cannot use metal armor and will not use leather armor. They may, however, use wooden shields.

Oracle

The Oracle is the halfling cleric who deals with spiritual matters, the will of the gods, auguries and prophecies, and the like. Whereas the Healer's emphasis is on spells that affect his or her people directly, the Oracle is more concerned with interpreting the gods' will to the people.

Roads to Adventure: The Oracle can be drawn into a quest by a prophecy that he or she interprets as the will of the gods; alternately, like the Healer, he or she will accompany his or her companions on their own adventures out of a sincere belief that, without his or her help, they are doomed.

More than any other halfling type, the Oracle is driven by a consuming desire to learn, to answer great questions, to complete some great quest. The drive for such activities originates as a spiritual calling, but the Oracle with typical halfling common sense will follow up such motivations with very practical determination and drive.

Role: The Oracle seeks to be an interpreter who looks for signs of the gods' will and then teaches his or her people what they should do. As part of that role, he or she casts spells designed to communicate with those deities. He or she will usually be chosen to preside over the community's occasional religious ceremonies and festivities.

Secondary Skills: The Scribe secondary skill is useful to the Oracle.

Weapon Proficiencies: An Oracle can use any weapon allowed for the standard cleric.

Bonus Nonweapon Proficiencies: The Oracle receives Astrology as a bonus proficiency.

Recommended Nonweapon Proficiencies: Heraldry, Ancient History, Religion, and Spellcraft are recommended for the Oracle.

Equipment: Any he or she desires.

Special Benefits: When the Oracle performs any spell of the sphere of divination, he or she will receive (from the DM) unusually reliable and accurate information. The specifics of this benefit vary by spell, of course.

Oracles also occasionally receive visions directly from their deities; however, these visions are usually cryptic, requiring time and thought to unravel their significance.

Special Hindrances: The Oracle is very unwilling to compromise—he or she is more stubborn than the typical halfling. He or she treats every mission as a quest and will never abandon a task no matter how many difficulties stand in the way.

CHAPTER

5

Lindendale—A Typical Halfling Village

Lindendale is a small community, a town of halflings that could exist in almost any campaign world. It is presented here for two reasons: (1) it provides a look at a typical halfling village, with examples of households and the various trades and skills represented there, and (2) it can be used as a home base for launching an all-halfling campaign, as it can easily be dropped into any ongoing campaign.

The village is mapped on page 123. It lies in a sheltered valley on the south side of a long, forested ridge. About a mile to the south of the map, a major road runs from east to west. A small dirt track leads from this highway to the village.

A placid stream, the Lindenbrook, winds along the base of the ridge. While no more than three or four feet deep, the creek's silty bottom makes fording difficult.

1. Inn of the Brass Tankard

This homey place is the first building a visitor sees upon approaching Lindendale. It is a two-story structure of whitewashed wood with brown shutters and a round, oversized door. The common room is large enough for humans but still cozy to halflings. The guest rooms come in two sizes, for Big Folk (upper level) or small folk (lower level), with appropriately-sized furniture in each.

The innkeeper, Gwiston Shortwick, lives here with his wife Lucretia, their four daughters, and Lucretia's elderly mother; the family quarters are in a burrow at the south end of the inn. Several other halflings work here as stablehands and waitresses, but they live in the village with their families.

2. Mill and Bakery

Dottery Dale is a bawdy halfling wench who runs the village mill and also bakes fabulous bread and cakes. She has two brothers and a sister who live here as well, each of them married with several children—but the unmarried Dottery is unquestioned head of the household.

The Millbridge is attached to the great wooden building and is the only dry means of crossing the Lindenbrook for more than a mile in either direction.

3. Cheese Factory

Hofflik Kaese is the master cheesemaker here. He takes all the milk that the local dairies can provide and turns it into a sharp, white cheese (called "Lindenbrook") that is highly prized within the local area and beyond. It is the village's major export.

Hofflik, a bachelor, lives in a small set of rooms beside his factory. Two small compartments within the shop itself provide quarters for the one to four full-time apprentices (both male and female) he's likely to have working with him at any one time.

4. Dairies

These three prosperous concerns each own a dozen or more cows and graze them in these distinct pastures. The animals are sheltered in neat, low-ceilinged barns. Each herd includes a half-dozen calves; a great bull occupies his own pen on the Kalliwart farm north of the stream.

The clans that run these dairies are friendly rivals, striving to outdo each other in milk production—most of which is bartered or sold to the cheese factory.

4a. Kalliwart Farm, the largest of the three, is managed by Glenvius and Blythi Kalliwart, who recently celebrated a complete century of marriage. Ten children and their spouses, twenty-two grandchildren, and five great-grandchildren make up the rest of the household. The family is known for its slightly rambunctious youngsters—they are charismatic and popular, but prone to be troublemakers. The farm boasts twenty-two milk cows and the village's only bull.

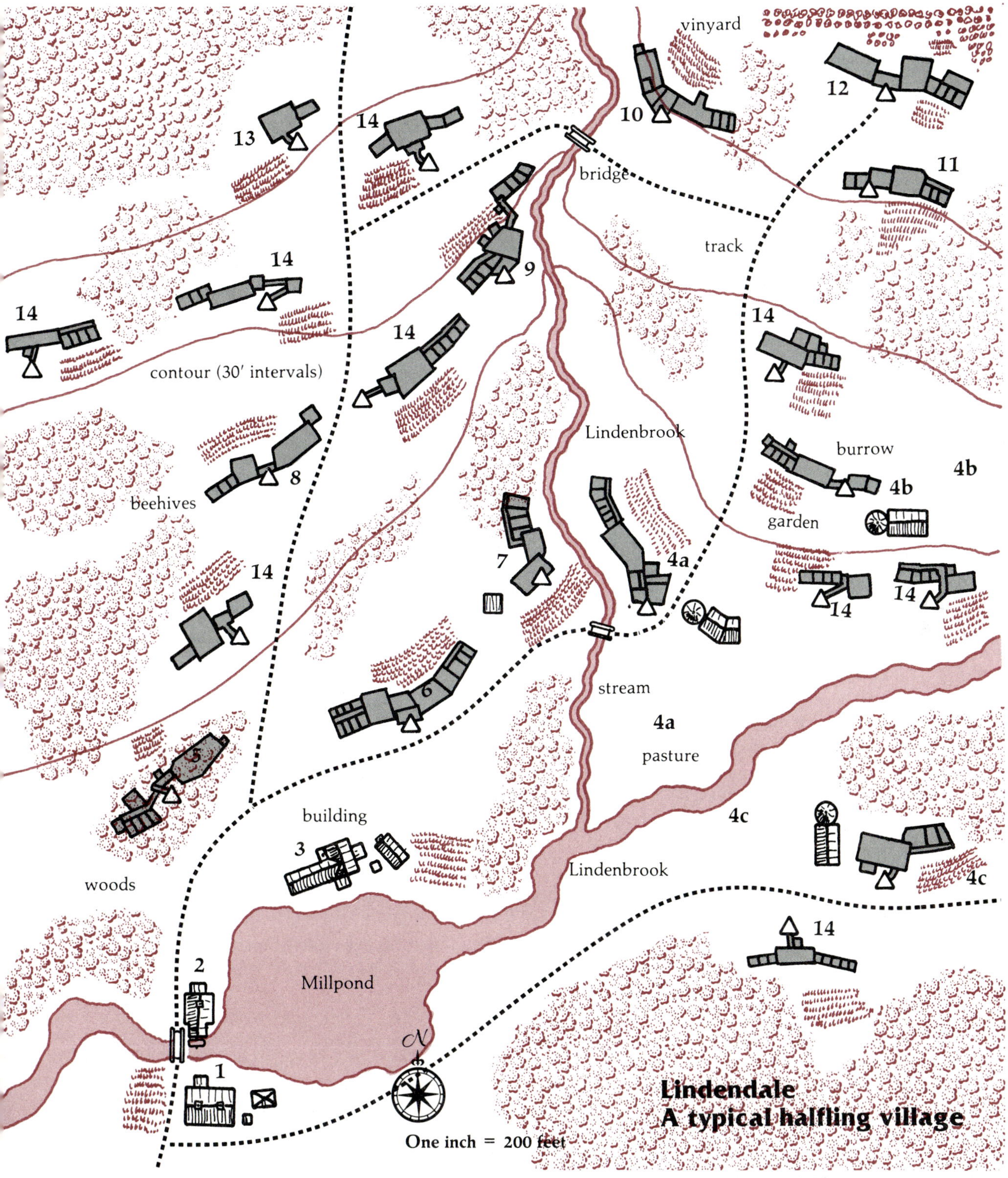
vinyard
12
10
13
14
11
bridge
track
14
14
9
14
14
contour (30′ intervals)
Lindenbrook
8
burrow
4b
4b
beehives
garden
7
4a
14
14
14
6
stream
4a
pasture
5
building
4c
3
Lindenbrook
4c
woods
14
2
Millpond
1
One inch = 200 feet
Lindendale
A typical halfling village

4b. Bandawax Farm, with its fifteen cows, is tended by a smaller clan with a reputation for thrift, even tightfistedness. Gammer Bandawax is a venerable matriarch who keeps tight control over the family purse strings. Her five daughters and their husbands, together with fourteen grandchildren, live in a sprawling, multi-roomed burrow.

4c. Lily Hectare, the third farm, is where the Jallisall family tends a herd of twelve cows. A trio of brothers, all widowers, head the family, sharing the house with a dozen descendants. The farm is most noted for the gorgeous flowerbeds that surround not only the house but the barn and pasture as well.

5. Trading Stump

The arched bridge descends from the mill into a small grove of towering oaks. Among them is centered the hut of Filbert the Trader. Before his ramshackle dwelling is a flat stump, more than four feet in girth, where a tree struck by lightning was cut down. Here, in the shade of the arching branches, the wily halfling merchant sits and barters with his many customers.

Filbert Oldfur is a well-traveled halfling, a former adventurer and a famous character in the village. His home sprawls through several underground tunnels around his shop, and he shares his burrow with seven nieces and nephews, and a vivacious "housekeeper" named Milliciny. This attractive halfling lass returned to the village with Filbert following one of his travels and has been the source of considerable gossip and raised eyebrows among the good citizens of Lindendale.

Filbert maintains a regular stock of the village's major products, including Lindenbrook cheese, Amsterbock ale, and Daleside red wine. He also offers samples of Dwilcath Batel's woodcarvings, including well-turned cups and bowls.

The trader also keeps a number of goods of human, dwarven, and elven make in stock, including metal pots, pans, utensils, tools, arrowheads, and knives; salt, spices, tobacco; wines, ales, and cheeses from surrounding villages; and an extensive collection of fabrics, including wool, cotton, and even bolts of bright silk.

6. Mayor's Mansion

This large burrow belongs to Fairweather Montajay, Lindendale's esteemed mayor. An adventurer in her youth, she lived for ten years in a large city not too far away. A first-class Burglar, she eventually rose to become head of the local Thieves' Guild before retiring and returning to her home town. Her clan is numerous, including her husband Ashworthy (whom she met in the city and brought back to Lindendale), five children and their spouses, and fifteen grandchildren.

7. Sheriff Greenspan's Burrow

The primary force for law and order in Lindendale is this stocky warrior with graying hair and grizzled sideburns. He and his wife live in this comfortable burrow, together with their six children, two daughters-in-law, and their first grandchild (who is perhaps a trifle spoiled).

The sheriff is a calm fellow who enjoys the comforts of life, slow to respond in an emergency but level-headed and dependable in a crisis. His chief secret in keeping the peace is to always allow everybody to have his or her say before passing judgment. Just downhill from the family home he and his sons have constructed a small, partially buried shed. He uses this for storage, but it can be securely barred on the outside if it's necessary to lock someone up.

8. Carissa Candlemaker

The elderly Carissa is a widow famed for her stubborn determination and unwillingness to compromise. She is kind-hearted but cranky, unusually crotchety for a halfling. She lives her with two sisters (also widowed) and a dozen children and grandchildren. The burrow is surrounded by clover, as the family maintains a row of beehives from which they harvest honey and wax. They barter with the honey and use the wax to make fine candles which are prized throughout the village.

9. Benden Sire, Locksmith

This halfling is something of a hermit. He is also the wealthiest halfling in Lindendale, having made a fortune designing the locks to protect an emperor's hoard that foiled the attempts by heads of three thieves' guilds to pick them. His burrow is extensive and mostly underground, with stout shutters over the windows and an iron-barred door of heavy planks. Benden lives here alone, never having married and being totally absorbed in the pursuit of his art; he spends almost all his time working on his dream of creating a lock that cannot be picked. To test his creations, he has amassed the finest collection of lockpicks for many miles around.

10. Amster's Brewery

This hardworking family of seven brews the dark ale called Amsterbock here. The business was started by a famous ancestor, Alberti Amster; today, his granddaughter Jess carries on the family tradition, added by several cousins. This beverage is one of Lindendale's most popular products, allowing Jess and her cousins to live quite comfortably, although rumor has it that she has succumbed to the adventuring bug and may soon head out into the world to seek her fortune.

11. Woodcarver's shop

Dwilcath Batel is the premier woodcarver of Lindendale, living in this burrow near the fringe of forest above the town. He is a benign patriarch, still skilled with his knife, though much of the heavier work (woodcutting and carpentry) is now done by his four sons. They are all married, and three grandchildren live here, with the fourth on the way.

12. Vintners

Pally and Dorith Quettory are a cheerfully robust couple, middle-aged and childless, who have devoted their energies to the sweeping vineyards which cover the hillside below their front door. Their primary vintage is called Daleside Red, though they make a rarer Pale version that is also highly prized.

13. The Fletchery

This new burrow is inhabited by Wally and Sass Talbot, a young couple who only recently married and got a home of their own; they are now expecting their first child. Comfortable if not ostentatious, it is crowded with arrows finished and unfinished (Wally's handiwork) and Sass's latest bow. Sass only makes bows to order, carefully crafting each one for the person who commissioned it; so well made is her handiwork that the original owner receives a +1 bonus to his or her chance to hit when using it.

14. Farms

These nine burrows range from modest to capacious and are the home to the families of farmers who tend the fields surrounding Lindendale: the Baldorfs, Byttnis, Dudleys, Heathertoes, Newters, Ostgoods, Trills, Tucks, and Weatherbees.

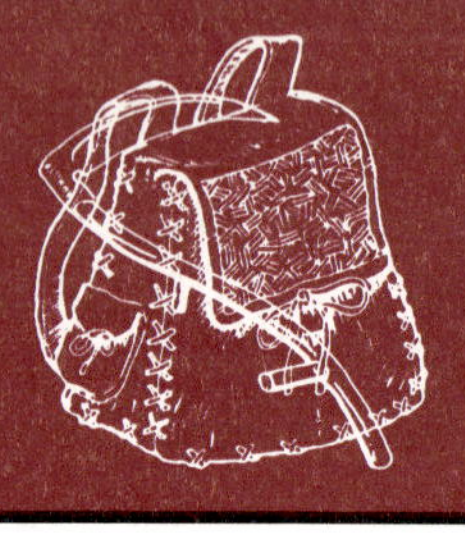

Adventure Suggestions

It is important to remember when playing a gnome or halfling character that halflings are not short humans, nor are gnomes scrawny dwarves: each is an entirely different race, with different perspectives on the world and different motivations.

Opportunities that might bring human or dwarven characters bounding to their feet, eyes gleaming in anticipation, can bring quite a different response from a halfling—e.g., "So what if the old castle's full of treasure? I've got a warm fire, a jug half-full of ale, and my bread's almost done rising!" However, the same halfling might change his or her tune upon learning that the only known copy of a legendary chef's cookbook was rumored to be in the castle as well. Likewise, whereas the Big Folk would avoid a tomb if at all possible once they learned it was heavily-trapped, a gnome might well want to explore it for the same reason in order to see how the traps work and employ the same principles in his or her next practical jokes.

In any adventure involving a gnome or halfling character, the player must ask himself or herself "Why is my character here?" Gnomes love gems like halflings love good food, and most gnomequests will involve searching for fabled gems and lost mines. A halfling will be more likely to join an adventure out of a sense of duty (e.g., an old friend is in trouble) or pure curiosity than from greed for treasure or a desire to go out and fight monsters.

The following outlines are kernels for adventures specifically designed for an all-gnomish or all-halfling campaign. They can easily be adapted to almost any AD&D® campaign world and level of experience.

Gnome Adventures

Goblin Infestation: This begins as isolated and mysterious attacks against lone gnomes, who are either killed or otherwise unable to describe their assailants. During these raids the goblins capture something very valuable, whether it's the community's prized gemstone artifact or a well-liked gnome NPC.

The characters must anticipate where the attackers will strike next, lay illusionary bait for them, and then follow the raiders back to their lair. Once they've located the attacker's home base, they must infiltrate it, rescue the missing treasure or hostages, find a way to disrupt the goblins so badly that it will put an end to the ambushes, and escape.

Festival of the Starmelt: The clans are scheduled to gather for an important, once-in-a-decade observation. An old and evil dragon gets wind of the plans and decides to make an attack against the assemblage with the aid of a tribe of kobolds. Gnomish adventurers must discern the plan from captive kobolds and then take steps to confuse or divert the dragon before the festival begins.

City of Illusions: Gnome illusionists begin to find that sometimes their spells don't work, while at other times they behave in unexpected ways. Investigation will eventually trace the source of the problem to a strange village peopled entirely by intelligent illusions created for company by a since-deceased master Imagemaker. They resent the "involuntary servitude" of their fellow illusions and are trying to nudge them into rebellious sentience, with some success. The PCs must find a way to placate the angry illusion-people; with luck and tact, they may gain some unusual allies in the process.

Gemquest: A strange gnome comes to the village, badly wounded by some bizarre and magical force. He collapses and dies, but not before he drops a huge and stunningly beautiful gem of a type none of the gnomes have ever seen before, together with a gasped-out description of a "Mount Crystal" that lies somewhere in the distance. In truth, the gemstone is an intelligent parasitic quartzite creature from the elemental plane of earth that

sapped his strength with its baneful magic, but not before he served as the bait to lure more gnomes into its trap.

Gnomes who make the journey will find Mount Crystal, a shining hill of white quartz. Inside, they find abandoned mines holding an incredible wealth of gems of all types—unknown to them, more of the creatures. Each creature forms a bond with a single gnome and drains 1d4 points of his or her Constitution per day. The characters must realize what is going on, find a way to break the charm which prevents each gnome from throwing away his or her own stone, and make a desperate break for freedom.

Halfling Adventures

Meddlesome Officialdom: A nearby human lord decides to charge the small folk a toll for using a road, bridge, or river passing through their town, as well as a tax on all transactions, sending guards and tax collectors to make sure that his commands are followed. The halflings must find a way to avoid paying the tariffs and eventually rid themselves of the pestering presence without resorting to violence.

The Bully: A tough human knight, or perhaps even an ogre, troll, or giant, takes up residence nearby. He or she appoints himself or herself the village's "protector" and demands food and drink, and eventually treasure, from the small folk in return. He or she is too strong for the villagers to defeat in combat, forcing the halflings to use their wits to come up with a clever plan to chase the brute away.

Kidnapped: All the human children from a nearby community are captured by goblins or kobolds and taken to the humanoid's lair—a lair with ceilings too low and passages too narrow for adult humans to enter. The humans approach the halflings and beg them to rescue the children, offering whatever inducements they can to gain the aid of a brave band of small folk.

A Tinker Comes to Town: A strange peddler rolls into the village with a wagon full of wondrous gew-gaws and trinkets. He or she sells many of these and gives others away. Shortly after the stranger leaves, the villagers start to change their lifelong patterns of behavior—some become short-tempered or depressed; others frivolous and irresponsible.

The trinkets are *not* the cause of the changes, however. There's an evil wizard at work, and the tinker's gifts are charms against her enchantments. The halflings must first find out what's going on, and then find a means to drive the wizard away.

Monster Depredation: A tribe of monsters, such as gnolls or orcs, begins to ravage the area. Only if halflings and their human and demihuman neighbors unite do they stand a chance to defeat the menace. The halflings must convince rival groups of humans, dwarves, and elves to work together in a common cause. When it comes to actually facing the foe, the halflings should try to defeat them through cleverness and deception rather than an outright attack.

The Forest Plague: A mysterious malady begins to affect the surrounding woods, causing trees to wither and die, crops to fail, and a general blight to settle across the land.

After some investigation (which can be an adventure in itself), the halflings determine that the plague results from losses suffered by local treants and dryads due to indiscriminate logging. The small folk must then find a way to deter the woodcutters until the people of the trees have a chance to recover, while at the same time avoid causing the woodcutters from losing their livelihood.

JOIN THE ADVENTURE!

ENTER NEW WORLDS OF EXCITEMENT AND FUN IN EVERY ISSUE!

Dragon® MAGAZINE

The leader of the role-playing world offers gaming advice, new ideas, reviews, monsters, cartoons, and treasures not found anywhere else!

Dungeon®
ADVENTURES FOR TSR ROLE-PLAYING GAMES

The module magazine for AD&D® and D&D® game players leads you to the limits of the known gaming universe!

FILL OUT AND MAIL THE SUBSCRIPTION FORM BELOW to receive the world's greatest gaming magazines.

DRAGON® Magazine

Subscription type:
☐ New ☐ Renewal (enclose mailing label)

Amount of payment (send U.S. funds only!)

To U.S. address	To Canadian address
☐ 1 year (12 issues) for $30	☐ 1 year (12 issues) for $38
☐ 2 years (24 issues) for $57	☐ 2 years (24 issues) for $66
☐ 3 years (36 issues) for $84	☐ 3 years (36 issues) for $95
	(prices include GST)

To foreign address
☐ 1 year (12 issues), by surface mail, for $50
☐ 1 year (12 issues), by air mail, for $90

DUNGEON® Adventures

Subscription type:
☐ New ☐ Renewal (enclose mailing label)

Amount of payment (send U.S. funds only!)

To U.S. address	To Canadian address
☐ 1 year (6 issues) for $18	☐ 1 year (6 issues) for $24
☐ 2 years (12 issues) for $33	☐ 2 years (12 issues) for $40
☐ 3 years (18 issues) for $48	☐ 3 years (18 issues) for $56
	(prices include GST)

To foreign address
☐ 1 year (6 issues), by surface mail, for $35
☐ 1 year (6 issues), by air mail, for $52

Check the appropriate boxes under the publication(s) to which you are subscribing. Then, mail this form with payments to: TSR, Inc., P.O. Box 5695, Boston MA 02206. (All payments must be in U.S. funds.)

(Please PRINT clearly.)

Name ____________________
Address ____________________
City ____________ State/Prov. ____________
Country ____________ Zip/Postal Code ____________

Method of Payment
☐ Check ☐ Money order ☐ MasterCard ☐ VISA

Credit card no. ____________________
Expiration date ____________ MC bank no. ____________
Signature ____________________ Date ____________

Your first issue should arrive within 8 to 10 weeks in the U.S. and Canada. All prices are subject to change without notice.

(ASB)